How to Woo a Wallflower

Also by Christy Carlyle

Romancing the Rules series
A Study in Scoundrels
Rules for a Rogue

The Accidental Heirs series
One Dangerous Desire
One Tempting Proposal
One Scandalous Kiss

How to Woo a Wallflower

A Romancing the Rules Novel

Christy Carlyle

AVONIMPULSE
An Imprint of HarperCollinsPublishers

Excerpt from *Rules for a Rogue* copyright © 2016 by Christy Carlyle. Excerpt from *A Study in Scoundrels* copyright © 2017 by Christy Carlyle.

HOW TO WOO A WALLFLOWER. Copyright © 2017 by Christy Carlyle. All rights reserved. Printed in the United States of America. No part of this book may be used or reproduced in any manner whatsoever without written permission except in the case of brief quotations embodied in critical articles and reviews. For information, address HarperCollins Publishers, 195 Broadway, New York, NY 10007.

Digital Edition NOVEMBER 2017 ISBN: 978-0-06-257239-4

Print Edition ISBN: 978-0-06-257240-0

Cover art by Christine Ruhnke

Cover photograph © Mary Chronis, VJ Dunraven Productions & PeriodImages.com

Avon Impulse and the Avon Impulse logo are registered trademarks of HarperCollins Publishers in the United States of America.

Avon and HarperCollins are registered trademarks of HarperCollins Publishers in the United States of America and other countries.

FIRST EDITION

17 18 19 20 21   HDC   10 9 8 7 6 5 4 3 2 1

To my husband.
You're my real-life hero, and
I'm so grateful for your patience and support.

ACKNOWLEDGMENTS

Thank you to my editor, Elle Keck. You help make every book better, and I'm so grateful for your encouragement and insight.

How to Woo a Wallflower

CHAPTER ONE

"Don't assume every young lady is in need of rescue. Some of us wish to be a heroine who fights her own battles."

—JOURNAL OF CLARY RUTHVEN

London, 1899

Whitechapel repulsed Gabriel Adamson.

Grime and smoke hung so thick in the air that he could taste grit on his tongue. Narrow lanes conspired to trap the neighborhood's fetid stench, and its tenements loomed above his head as if they'd crush him under the weight of their cramped, miserable inhabitants.

Now that he could afford proper togs for the first time in his life, he took care selecting the finest fabrics for his tailored suits and shirts. Today, he feared every stitch he'd donned would reek from the East End's noxious stew of ash and muck.

The rain had been on and off and on all morning, but the heavens showed no mercy in a place like this. The sky opened the moment he alighted from the hansom cab, fat drops pelting his hat like the clatter of horses' hooves on cobblestones.

Tugging up his fur-lined collar, he lengthened his stride and ducked under the awning of a grimy-windowed shop. He stared across the lane at Number 12 Doncaster.

The building slouched toward the street, its wooden frame worn by time and eaten away by moisture. The brick buildings buttressing each side were smart and modern by comparison, though their red bricks had been smoked to an oily black too.

As he gazed up at the house, echoes rang in his head. Raging shouts and desperate cries. The thud of fists on flesh. Bone meeting bone.

Peg Delaney was a cruel woman, but she was nobody's fool. Gabe doubted she'd still be eking out a living in the last place he'd seen her. This venture was a fool's errand.

He drew in a ragged breath, biting back a curse.

At least he'd had the good sense not to tell Sara of his trip. He couldn't bear to dash his sister's hopes, nor could he stand watching her fret over their mother's fate when she should be focusing on her future and finally securing a bit of long-delayed happiness.

When the rain slowed to a sparse patter, he dashed across the narrow lane and knocked at the door. No answer came, and he suspected the landlord was far in his cups by this hour. The man had always been a wastrel. Trying the latch, he found the door unlocked and stepped into the dark, musty vestibule, choking on memories and stale air.

A discordant strain of music—a bow scratching at violin strings—echoed from upstairs. Gabe started up the worn slats. The wood creaked under his weight.

His mother's door stood ajar, and nausea clawed its way up his throat when he caught a hint of her cheap perfume on the air. Bracing a gloved fist against the wood, he pushed inside and held his breath. Amid dried leaves and a cascade of cobwebs, the stench of rot turned his gut inside out.

Except for a single overturned chair, the room contained no furniture. Nothing hung on the walls. No personal effects decorated the space. She'd abandoned this place long ago, and no one had given a damn about the miserable lodging room since. Water ran down the walls, leaking from loose roof tiles.

Gabe strode to the back of the room and gripped a moldy edge of loosened wallpaper. Peeling back the paper revealed a gaping hole in the plaster. Reaching inside, he scraped his fingers around in the dust and dark until he felt a rounded shape. He tugged the object forward, grasping the tiny horse head in his hand.

Years ago, he'd found the knight chess piece in the gutter and had squirreled it away like a treasure. Even now, the chiseled quartz glinted in the weak light from the room's single, cracked window.

"Wot you after?" A woman's gruff bark sounded from the threshold, and Gabe turned, fists balled, muscles tensed.

"Mrs. Niven." She'd been wrinkled and gray when Gabe was young. Now his old neighbor had the aspect of a wizened crone. If wizened crones wielded a violin bow in one hand and a revolver in the other.

Squinting until her eyelids were little more than creased slits, she shuffled forward. "Is it you?"

Gabe's pulse slowed as he watched the old woman's drooping mouth curl up in a toothless smile.

"Ragin' Boy." She drew close, reeking of smoke and soiled wool. "Never fought I'd see those eyes of yours lookin' back at me again. 'Ow many years gone now, child? Five? Ten?"

Nine and a half years. He'd left Whitechapel at sixteen and never looked back. Never intended to step foot in the godforsaken place again either.

Tipping her chin, Mrs. Niven examined Gabe down the length of her bulbous nose. "Judgin' by those fine togs you're sportin', I'd wager you're not frowin' punches for your supper these days, are ya boy?"

"Where is she?" He wasn't here for small talk.

"Peg? 'Aven't seen 'er in ages, boy."

Gabe flexed his fingers. He fought the urge to throttle the old woman every time she called him *boy*. Mrs. Niven was thinking of another person. A child discarded long ago. An imp who woke angry every morning and spent his days fighting, striking out at anyone, anything that stood in his way. Bloodthirsty men had once had a use for him, betting on his skills in the ring. But he'd escaped. Taken a new name. Made a new life. Never looked back.

Until now.

"You've no idea where she's gone?" He couldn't lose sight of why he'd come. If he thought of anything else, the memories would break in, and he'd lose control. Control was how he survived. Imposing order on chaos had been his salvation.

"Not a clue." Mrs. Niven choked before bursting into a racking, hollow cough. "Wot you need 'er for?"

"I don't need 'er at all." Neither did Sara. This ridiculous venture was what happened when he gave in to sentiment. He needed to stop making that mistake. Reaching into his coat pocket, he extracted a silver sixpence. The woman's rheumy eyes widened, nearly bursting from their sockets, when Gabe deposited the coin in her grimy palm. "Don't drink it all at once, Mrs. Niven."

He started across the leaf-strewn floor, stopped, and turned back. After extracting a calling card from his waist-coat pocket, he offered the cream rectangle to her. "Send word if you hear anything of my mother."

Mrs. Niven was decidedly less eager to claim the slip of paper than she'd been to take his money, but she finally hobbled forward and retrieved the card from his fingers.

Gabe didn't look back as he descended the stairs and made his way onto the rain-drenched street.

Let his mother find them if she wished. Nothing would ever compel him to return to this godforsaken place.

The downpour had diminished to a drizzle as he started down the lane, heading for the busier cross street, praying for a stray cab rattling by in search of a fare. Strangely, this area of Whitechapel had begun to transform. Run-down buildings had been replaced by newer brick structures, and a few thriving shops lined the streets. Outside of a tea room, the pavement had been painted in whitewash, and chairs were arranged outside, awaiting diners and a drier, sunnier day.

If he'd possessed no memory of these streets from a decade before, he could almost be lulled into believing the neighborhood a respectable one.

At the precise moment such hopeful nonsense teased at his thoughts, a screech rent the air. A rowdy brothel had once thrived around the corner, but the sound echoing in the narrow lane wasn't one of pleasure. More like agony. A man's bleat emerged again, high-pitched and pained.

Gabe's body responded like a soldier's on the eve of battle—muscles taut, instincts sharp, pulse throbbing in his ears.

"You bloody bitch!" the man squeaked.

Gabe rolled his shoulders and tugged off his gloves. Whoever the man was, he'd chosen to menace the fairer sex, and Gabe never had been able to stomach a bully. Too many times as a child, he'd watched helplessly as his mother cowered on the losing side of a man's fists.

Until he was old and strong enough to beat them off himself.

Rounding the corner, he expected to find a man overpowering a woman with his height and strength. A sight he'd seen a thousand times in these streets. Instead, he spotted a man bent at the waist, clutching his groin, glaring toward the entrance of the Fisk Academy for Girls, according to the sign above the door.

"I'll smash that pretty face of yours," the wounded blighter cried.

"I don't think you will," a feminine voice countered. "And don't let me see you darken this doorstep ever again."

A croquet mallet emerged through the doorway first, the cylinder of wood painted with jaunty blue stripes around the edges. Purple ruffles came next, the edge of a skirt kicking up as a diminutive woman stomped out to face the wounded man.

Gabe rushed forward to assist her and jerked to a dead stop.

Clarissa Ruthven.

Pert nose. Guinea-gold hair. Wavy strands glinting in a beam of afternoon sun that managed to break through the clouds.

He recognized her, yet he squinted, unwilling to believe the evidence of his eyes. Queen Victoria parading down the sodden streets of Whitechapel wouldn't have shocked him more. What business could the young woman have in this soot-smeared place?

She was a country girl. Gently bred. And on the occasion of her twenty-first birthday, the little hellion would become his employer. Though when Leopold Ruthven entrusted Gabe with the running of his publishing enterprise, Gabe had never imagined answering to the man's children one day.

Clarissa Ruthven couldn't see him here. She wasn't privy to his history, and if he had his way, she would never know he hailed from these grimy streets.

As surefooted as he'd been as child when he'd served as lookout to a notorious housebreaker, he retreated. One boot placed silently behind the other.

Then the bullying fool made an awful choice. Tucking his head, he hunched his shoulder forward and heaved toward Miss Ruthven. She lifted her mallet for a defensive swing, but the man moved quicker.

Gabe surged forward, one boot slamming down to break the man's stride. With a muffled yelp, the fool pitched forward, striking the wet pavement with a satisfying thud.

Clarissa's mallet whisked through the air, and Gabe arched back just in time to keep the bloody thing from breaking his nose.

"Mr. Adamson?"

Ignoring her dumbfounded query, he pulled her nemesis to his feet. "Is this wretch troubling you, Miss Ruthven?" He didn't glance at her, couldn't bear to meet her inquisitive gaze.

"He's infatuated with one of our students." Her bodice brushed Gabe's coat sleeve as she leaned toward her attacker. "And Sally has no interest in receiving your attentions, as she's made clear on multiple occasions," she barked, seemingly undeterred by the man's murderous glare.

"Go," Gabe said more succinctly, emphasizing his point by squeezing the man's shirt front in his fist, twisting and tightening until the scalawag began to gasp. "Never come back." When he released the bastard, the man stumbled forward, clutching at his neck and casting them a withering scowl before limping up the lane.

Gabe was intensely aware of Miss Ruthven's perusal. He would have preferred to don a mask and disappear into the fog, like Spring-heeled Jack or one of the other characters in the penny dreadfuls he'd read as a child. When he finally met her gaze, her face puckered in a frown.

"What is it?" He should have spared a thought for what damage might have been done before he arrived on the scene. "Did he hurt you?"

"No," she assured, though she continued to study him closely.

He swept a hand across his head and pulled at the lapels of his coat to straighten them. Dust and muck had soiled his pristine cuffs. He shoved his hands behind his back to conceal them.

"I've never seen you with a hair out of place," she mused. "Dishevelment quite transforms you, Mr. Adamson." From her expression, he couldn't determine if she intended to praise or insult. "Thank you," she finally said, waving her hand in the direction her assailant had gone.

Her clipped tone and taut expression didn't surprise Gabe. Offering him gratitude must have galled her. The one fact he knew for certain about Clarissa Ruthven was that the young woman loathed him. On the few occasions they'd met, she'd refused all his attempts at gentlemanly civility—whether opening a door or pulling out her chair.

He suspected she was the last woman who'd wish to play the role of damsel in need of saving.

"You're welcome, Miss Ruthven." He spoke slowly, enunciating each syllable, taking care not to lapse into the Cockney accent he'd used with Mrs. Nivens. "Though I'm sure your mallet would have been an effective deterrent."

She glanced down at the sporting equipment, more suited to a posh lawn party than fending off an East End thug, then narrowed an eye. "Why are you here?" Balling a fist at the swell of her hip, she demanded, "Did my brother send you to spy on me?"

"Of course not." Like a match to dry tinder, his irritation sparked into flame. "Today I am master of my own hours."

How dare she look down her pert little nose at him? As if he were some lackey sent on her brother's errands. He'd been running her family's business for years, keeping the income flowing so that she could afford her fine dresses decorated with satin ribbons.

He stared at the unfastened length of ribbon at her neck, the cleft in her chin, and the tremor in her full, flushed lips. Then he found himself caught in the glare of violet eyes.

She was irritatingly pretty, with pale freckled skin, peach-plump cheeks, and a thick fringe of dark lashes over those unique lavender-hued eyes. He might be a ruffian playing at being gentleman, but he never lied to himself. Both the Ruthven sisters were lovely, but the younger Miss Ruthven stood out. If only because she was the most vexing female he'd ever met in his life.

Ridiculously independent in her views and behavior, she fully embodied the "New Woman" London newspapers lambasted with glee. Strident in her opinions about politics, society, and everything in between, she took special delight in discomfiting him—whether it was her annoying habit of leaving flowers, ribbons, or some scribbled scrap of paper in her wake, interrupting his sentences, or laughing at his need for order.

Beyond her beauty, she was precisely the sort of woman who held no appeal. What man wished to spend his life distracted by the mere sight of his wife? Or vexed by her quirks and odd habits? When he married, he wanted what he'd never had—peace and simplicity. Give him a plain woman with domestic inclinations and impeccable behavior any day of the week over a reform-minded harridan.

"What are *you* doing here, Miss Ruthven?" Gabe shoved his fingers into his gloves and scanned the streets for any sign of a cab. "Does your family know you spend your days fending off brutes in Whitechapel?"

"I'm not a child in need of a minder, Mr. Adamson. Kit and Sophia are aware of my charitable work." She folded her arms over her chest and pursed her mouth. She'd make the worst sort of gambler. Her lying tells were far too obvious.

"But do they know where? This is hardly the place for a lady to spend her spare hours."

She huffed at him and pivoted on her boot heel, not bothering to favor him with a reply.

He noted the mesmeric swish of her purple skirt and the wavy strands of gold hair escaping a messy bun at the back of her head. She spun to face him, catching his perusal. Heat infused his skin.

"Well? Don't you wish to see how I pass my Saturday afternoon?"

From the first moment he'd set foot in Whitechapel, he'd wanted to depart. Yet he was curious to see the enterprise that brought a well-bred young lady to these streets.

A milling group of girls greeted them on the threshold, eyes wide, mouths agape.

"Shoulda landed him a facer," one mumbled as he passed.

"All right, ladies. Mr. Keene has gone. I don't think he'll trouble us anymore." Miss Ruthven clapped her hands together lightly. "Everyone back to your lessons."

They scattered like dandelion fluff, floating off in different directions. Each girl seemed to know where she belonged, and they resumed their tasks swiftly.

"There are twenty girls here now," Miss Ruthven informed him, her voice ringing with pride. "We hope to admit at least five more if we can convince the landlord to rent us every floor in the building."

Gabe had been responsible for the welfare of his older sister for years. The notion of being responsible for twenty young women made his skin itch.

"Seems an enormous enterprise to take upon yourself." The ragged school he'd attended as a child hadn't provided lodgings, and only a handful of boys had been admitted.

"Oh, I don't administer the school, nor did I start the enterprise. I was recruited as a volunteer and patron by one of my friends at college." She turned and called over her shoulder. "Helen?"

A tall, spindly-limbed young woman stepped forward, assessing Gabe over the top of metal-rimmed glasses. "I heard Clary call you Mr. Adamson. Thank you for scaring Mr. Keene away. He's a menace we're glad to see the back of." She offered him her hand in greeting.

"Welcome to Fisk Academy. As you can see, our young ladies keep busy here. Most attend for the day, though two are parentless and lodge at the school. They're also the oldest and will be graduating soon. We'll miss them." She cast him a sad glance, as if expecting him to offer sympathy. "Oh goodness, I almost forgot to say, I'm Helen Fisk." The lady spoke in a rapid-fire patter, as if she needed to impart as much information as quickly as she could. When she finally stopped, her breath whooshed out in a gust and color splotched her cheeks.

As he examined the schoolroom, he sensed her gaze on him. He turned back to find her watching him, as most women did. With a glint of interest in her pale green eyes.

Most women, that is, aside from Clarissa Ruthven.

"The school seems to be...thriving," he said, attempting politeness, despite the chaos around him.

Unlike the dusty, unadorned rooms of the ragged school where he'd taken lessons as a child, Fisk Academy sported a riot of colors. There was far too much noise in the overcrowded room. Even the tables were oddly arranged, some pressed close together, others set apart, as if they'd been placed at students' whims. Several girls bent over desks, but a cluster of others stood in a corner, working at canvases, applying seemingly random washes of paint. In another corner, three girls sat with their backs to him, carefully printing letters in cursive script. Another trio crouched at a low table with test tubes, a tiny gas burner, and a boiling liquid that smelled of metal and rotting sewage. They all chattered to each other as they worked.

He appreciated the efforts of Miss Ruthven, Miss Fisk, and other charitable ladies of their ilk. However, they desperately needed the input of someone with a sense of structure and efficiency to impose a bit of order.

"We ensure the girls are kept busy and challenged with a variety of tasks throughout the day." Miss Fisk beamed beside him as she took in the disorganized mess. "I teach mathematics and composition. Miss Ruthven guides the girls in art." She pointed merrily to the trio concocting God knew what over an open flame. "And sometimes chemistry."

"Every lesson at once, apparently." He cast her a dubious glance. "Why not one task at a time and then the next? In an orderly fashion."

She frowned, and her glasses scooted up to meet the line of her brow. "Every student has her own unique aptitudes, Mr. Adamson. Not every task suits every girl."

Gabe nearly choked on the chuckle tickling in his throat. Miss Fisk's sincerity was almost as amusing as her naïveté.

He preferred to deal in reality, not fantasy.

"If you'll excuse me, Miss Fisk, I have a prior engagement in the city." He'd had enough. Of chaotic spaces. Of prim ladies and their charitable urges. Of rotting wood and the potent memories lurking around every corner.

Miss Fisk looked worried she might have caused offense, and Gabe sketched a gentlemanly bow to assuage her feelings. She managed a tight smile before he spun on his heel and headed for the door.

Being in Whitechapel again reminded him of how hard he'd worked to escape. To embrace a new life. One day he'd marry, have a home and business venture of his own. One day he'd forget the pit he'd dragged himself out of.

Halfway to the door, Clarissa Ruthven stopped him in his tracks. "I'm heading back too, Mr. Adamson. Shall we share a cab and save on fare?"

Her voice sent a strange shudder of awareness down his spine. She was, as the sister of his employer, a young lady he could not deny. Yet every instinct told him being near her would bring no end of trouble his way.

Turning back, he forced down the ire that came naturally and practiced the polite civility he'd spent years struggling to master.

"Very well, Miss Ruthven." He lifted his arm as he'd been taught a gentleman should when escorting ladies. "Shall we set off?"

She raised her chin, eschewed his gesture, and swept past, as if determined to show him that a woman could and should lead the way.

CHAPTER TWO

---

*"There is nothing quite as an intoxicating
as a man who sees a ~~wallflower~~ woman
as she is, with all her merits and all her
flaws, and smiles at her as if she's the only
one worth noticing in the world."*

—JOURNAL OF CLARY RUTHVEN

Clary's foot bounced against the carriage floorboards as she watched Gabriel Adamson give directions to the hansom cab driver.

Ruthven Publishing's office manager made her miserable.

Beyond exuding insufferable pomposity, the man never smiled. He was as stiff as a statue. Admittedly, a gorgeous statue. One with all the beautiful symmetry of a Greek god. Assuming the god in question had oak-plank shoulders and a chest as broad as a doorway.

No matter how well-tailored his clothing—and it always was—the fabric showcased his muscled frame.

Not that she'd spent an excessive amount of time studying the man or his muscles.

Only enough to know he disturbed her with his flawlessness. Perfect features, perfect hair, polished accent. Yet his cool blue eyes and ink-black lashes were too striking. And he was far too tall and definitely too bulky. Most disturbing of all, Mr. Adamson seemed to lack any joy.

Of course, he always noticed *her* imperfections. His displeasure was evident every time they met. When she spoke too quickly, he grimaced. When she laughed too readily, he turned away. When she unsettled some item on his spotless desk, he eyed her with disdain.

What on earth was the point of having a desk if one's intention was to give the appearance that no one ever used it?

In the four and a half years she'd known Mr. Adamson, they'd only been forced into close quarters on a few occasions, during rare visits to her family's publishing business on Southampton Row and the single awful time her brother invited him to a family Christmas party. After five courses of glaring at her, he'd made a ridiculous excuse and bolted the moment Phee suggested he and Clary partner for a dance.

In short, he was the last man she wished to accompany on a stop-and-start crawl in a cramped carriage through London's crowded streets, but she needed time with him. It wouldn't do for Kit to hear of her run-in with Mr. Keene. Her brother's concern was already suffocating. The last thing he needed was fresh fuel to stoke his worry.

When Adamson turned toward the carriage, Clary scooted across the bench and plastered herself against the cab's wall, wishing for narrower hips and slimmer thighs.

He climbed up and squeezed in next to her, taking care not to allow their bodies to collide in any but the most unintentional of ways. "Pardon me."

His voice had a low, smoky quality that Clary never understood. She couldn't imagine him partaking of anything as messy as a cigarette or pipe.

She tried to ignore his enticing scent underneath the starch of his clothing. She prayed she didn't reek of the vinegar mix she'd used to clean one of the schoolrooms.

Every time the carriage took a turn, their arms and hips and thighs pressed together. Every place their bodies met, he was hard and warm.

"I hope you'll make your engagement in time, Mr. Adamson." If she was going to convince him to keep mum about her activities in Whitechapel, establishing a polite rapport seemed a good start. Never mind that they'd never managed this in all the years they'd been acquainted.

"As do I."

Ah yes, she was used to that note of irritation in his voice.

"If you're late, will you blame me for your tardiness?" She lightened her tone, though teasing Gabriel Adamson felt a bit like baiting a bear.

"How could I, Miss Ruthven?" Sarcasm dripped from every syllable.

"You needn't have stepped in, you know."

"What should I have done? Watched as you bludgeoned a man to death with a croquet mallet?" He wrenched off his gloves, then assembled them, one on top of the other and every finger aligned with its mate, before slipping the pair inside his coat pocket. "I have no tolerance for men doing violence to ladies."

"Nor do I." Clary nibbled the edge of her lower lip. "Though I must admit, Mr. Keene never laid a finger on me. He tried, but before you happened upon us, I kneed him in the groin."

"I know." He cast her a quick glance, a single flash of his clear blue eyes. "No man could mistake that squawk of agony."

Clary recalled the effectiveness of the defensive jab with her knee. "I'm not usually given to violence. I wished to banish the man from lurking outside the school, but I never intended any permanent damage."

He didn't reply, but the lift of one perfectly shaped ebony brow spoke volumes.

"I don't care if you believe me or not." Clary lashed her arms over her chest, which proved impossible to do without brushing the side of his body. "May I rely on you to say nothing to my brother?"

"He doesn't know you waste your time in Whitechapel?"

"Is charity a waste?" Clary swung to face him, pressing her knees into the muscled thickness of his thigh. "You speak like a man who's never been charitable in his life."

She sensed a tremor rippling through his body, felt the jump of his leg against hers. He clenched his fingers into a fist against his thigh. For a moment, she thought he might leap from the moving vehicle. Bolt, as he had the night of that dinner party months ago. Just to get away from her.

He turned his wintry gaze her way. "You know nothing of my life, Miss Ruthven," he finally said, his voice tight and even. "Even when you've come of age and call yourself my master, you won't be privy to my past."

Clary's breath caught in her throat. Despite the forced calm of his voice, fury sparked in his eyes. Not his usual ill humor but something fiercer. Pain? Fear? Sitting here, closer than they'd ever been to each other, Clary wanted to know why Gabriel Adamson seemed a man forever fighting for control.

What did he fear unleashing?

She told herself he was cold, unfeeling, but she'd glimpsed something more too. Only intermittent peeks. But now she saw it again. Sparks of fire beneath his icy facade. She couldn't help but wish to break through.

They stared at each other so long that embarrassed laughter bubbled up Clary's throat. She fought the impulse, but a sound escaped. Not quite a gasp, more like a gurgle. Mr. Adamson's gaze dropped to her mouth, and her lips warmed under his scrutiny. Heat spread down her body, pouring across her belly like warm syrup, gathering at the center of her thighs. Her cheeks caught fire.

Then it was as if the rain battering the carriage roof had rushed in to douse all the fire in Mr. Adamson's gaze. He turned away from her and retreated toward his side of the carriage.

Clary drew in long steadying breaths as all the heat between them chilled. Retorts stewed in her mind, from scathing to impolite. Instead, she tried on an imperious tone and informed him, "The *when* you speak of has arrived, Mr. Adamson."

"Pardon?" His handsome face crumpled in confusion, and he frowned at her as if she'd gone completely dotty.

"Today is my twenty-first birthday. I may not be your master, but as of today, I am your employer."

For a fleeting moment, she thought he might let his fearsome expression slip. That he might be jovial or kind. Offer her felicitations. Crack a smile.

But after a moment of dumbstruck confusion, his glower deepened, and he banged on the carriage roof. The vehicle immediately swerved before rattling to a stop.

"What are you doing?"

"Leaving." He pushed the door open and stepped out. "Good day to you, Miss Ruthven." Just like that, he escaped her presence, as he'd proven quite skilled at doing.

"I thought you had an appointment," she shouted.

"I'll walk."

"You'll be late." One hand braced against the open door, Clary leaned out to urge him back. Rain poured down in a steady shower.

"Then I'll walk quickly."

"You'll be drenched by the time you arrive."

"It's only a bit of mist now," he insisted, contradicting her, as he liked to do almost as much as finding fault with her.

Why did it matter whether he appeared at his meeting sopping wet? Nothing about the man was her concern. She settled back in the carriage and was just on the point of knocking on the wall to urge the coachman into motion.

She leaned out and watched Mr. Adamson rushing away. Perhaps he was, in some sense, her concern. She was his employer now. Learning more about Ruthven's was one of her goals. Getting along with the man who managed the whole enterprise seemed a logical first step.

"I'm happy to take you wherever you wish to go," she called to him.

"No." He turned back. "Be on your way, Miss Ruthven. The driver will take you wherever *you* wish to go."

"I'm going to my brother's townhouse in Bloomsbury Square." Clary scrambled out of the narrow carriage door before the vehicle could depart. "Would you like to come with me?"

His face shuttered, wiped clean of emotion, and then one dark brow winged high.

She'd probably come to regret it, but she couldn't deny the value of ending the animosity between them. What if she offended him so thoroughly he quit? Kit would have no end of questions.

"My sister-in-law is planning a special dinner for my birthday. Would you care to join us?"

For a moment, she thought he might agree. The prospect set her pulse racing.

"No," he finally said. "I have a prior engagement."

Striding forward, he came close enough for her to see a scar she'd never noticed, a faded line running through his right brow. Then she spotted another, a tiny faint slash at the edge of his evenly shaped upper lip. How had she missed those flaws in his otherwise perfect face?

One more step, and they stood toe-to-toe. "May I offer you a piece of advice, Miss Ruthven?"

"If you must." Clary braced her arms across her chest.

"Don't go back to Whitechapel. It's not fit for a lady such as yourself." His accent changed, syllables spoken with different emphasis than his usual clipped tone. "Not sure the place is fit for any living creature." He straightened, rolling his shoulders, and lifted two fingers to tug on the edge of his hat. "Good day to you."

Without another word, he strode away.

"Like you, Mr. Adamson," she called to him, "I am my own master and will go wherever I please."

"As long as your brother doesn't find out, of course." The smirking glance he shot back at Clary pinned her in place, while he picked up his stride and carried on with his day.

Miserable, insufferable man.

His advice could be damned, along with his curt manner. He met the strict requirements of being polite without offering anything more.

Except for that flash of heat she'd seen in his gaze, the man was a devil to read. Had she truly offended him? Would he tell Kit he'd found her swinging a mallet at Mr. Keene? She wouldn't put it past Gabriel Adamson to quit his job at Ruthven's just to keep her from being his master, as he put it.

As she climbed back into the cab, Clary vowed that, in future, she'd exhibit more poise in her role as a freshly minted lady of business.

A pity, since she rather liked sparking a reaction stronger than cool civility from Mr. Adamson.

Chapter Three

"Nothing?" Clary swallowed against the lump of disappointment lodged in her throat. "He left me nothing?"

Time slowed to the speed of treacle dripping from a teaspoon. Only Kit and Ophelia's drawing-room mantel clock continued on, ticking steadily as if nothing had changed. As if all her hopes and plans weren't evaporating before her eyes.

"On the contrary, Miss Ruthven, your father provided a prodigious sum to secure your future." The family solicitor, Mr. Whitaker, tapped a finger against the document in front of her. "Just there, second paragraph. Shall I read that portion again?"

"No, thank you." Leaning closer, her eyes blurred as she skimmed the minuscule print, but the opaque legal language was shockingly clear.

Her father had left her no money of her own.

"As the will states," Mr. Whitaker continued in his dry, no-nonsense drone, "the entire dowry will be paid once you marry."

Once you marry. He might as well have said, "Once you climb Mount Kilimanjaro" or "Once you become the most feted debutante of the Season." Neither of which was going to happen. Marriage wasn't possible. At least not yet. Perhaps not ever. There was too much she wished to do.

A folded square of foolscap in Clary's pocket contained a list of goals she wished to accomplish and causes she wished to promote. First of which was the Fisk Academy. The rest of her inheritance she'd planned to invest, so that she could preserve her independence, travel widely, and continue doing as she pleased into her dotage.

Among a thousand interests, she couldn't bear the notion of confining herself to one singular pursuit.

Rather than mediocrity spread among many tasks, pursue excellence at a single undertaking.

The admonition, a line from one of her father's etiquette books, stuck in her head but never altered her essential nature. Her brother and sister said she lacked patience. Perhaps they were right, but she never lacked energy. Or grand plans.

For too long she'd been a dabbler. A trifler. An armchair explorer. She read voraciously of fearless young ladies in novels, but she'd yet to make her own mark on the world.

"I don't wish to be indelicate, Mr. Whitaker, but surely my father left me something. Are there no funds that come directly to me? To do with as I wish?"

Freedom would only come when she could control her own funds.

"I'm sorry to bring distressing news, Miss Ruthven." Whitaker began to withdraw, turtle-like, his neck disappearing and shoulders sinking as his barrel chest deflated.

"For years, I've served your family and still recall your father contacting me to alter his will on the occasion of your birth." He regarded her solemnly for a moment. "He did wish to provide for you."

"I know." As with everything her father did, he assumed his children would conform to his expectations.

Whitaker busied himself, pulling out another oblong legal document from his leather satchel. "Shall we ask your brother and sister to join us for the signing of the partnership document? Their signatures are required too."

"Yes, of course."

Whitaker sprang from the settee like a man half his age.

"And thank you for your years of service to the Ruthvens," Clary called after him. She couldn't blame the solicitor for wishing to carry out his duties and be on his way. The poor man was probably used to young ladies who were grateful for their dowries and eager to put the sum to use securing an appealing suitor.

Clary could only think of everything she could achieve with the money.

Her older sister, Sophia, stepped into the room first, her expression faltering before she shot straight toward Clary like an arrow of sisterly concern. "What's happened? You look pale and miserable."

"Father left me a dowry."

"Were you expecting him to do otherwise?" Sophia's brow puckered under the artfully arranged wave of honey-blonde hair across her forehead.

"I thought he might have left me something of my own."

Sophia laid her palm against Clary's cheek. "Marriage was the fate Papa imagined for every woman." She ducked her head until Clary looked her in the eye. "You have heard of the *Ruthven Rules*, haven't you?" she teased.

They'd all been forced to read them. Every single word.

Their father's dry, traditional etiquette books were so successful that they were the reason there were dowries and a publishing business for Clary and her siblings to inherit.

What a fool she'd been to think Papa—who loathed change and progress and any notion that women longed for accomplishments of their own—would set aside funds to allow her a measure of independence.

It didn't matter. She'd find another way.

"Is everything in order?" Kit entered and closed the drawing room door behind him. Clary got a glimpse of her sister-in-law, Ophelia, in the sitting room across the hall. She longed to join her. She'd had enough of legal documents and disappointment for one day.

Her encounter with Gabriel Adamson came to mind. Just the thought of the man—his spotless suit, chiseled jaw, and icy gaze—was sufficient to ruin her day.

"The document only awaits your signatures." Mr. Whitaker gestured to a low table that had been placed in the center of the snug room.

Sophia settled on the settee and patted the spot next to her, urging Clary over. Kit balanced on the edge of a chair, leaning forward, appearing almost as eager as Mr. Whitaker to have the matter resolved.

"Your one-third share of Ruthven Publishing is herewith declared in perpetuity, Miss Ruthven, and will eventually pass to your heirs, barring liquidation of the business."

Mr. Whitaker uncapped a fountain pen and held it out to her, barrel first.

Clary leaned forward, scanned the document, and signed her name before handing the pen to Sophia.

"Of course," Whitaker added, "you may wish to pass ownership to your husband once you marry." He glanced at her, a smile causing his neatly trimmed mustache to quiver. "See me, and I shall be happy to add a codicil to the agreement."

"I have no wish to marry, Mr. Whitaker."

The solicitor drew back as if she'd struck him. Sophia emitted a little gasp.

Kit turned to face her. "Clary, you've just come home after four years away at college. You needn't make such a decision now."

He implied she hadn't given a thought to her future until this moment, but Clary had been looking forward to this day for years. Turning one and twenty meant reaching the legal age of majority, but for Clary, it had always been more. A prospect of the independence she craved.

"There is another possibility." Sophia's soft voice stopped Clary from saying something to her brother she'd likely regret. "My dowry was transferred into an annuity. Is such an arrangement possible for my sister, Mr. Whitaker?"

Clary let out a sigh of relief. Sophia had a knack for finding solutions to dilemmas.

The solicitor nodded hesitantly. "Your situation was quite different, Lady Stanhope." The patches of skin above his thick side whiskers began to redden.

"How so?"

"Well, you…your situation." The solicitor tugged at his ascot. "My lady, you activated the spinster clause."

"I see." Sophia cast the older man a rueful smile. "Father finally had given up on the prospect of my ever marrying."

"Yes, that's the provision I want." Clary bolted up from the settee, too tense to stay still. "I'll take the spinster clause, Mr. Whitaker."

"You've just turned one and twenty." Kit held out his hands, palms up, beseeching her. "How can you be eager for spinsterhood already?"

"I'm afraid I cannot assist you, Miss Ruthven." The solicitor pressed his lips together and shook his head. He looked truly bereft. "The clause is only applicable if a Ruthven daughter remains unmarried at the age of five and twenty."

Four years. An unbearable delay when an eagerness to start her life burned inside her like the sun.

"Much can change in four years." Kit's voice had softened. "At least wait and see what the coming year brings."

What Clary saw was doubt in her brother's eyes. He knew she wasn't patient and that waiting had never been her way.

"I wish you birthday felicitations, Miss Ruthven." Whitaker began collecting his documents and carefully recapped his fountain pen. "If you remain unwed, perhaps we shall meet again in four years."

After the solicitor departed, Clary slumped beside Sophia on the settee. Her sister wrapped an arm around her shoulders.

"We have a suggestion." Kit stood as if he'd been waiting for the moment since Whitaker's arrival. "What would you say to a Season?" His voice rose on a cajoling lilt, the way he'd spoken to her when she'd been obstinate as a child. "Balls, gowns, dinner parties. Sophia and Grey will sponsor your coming out."

To the surprise of the family—and Sophia herself—she'd fallen in love with a viscount, Jasper Grey, Lord Stanhope. A man who'd pretended to be nothing more than an actor but was heir to an earldom. Sophia and Jasper had gained many friends among London's aristocratic set, but Clary had no interest in following in her sister's footsteps.

If worry wasn't gnawing at her insides, Clary would have laughed at Kit's suggestion. "Did you forget who I am in the years I've been away? Odd, unusual, never quite fitting in." At her ladies' college autumn ball, she'd been a wallflower, content to read while others danced. "I'm not a debutante. I don't wish to be."

She only wished to be free.

"I know you mean well, but I don't want a Season." Rising from the settee, Clary tugged loose the strangling knot of a ribbon at the high neckline of her gown. "What I need is employment."

A far better choice than relying on her father's money. She'd earn her own.

"Why would you need employment?" Kit's voice rose to incredulous pitch. "We can increase your allowance."

"An allowance comes with expectations and judgements about how I spend my pounds and pence." Clary drew in a breath. She sounded ungrateful, and that wasn't at all what she intended. Kit and Ophelia had been generous, opening their home to her when she returned from college. "You and

Phee have been wonderful to me. It's not a matter of expecting you to do more. I simply wish to provide for myself. To make my own way."

"You will, of course, receive a portion of the earnings from Ruthven's." Sophia tempered the news by adding, "Though they are only paid out twice a year, and Kit and I have been investing most profits back into the business to expand our offerings."

Clary tapped her lower lip. Learning more about the family business was on her list of goals. "I would like to spend more time at the office and learn how everything works." Perhaps a skill learned there could aid her in finding employment elsewhere.

Kit let out a strangled sound, part shock, part chuckle. "You needn't worry about the day-to-day workings of Ruthven's."

"But I wish to. I plan to take my responsibilities to heart."

"Mr. Adamson has the business well in hand."

Clary's teeth snapped together, and her fingers clenched into fists. "I'm sure he manages Ruthven's well, but we cannot forfeit all responsibility. Father wished the business to remain in the family." Of course, he'd never expected his daughters to share in its ownership. That had been Kit's idea.

"As a member of the administrative board, you may bring any suggestion you have for Ruthven's." Kit looked her, the seriousness in his gaze replaced with the warmth she was used to. "Sophia and I both have been looking forward to your input."

"And Mr. Adamson?" Kit and Sophia had allowed the man complete independence to establish iron control over the publishing office, and Clary would never forget the way Adamson bristled at the prospect of her involvement in the business. "Will *he* welcome my suggestions?"

"He's a practical man." Kit lifted his shoulders in a shrug. "There's a board meeting next week. A good opportunity for you and Mr. Adamson to become reacquainted."

"Yes." Though of course they already had, and Clary tried not to think of how badly that encounter had gone. Most of all, she prayed Kit never learned the details. "But I still wish to seek employment."

Kit pinched the skin at the peak of his nose.

"I wish to find my own lodgings too." Clary got the words out quickly, fearing how Kit might respond to this detail. To her surprise, he seemed more sad than disapproving.

"You know Phee and I enjoy having you here. You may stay as long as you like. We'd like you to consider this your home too."

"I know." Clary took a step toward him, yearning to erase the hurt in his eyes. "I do. But I still long for a space of my own."

"Are you in some sort of trouble that requires funds?" His golden-brown eyes took on a haunted look, as if he feared hearing her confess the very worst. "Is there something you're not telling us?"

"Not at all." Only that she'd fended off a bully with a croquet mallet and irritated their trusted business manager to the point he'd practically leapt from a moving carriage. "Please don't fret." She knew her brother meant well, but his protectiveness felt stifling.

Clary gazed out the window where a few shafts of sunlight were bursting through the rain clouds. She needed movement and fresh air. To stretch her legs and begin formulating fresh plans.

"I think I'll go for a walk." Clary kissed her sister on the cheek and offered Kit a grin. "Thank you for arranging for Mr. Whitaker to come."

Sophia stood and followed her toward the door. "Don't forget that we've planned a special dinner for your birthday."

"I'll be back in time for dinner; I promise."

Two steps from the threshold, Kit's voice rang out. "Tell me you're not headed to Whitechapel." He hated her trips to the East End, but, to his credit, he'd never insisted she stop her volunteer efforts at Fisk Academy.

"Trust me a little." Clary hated that his worry led him to exert so much control. "I haven't caused any scandals yet."

Chapter Four

Gabe shifted on the plush chair underneath him and tried to think of anything but the envelope tucked in the pocket of his waistcoat. The letter's contents nagged at his thoughts.

Wellbeck Publishers had been competing with Ruthven's for years. On several occasions, they'd tried to lure him away to manage their enterprise, and now they were after him again. This time with the enticement of higher wages, opportunities for advancement, and an additional sum for quick action.

Why was he even considering turning them down?

For a nearly a decade he'd convinced himself honest work would pay off. Turning his back on stealing and brawling allowed him to look in the mirror without loathing the man staring back. With diligence, he'd eked out a measure of respectability for himself and his sister. Not wealth. They needed nothing lavish. Savoring the slide of quality linen against his skin was his only indulgence. Yet now, a decade on, he and Sara still resided in a run-down flat in Cheapside.

In all his time at Ruthven's, he'd never arrived late or departed early, often doing the work of others who failed to carry their load. But rather than achieving the success he craved, the elder Ruthven had paid Gabe only enough to keep him coming back year after year. When the son took over, they'd loathed each other on sight, though a truce had been struck in recent months. Still, Gabe had yet to demand higher wages. He knew the strained state of the business's coffers better than anyone.

"You'll have to do better." Sara nudged his elbow, dragging him from his wandering thoughts.

"Better at what?"

"Pretending that you enjoy Miss Morgan's singing." His sister chuckled under her breath, and the sound lightened Gabe's mood.

After a bout of illness, she'd been stronger of late, less fatigued and eager to spend part of every day out of doors. This evening marked her first social outing in months.

And she was right. He owed their host his full attention.

In truth, he owed Sir Eliot Morgan's daughter, Jane, more than he could ever repay. He'd come to her father for elocution lessons the year he'd left Whitechapel, determined to shed his Cockney dialect. In Sir Eliot, he'd found a mentor and friend, and Jane had proved an excellent conversational partner, allowing him to practice his polished pronunciation. She'd also befriended Sara. After Sir Eliot's death, remaining friendly seemed the natural course. Lately, however, the demure spinster had developed a terrible habit of flushing to a feverish crimson whenever he was near. She also sang poorly, in a pitch that clashed with her cousin, Dorothy, who accompanied her on the piano.

Out of loyalty to the late Sir Eliot, Gabe lifted his head and offered Jane an encouraging grin.

"Much better," Sara praised under her breath. "Look, she's blushing now."

She was, and Gabe wished he could ascribe her high color to the overheated room rather than a blooming infatuation he had no interest in encouraging.

"Have you considered asking her to marry you?"

Gabe choked on the sickly-sweet cordial he'd been sipping from a ridiculously tiny crystal glass. "Never, and don't you dare put the thought in her head."

"I'm content putting the notion in yours." Sara set down her teacup and offered Miss Morgan a round of hearty applause as she finished one song and launched into another. "She's respectable, polite, mild mannered. Everything a man might wish for in a wife."

Indeed, she was. If he'd made a list of qualities a bride should possess, Miss Morgan would tick every box. Unfortunately, she didn't interest him in the least. Nothing about Miss Morgan moved him. Not a single part of him. There was also the matter of her being the daughter of a baronet. Despite their long friendship, he wasn't at all certain Sir Eliot would have encouraged his suit.

"It's time for you to marry. I can't bear the thought of your being alone." Sara worried a great deal about his being left on his own after she married.

"I can't afford a wife yet." He lightened his tone, forcing his mouth to curve in a smile.

She planned to marry a young man she'd met by chance in a coffee shop, a young law clerk who had the good sense to become smitten with her. What she didn't know was that Thomas Tidwell had come to Gabe soon after, explaining his desire to further his legal studies and inquiring about the possibility of a dowry.

Gabe was hesitant to discuss the matter bluntly with Sara, for fear she'd believe Tidwell's intentions weren't pure. Yet Sara had always been the practical one. Her good sense had stretched a few shillings into weeks of food. When their mother disappeared for days, she'd been the one to bring in wages to keep a roof over their head. Sara's sensible, hard-working nature had kept them alive.

After a few more sips of tea, she leaned closer. "I thought you planned to speak to Mr. Ruthven about higher wages."

"I need to find the right time."

"Now or never, I always say." Sara viewed time differently than Gabe. She was impatient, eager for life to proceed, never willing to wait.

He reached for her hand and promised, "I'll speak to him tomorrow."

"And once you're earning enough, you'll get yourself a wife?" Sara gripped his fingers fiercely. "Promise me you will."

"I'll begin considering matrimony. Will that do?" He gave her a reassuring squeeze. "I suspect searching for a bride won't be a simple matter." Ladies weren't lining up at his office door, after all. And even if a fetching one appeared, she would judge him based on the gentleman he'd spent years trying to become.

What if the day came when a lady he courted discovered the creature he'd once been?

"Nonsense." Sara released his hand and nudged her chin toward Miss Morgan, whose voice cracked as she hit the song's crescendo. "Finding a wife will be as easy as allowing yourself to see what's been in front of you all along."

"Why have you planted yourself over here in the corner?"

Clary looked up from the notes she'd been making in her journal as Helen approached, bearing ruby-hued punch in dainty cut-crystal vessels. Phee and Kit had invited a few friends to her birthday dinner, and the crowded drawing room was filled with pleasant chatter interspersed with laughter.

Clary had indulged too freely in sweet wine and dessert. "I think the seed cake did me in, and I fear they'll start in with music and dancing soon."

"I thought you were fond of music." Helen passed Clary a cup before settling next to her. "Sitting together like this reminds me of Rothley's autumn dances."

"We did all of our best plotting while sitting along the wallflower wall."

Helen cast her gaze at the open notebook in Clary's lap. "What are you plotting this evening?"

"Employment and where I might seek a position. I'm also working up an estimated budget of expenses. I wish to secure my own lodgings as soon as I'm able."

"I'm glad you've shifted from misery to plotting." If Helen was worried Clary's change in fate would affect their plans for Fisk Academy, her expression revealed none of it.

"What's most disappointing is that my father only thought me worthy of a bounty for whatever man wishes to bind himself to me in wedlock." Clary slapped her journal shut and settled against the back of her chair.

"You cannot be surprised." Helen lowered her voice to a confidential tone. "Your father valued tradition. Marriage is what our fathers expect of us."

"Even yours?"

"My father planned my marriage when I was still a child." Helen's voice softened. "The son of his business associate was to be my groom."

"Who?" She and Helen shared a desire to work and improve the lives of others, and Clary assumed her friend also shared her desire to postpone marriage.

"Nathaniel Landau."

"That handsome doctor from the Royal London Hospital? The one who came to visit the school?"

"He is handsome, isn't he?" Helen removed her glasses and blew a bit of lint from one lens.

"Half the girls wanted to follow him out the door when he spoke of employment opportunities at the hospital." With his dark wavy hair, easy smile, and natural charm, Dr. Landau had been an instant favorite at Fisk Academy. Clary's chief memory of his visit was how difficult it had been to keep the girls from giggling every time he said something amusing.

"Nate has a heart for helping his patients in the East End," Helen confided. "He's passionate about making a difference through medicine."

"And you're besotted with him."

For a young woman who usually excelled at concealing her emotions, Helen was failing miserably. Her cheeks had taken on a peachy hue and her green eyes glinted in the gaslight.

"I never planned to be," she said defensively. "We've known each other since childhood. He'd always been a friend but never more until…well, until the last few months." She swallowed down the last of her punch and took a deep breath. "I'm quite independent. You know that. But lately I find that I miss him when we're apart. Quite a lot."

"So you'll chain yourself to him forever?"

Helen's brow pinched in a frown. "I don't recall anyone mentioning chains." She turned a scrutinizing gaze Clary's way. "When did you become so averse to marriage?"

"I can't pinpoint a date." Perhaps it had simply been her parents' example of how miserable wedlock could be. Her father had carried on exactly as he pleased, while her mother frittered away her days, planning menus and selecting gowns. She'd seemed more miserable with each passing year.

"Surely in twenty-one years, some gentleman caught your eye, if not your heart."

"Plenty catch my eye. I can acknowledge a handsome gentleman's appeal easily enough." Even if the man in question was boring and boorish and managed her family's publishing business. "But the notion of vowing my life away, my choices, my freedom." The thought ignited a panicky flutter in the center of her chest. The panic of being trapped with no way to escape. "I cannot imagine any man who could persuade me to forfeit my independence. At least not yet."

Helen's mouth puckered in a thoughtful moue. "You've never fallen in love? Not even a little?"

A nervous laugh burst from Clary, but Helen continued to stare. A sandy-brown brow arched up. A sure sign that she'd keep pushing for an answer.

"There was someone once."

"I knew it." Helen's excited pitch drew a few gazes their way.

"Digby Smythe was twelve when I turned ten, and I thought him the most interesting boy in our village."

"And?"

"I gave him a drawing I'd made for him." A chipmunk in a top hat. She'd gotten quite skilled at drawing the little creatures and thought the fancy headgear a nice touch. "He called me 'pudgy Clary' and tore my sketch in two."

"Digby sounds dreadful."

Clary laughed to think of her foolishness. How nervous she'd been. How much care she'd taken with the little chipmunk, which, thinking back, was quite like Digby, with his sleek brown hair and beady eyes.

"You should take another chance," Helen whispered. "Not all men are as rude and thoughtless as Digby Smythe. Your brother is happily married, and your sister."

"My brother broke his wife's heart before finally having the good sense to marry her, and my sister happened to find the one man in England who suited her. She waited a long time. I can wait too."

"Perhaps a bit of dancing and less waiting is in order." The voice of Clary's brother-in-law, Grey, Earl of Stanhope, startled them both. "Forgive me, ladies, but I couldn't bear to see two such lovely creatures stuck in the corner. Which of you will partner me for the first dance?"

"I would be honored, Lord Stanhope. I'll join you directly." Helen smiled as Grey executed a dramatic bow before heading back into the gathering of guests.

"You were right," Clary admitted.

"Wonderful. I do enjoy being right sometimes. What was I right about?"

"I have no business lingering in the corner and grousing about my inheritance when we're in a room filled with potential philanthropists. Perhaps some of them would be willing to contribute funds toward the school." Clary nudged her chin toward her sister and a literary-minded couple Kit and Phee had befriended.

"No." Helen shook her head. Her voice had taken on the firm tone she used with the girls at Fisk Academy. "It's your birthday." Determination shone in her eyes. "A family gathering is no place for business."

"Have you forgotten that my family *owns* a business?" Clary tipped her friend a grin.

Helen's left eye began to twitch behind her spectacle lens, a sign that she was about to pull forth an ingenious idea. "Why don't you work for Ruthven's?"

"No." Clary shook her head with extra vehemence. "The point of finding employment is to strike out on my own. How can I be independent if I'm working for Ruthven's? A business I now own a piece of?"

"You want work, and quickly. Believe me, positions are hard to find and extremely competitive." Helen's cheeks went ruddy, as they always did when she was excited. "You said you wished to take part in running the company. Why not assist with managing Ruthven's or contributing to editorial decisions?"

"I can't just waltz in and take over." Though imagining the look on Gabriel Adamson's face if she did so was almost worth trying it.

"I'd never suggest you be quite that high-handed. But think of what you might learn. We've both talked about purchasing typewriters for the girls at Fisk. If you became proficient, you could teach them."

Helen was making sense. Rational arguments were Clary's weakness.

"I suspect Mr. Adamson wouldn't want me underfoot." The man couldn't even manage to endure an entire carriage ride with her. "If I'm going to be there, I'd want to contribute. What could I contribute to the running of Ruthven's?"

"You're one of the cleverest young women I know, creative, thoughtful. I'm not sure you'll know until you get there." Helen leaned over and whispered, "But first you have to get there."

"He won't like me lingering about the office, I suspect." Mr. Adamson's glower was fresh in Clary's mind.

"You are co-owner, and you won't be lingering; you'll be applying your time and talents. After spending four years at study, surely you're as competent as Mr. Adamson."

Now *that* had a nice ring to it.

CHAPTER FIVE

*"There is no victory quite as sweet as turning
disappointment into determination."*

—JOURNAL OF CLARY RUTHVEN

Few visited the Ruthven offices who were not expected.
Workroom employees were due at half past seven. Vendors
arranged appointments weeks in advance. No meeting was
ever scheduled before nine. Gabe imposed order efficiently
and effectively on the daily goings-on of the business. If some
random Londoner happened across their threshold, it was
usually because the poor sod got lost.

Over the years, Gabe had learned the rhythms of the
workroom floor by heart, memorizing the clatter of the printing presses and the patterned strikes of Daughtry, his assistant, and other clerks tapping at their typewriters. When
productivity waned because of inane chitchat, he caught that
too. And immediately cut such nonsense short.

So when he settled behind his desk on Monday morning, a half hour before any other employees were due to arrive, as was his habit, he savored the bliss of quiet. He felt something akin to peace. After weeks of mulling, he'd made a choice. He would inform Kit Ruthven of his plans to leave Ruthven's and take the position offered by Wellbeck Publishers.

Why shouldn't he go? He owed no loyalty to the late Leopold Ruthven. The man had been a reprobate, far worse than his family suspected. Only grudgingly, Gabe had come to respect the son. Kit Ruthven trusted him to carry out his duties, rarely questioning or interfering with his management. He even admired the man's determination to share ownership with his sisters. If he'd been lucky enough to inherit anything of value, he'd have happily shared with Sara too.

Of course, Gabe didn't believe in luck. Only in scrabbling and fighting for every scrap of good fortune that came his way.

Change was necessary. He needed the higher salary Wellbeck's offered. He'd been beholden to the Ruthvens for long enough.

Unfolding the letter from Wellbeck's, he smoothed the document on his desktop. Beside it, he poised a nib pen over a fresh sheet of foolscap and began scratching out a formal reply. A moment later, a noise in the outer workroom jolted his attention, and his nib sputtered blots of ink across the paper.

Hell and damnation. Gabe crushed the ruined page in his fist and shot up from his chair. No one ever arrived this bloody early, and he'd secured the door behind him when he'd let himself in.

After shrugging out of his suit coat, he rolled up his sleeves and moved slowly toward the door. He took care to land his boots softly on the polished wood. A distinctive sound froze him in place. Not the rustling that had initially drawn his notice but a steady, rhythmic tick of type bars hitting the platen of a typewriter.

Plastering himself against the frame of his open office door, Gabe gazed across the workroom to get a glimpse of the early morning typist. Irritation flared, and his chest collapsed in a long sigh.

Bent over Daughtry's typewriter, Miss Ruthven swiped a strand of hair from her face and then proceeded to jab haphazardly at the keys. With her back to him, her body curved in a perfect hourglass shape. A single loose curl had slipped its pin, hanging down her back in the same sinuous line. Despite the fact that he'd never entered the workroom to find a lovely woman working away at one of the desks, she looked strangely right perched on Daughtry's chair.

He couldn't lambast her for skulking into the office and commandeering the old man's typewriter. This was her office now. Her business. Her typewriter, if she damn well pleased to use the machine. Apparently, she did.

Gabe cleared his throat as loudly as he dared.

She jumped before turning an irritated glare his way. "You startled me." After an enormous gulp, her tone softened. "I didn't expect anyone so early."

"Likewise."

"Do you always arrive before everyone else?" She collected whatever she'd been composing from the typewriter and turned to face him.

"Always." Gabe gestured toward Daughtry's work space. "What required typing so urgently?"

"Nothing." She shoved the paper behind her.

The movement amused him. How many filched objects had he pushed behind his back or stuffed into his pockets as a child? Once he'd even hidden a stolen pocket watch in his mouth while a constable passed on his nightly rounds. The bitter tang of tarnished metal had lingered on his tongue for days.

"May I?" he asked, palm out, much more politely than any copper had ever cross-questioned him.

She notched up her chin a moment and then relented, shoving the half-covered sheet in front of him. "It's nothing. Truly."

The page smelled of flowers. Gabe wondered if she imprinted her scent on everything she touched. Rows of letters typed over and over were broken with lines of text such as "There was no possibility of taking a walk that day." The words were familiar to Gabe, though he couldn't recall from where.

"I must become proficient with the typewriter. I came early so as not to disturb anyone." She stepped closer and snatched the sheet from his fingers. "Did I disturb you, Mr. Adamson?"

"No," he lied. But she did disturb him. Mightily.

His senses ignited in awareness, every nerve firing. She was the brightest spot in the room, her blouse a bright buttercup yellow that clashed with the darker gold of her hair. And those violet eyes of hers seemed to eat up everything they beheld. She had an eager way of gazing about, as if she was seeing the world for the first time, and every sight fascinated her.

She moved constantly too, like a flower swaying in a stiff breeze. Shuffling her feet, twisting at the hips, she behaved as if the act of standing in one place put a fearsome strain on her patience. "Would you mind if I continue, at least until the other employees arrive?"

Yes, I would mind quite a lot.

"As you wish, Miss Ruthven."

"Will you be at the meeting later this morning, Mr. Adamson?" she put to him over her shoulder after settling herself back into Daughtry's chair.

"Of course." The question irked him, almost as much as her sweet floral scent. Where did she think he'd be? This was his domain. At least for a little while longer. "I'm the one who called the meeting."

As he headed back to his office, a thought struck like a punch to the gut.

He'd miss this damned place—the tidy workroom, the hum of activity when a shipment came in or a new title started production, even the simple orderliness of his desk. Employees like Daughtry, who believed in working as hard as he did to make the enterprise a success, were a rarity. Would he find the same at Wellbeck's?

Then another thought came, and a chill spilled down his back like ice water.

"Will *you* be attending the meeting, Miss Ruthven?"

She shifted her enticing hourglass figure, glanced at him over her shoulder, and shot him an irksome grin. "Since I'm here, I might as well."

Wonderful.

When the bell over the front door jingled at ten minutes to nine, Gabe sprang from his desk, straightened his necktie, and smoothed a hand through his hair, eager to face Kit Ruthven. Requesting a private meeting before the general company weather report must have struck his employer as odd, but Gabe couldn't wait another day.

Sara was right. Time shouldn't be wasted. *Now or never.* That philosophy had saved his skin more than once.

"Is something amiss, Adamson?" Ruthven strode into Gabe's office and stuck out his hand in greeting.

"Not at all, sir, though there is a matter I wish to speak to you about."

Aside from height, they were opposites in every way— background, temperament, and, most starkly, how they viewed the publishing business. Mr. Ruthven pushed for change, regardless of financial prudence. Caution had been a hard-learned lesson for Gabe, but he'd become skilled at avoiding risk and fighting the instinct to run headlong into trouble.

"I have a proposal for you," Ruthven said, seating himself in front of Gabe's desk and hooking his hat over one knee. "But let me hear you out first."

The speech he'd planned petrified in Gabe's throat. Doubts swarmed in.

He should have given Ruthven a chance to pay him more before submitting his resignation. He deserved a higher wage. By any standards, his compensation was meager compared to the responsibility the elder Ruthven had heaped on his shoulders. Other men would have harangued their employer a dozen times already.

"Something's troubling you." Ruthven leaned forward, his elbows braced on his knees as he subjected Gabe to an irritatingly intense stare. "Is it your sister?"

"No, not my sister." In an offhand comment, Gabe had mentioned that Sara was unwell. He'd given no details, and Ruthven must have assumed she was ailing with more than the common cold.

"If there's anything you need. Time away from the office. More help. You need only let me know."

Gabe covered the letter he'd planned to present to Ruthven with his hand. "Mr. Ruthven, after due consideration, I have decided…"

"You seek an increase in compensation."

"Yes." Gabe clenched a fist over the resignation letter.

Kit leaned forward in his chair. "Precisely what I wished to speak to you about."

"Is it?"

"You keep Ruthven's running at a profit. Every member of my family is in your debt. I may not have agreed with my father often. Ever, to be honest, but he made a wise choice when he selected you as manager."

"Thank you, sir," Gabe said, biting out the words. He hated thinking of the elder Ruthven and how he'd acquired his job. But the son's words emboldened him. "What amount had you considered?" He'd carefully calculated the sum needed to provide Sara with a generous dowry and to begin saving for his own future.

"Fifty more pounds per annum?" There was uncertainty in Ruthven's tone, as if he was testing the waters.

The man would have made a rotten gambler. "And an additional sum too, if you're amenable to the project I have in mind."

This *project* made the man's voice rise an octave, and the sound was as clear an alarm bell as Gabe had ever heard. Lengthening his spine, he crossed his hands atop his blotter. "How much more?"

"Shall we say sixty pounds more per annum and an additional twenty pounds for the special project?"

More than Gabe expected. "Tell me of your project, Mr. Ruthven."

Gabe braced himself. If Ruthven meant to prattle on about the costly literary periodical he and his sister wished to start, he'd have difficulty refraining from rolling his eyes.

"My sister Clary..." Ruthven rose from his chair and began pacing.

Gabe's eye twitched.

"I would like you to mentor her, Adamson." Ruthven stopped to stare at him, awaiting a response.

"Mentor her?" Gabe shook his head. "I don't think—" His mind stopped dealing in words. Images arose instead. Clarissa Ruthven wielding her croquet mallet. Glaring at him in the close confines of a hansom cab as his body shifted against hers. Her scent, floral and innocent, sweetening the air of the workroom. The way her garish blouse cast a sunny glow over her pale skin.

He'd never played croquet, he loathed flowers, and yellow was his least favorite color.

"She's impetuous," her brother declared, turning up the palm of one hand to tick fingers on the other. "Reckless, impulsive, but good-hearted. Well-intentioned, even."

"Naïve," Gabe put in.

Ruthven frowned. "Yes, precisely. Since returning from college, Phee and I rarely see her at home. She pursues a thousand causes and busies herself with political meetings, charities, ladies' organizations." Real fear came into the man's eyes. "I worry for her safety and her reputation."

"I understand." Gabe worried about his sister too. "But where do I come in?"

Kit resumed his seat but only settled his bulk on the edge. "Clary wishes to learn more about the workings of Ruthven's. Employment is her true goal, though she has no experience whatsoever. Teach her. Show her how you manage the accounts and the employees. Hell, let her learn to operate one of the printing presses. She could sit in on meetings with vendors, review submissions. Assist you with your work."

For the first time since meeting the man, Gabriel realized how successful Ruthven must have been on the stage. How convincing his performances. He might have a terrible poker face, but he was managing to make a horrific idea sound utterly logical. Even beneficial, when Gabe knew with absolutely certainty that having Clarissa Ruthven underfoot would lead to nothing but trouble.

"I really don't think—"

"Seventy-five pounds more per year." Ruthven flashed a smile. "I should warn you that I'm tempted to keep upping the offer until you agree."

Gabe was glad he never let Ruthven near negotiations with vendors. And what he said wasn't entirely true. He couldn't keep upping his salary. Gabe knew better than anyone that the company's ledgers couldn't bear an overpaid office manager.

Still, the amount was tempting. Almost double his current income and far more than Wellbeck's offer.

"Clary can be a handful. I admit that."

Gabe didn't want to think of his hands anywhere near her. If he touched her, he'd no doubt come away smelling like violets or roses or whatever floral scent she wore. But at least he'd be warm. That energy of hers was like an ever-burning fire.

"An additional one-time payment of twenty-five for taking on what I know may be time-consuming." Ruthven crossed his arms, hardening his features. All the mirth was gone, replaced with steely determination. "I'm asking for your help, Adamson. I don't want her wandering into some unsavory situation. As you said, she's naïve. Too trusting. Too idealistic. She's going to make mistakes, as we all do, but I'd prefer she make them here."

"Where you can protect her from the consequences?"

"Where I can protect her, full stop."

If his own sister was as unpredictable and carefree as Miss Ruthven, Gabe would wish to protect her too. But he still didn't like the prospect of having Clarissa Ruthven here, in his space, garishly dressed and glaring at him with those odd amethyst eyes. Yet…he wasn't a man without strategies. Surely there were tasks he could find to occupy her time. She claimed she wished to master the typewriter. He could assign Daughtry to offer her instruction. If she wished to learn the workings of the presses, he could ship her down the road to the machines they leased, rather than observing those they kept on-site.

With a little effort, he could outwit a hellion.

"Perhaps—"

"Yes!" Ruthven whooped, nearly dancing a jig across the bare wood floor of Gabe's office. "I knew you'd see reason. Clary will come around too. Trust me."

Gabe rarely trusted anyone, but what disturbed him most was the man's reference to persuading his sister. "Mr. Ruthven, your sister is *aware* of this plan, isn't she?"

"Not every detail." Ruthven ducked his head to stare at the toes of his boots. When he looked up, his actor's mask faltered. Worry etched lines across his forehead. "She will agree. We'll convince her."

"We?"

"I'm willing to up your salary by as much as a hundred pounds. Surely, that will encourage you to take her on."

Gabe wanted the money, no doubts on that score. But he wasn't at all certain he was the man to convince Miss Ruthven to agree to her brother's scheme. He suspected she'd be more amenable if Ruthven promised she could avoid Gabe for the duration.

"How long do you intend this"—Gabe couldn't bring himself to refer to the man's sister as a project—"mentorship will last?"

Ruthven shrugged. "As long as it takes."

"Until?"

He sketched vaguely in the air. "Until she's matured and has learned a few skills. Until she's more sensible and less impulsive. Until I'm not worried every time she walks out the door."

While Ruthven fretted, Gabe surreptitiously pulled his resignation letter from the desk and crumpled it in his fist. One hundred pounds for a brief period of misery. No, that wasn't quite true. If Ruthven's stated goals were true, this project might last a very, very long time.

"So we've settled the matter?" Ruthven coaxed.

Gabe stood and offered his hand. "We have, sir."

"Excellent." Leaning in and lowering his voice, Ruthven added, "Best not to mention every detail to Clary. Especially the matter of the pay rise and additional bonus."

"Of course not, sir." Bribery might taste excellent when one's desired ends were achieved, but it never settled well in the belly. Gabe knew that better than most.

Just as they broke off their handshake, Daughtry burst into the office. "Pardon me, gentlemen. Mr. Adamson, you're wanted in the workroom, sir. Your sister is here and says she must speak with you urgently."

CHAPTER SIX

"This way." Gabe led Sara through the rain, lifting his overcoat over her head to provide shelter as they headed to a nearby coffeehouse. She'd refused to enter his office and carry on a conversation in front of the clerks in the workroom.

"I don't wish to disturb your workday." Breathless and shaking, she settled into the straight-back chair he pulled out for her. With a hand to her chest, she wheezed out her words. "I thought you should know straightaway."

"Tell me what's wrong." Gabe lifted two fingers in the air, and a waiter nodded. As a devotee of the shop's dark, smoky brew, most of the staff knew him well. A moment later, the young man deposited mugs that puffed like the stacks of a steam train.

"I ventured out for a bit of a wander," Sara started on a whisper. "Just around the square. They were cuttin' the grass. You know I can't resist that smell. Heavenly, it is."

There hadn't been much fresh-cut grass in Whitechapel, and they'd both come to treasure such a simple luxury.

She took a quick sip of coffee, wincing at the stinging heat. After another wheezing breath, she inclined toward him, leaning on the table. "I stopped to take in the spring flowers, and that's when I saw him. I swear it was him, Gabe."

Dizziness came like a wave, and he grasped the ceramic mug in front of him, letting its scalding heat ground him. Worry gnawed at his belly, a familiar chewing he hadn't experienced in years. He shook his head, trying to deny it, but he knew. He could see the proof in his sister's eyes. For so many years, they'd been safe. They'd forgotten the most important lesson of the East End: always watch your back.

"Did he speak to you?"

"Not a word. Soon as I seen 'im, 'e scarpered like the rotter 'e is." She always fell into pure Cockney when something got her back up. With a hand still pressed to her chest, she worked to steady her breathing.

"You're sure you saw *him*?" He had to ask. He wanted her to waver.

"Tried to convince myself I was mistaken. That I'd dredged up some nightmare." She tapped a finger against the table. "It was him, Gabe. The devil himself."

So this was the reckoning. The devil had vowed to come knocking. As soon as Gabe got his first taste of success. He'd promised to make whatever Gabe touched turned to dust. Swore to haunt him for the rest of his days.

Unfortunately, Malcolm Rigg wasn't a ghost.

"Go back home." Gabe removed a few coins from his pocket. "No more wandering today. Get a cab, and bolt the doors once you're inside. Answer to no one."

"I don't fear for myself. That old goat can't keep me trapped inside." Sara swept back a strand of dark hair, as black as his own, and gazed at him with sadness in her eyes. "Truth is, he never cared a farthing about me. Just wish I could keep him from causing you more misery."

Misery was just the start of what Rigg could bring. Pain, blood, death—they all followed in the old bastard's wake.

Gabe wouldn't let him destroy what he had. He'd escaped the cage of his past and made a new life. He'd be damned if he'd let Rigg snuff that out.

The man had already taken enough blood from him. He couldn't have any more.

Clothes wet, hair disheveled, the high cut of his cheeks flush with color, Gabriel Adamson stormed into the meeting room at Ruthven Publishing as if striding into battle.

Clary tipped her head and studied him.

The one constant every other time she'd seen Adamson was that he took care with his appearance, adding to his nature-given beauty by dressing in fine suits, tailored to fit as if the cloth had been stitched straight onto his bulk.

Today, he looked wild.

Clary couldn't take her eyes off him.

"Adamson," her brother called, "glad you could join us." Kit lifted his gaze to a wall clock.

Clary thought Kit's gesture unnecessary. Anyone watching could see that Adamson's tardiness horrified him more than it inconvenienced anyone else. He'd already extracted his pocket watch and shoved the timepiece back in his pocket, as if the sight made him ill.

"I was delayed," he explained.

"But you're here now," Sophia put in, always one to restore order and put others at ease. "Shall we begin?"

Adamson took the empty chair next to Clary and busied himself extracting a fountain pen from his pocket. Drops of the rain fell from his clothes and hair onto the stretch of table between them.

"Pardon me, Miss Ruthven," he muttered through clenched teeth, brushing the water from the table.

"You needn't worry." Clary leaned in and caught the scents of damp linen and sandalwood shaving soap. "I have a dreadful habit of being late."

"I don't," he snapped, casting her a fearsome glare, his clear blue gaze boring into hers. "I was unavoidably delayed."

"I hope you didn't intervene in another altercation," Clary whispered, unable to resist a bit of levity to ease the thundercloud he'd brought into the room with him.

"Next time I see a reckless young woman battling an intoxicated bully," he mumbled under his breath, "I'll be sure to walk the other way."

"Thank you all for being here. Today we have a new addition to the administrative board. Clary, as pleased as I am to see you take your place as co-owner of Ruthven's, the fact that you're old enough to do so makes me feel ancient." Kit shot her a toothy smile before gesturing toward their manager. "Adamson, please begin by reporting on the business's financial health in the last quarter."

Next to her, Adamson opened a folder full of papers and ran a broad finger across rows and columns of numbers written in ruler-straight lines.

Clary drummed her fingers on top of her own folder, stopping when her sister shot her a disapproving look.

"The accounts have taken a positive turn," Adamson began, his voice so deep the reverberation rumbled through her. "The updated volumes of *Ruthven Rules* have increased overall sales, and the new lines in popular fiction have, individually, outsold our main etiquette book lines. The collection of detective stories we've published is selling best, which includes Lady Stanhope's tales, of course."

He lifted his gaze briefly to acknowledge Sophia, whose lips parted before lighting in a smile, as if she was both pleased and shocked by the news of her books' success.

"For the coming year, we will proceed with plans to expand our fiction offerings and have invested in a chromolithograph machine, housed upstairs, for the publication of the literary journal. The chromo allows for a color printing process, and four of our clerks have been trained in its operation."

"What journal?" Clary leaned forward. The prospect sounded intriguing, but no one had mentioned a word to her.

Kit and Sophia exchanged a look, and Kit scooted his chair closer to the table, bracing his elbows on the edge. "We've been discussing the notion for some time. Since we're a family of writers and have come to know many more while living in London, we thought of creating a showcase for excellent writing."

"Perhaps you could submit one of your stories," Sophia suggested. "Or some of your art. We intend to include color illustrations."

Both of Clary's siblings knew she'd been writing and drawing for years, though as a child she'd been reluctant to show her work to anyone. The urge to publish had arisen off and on, but more than any acclaim for her creative endeavors, she wished to help the girls at the charity school.

She had a notion of how to do so and hoped others would see the merit in her plan.

"Actually, I have another idea." Her voice wobbled a bit, and she hated the quiver of uncertainty chasing through her body. Stiffening her back, she started again. "May I present a proposal?"

Sophia began to answer, but Kit cut in. "Is there anything more, Adamson?"

"Only to distribute these." He'd made duplicates of the quarterly report and passed copies down the table. After closing his folio and folding his massive hands on top, he cast Clary an expectant look. "Please proceed, Miss Ruthven."

His insistence that she take her turn to speak felt strangely like encouragement, though she doubted he meant it as such.

Unable to contain the nervousness buzzing through her body, Clary stood and pushed back her chair. She carefully extracted the sheaves of paper where she'd detailed her plan. "I volunteer at a girls' charity school in the East End."

Gabriel Adamson shifted his chair to watch her.

At the other end of the room, her brother braced his arms across his chest. "Where you disappear to all hours of the day and night."

"Kit," Sophia whispered, "this isn't the time."

"I would like to start a ladies' magazine, one that is organized, managed, and produced by women."

"Excluding men entirely? That seems unfair." The small, bespectacled Mr. Daughtry, assistant to Mr. Adamson, was a man of few words, but his burst of indignation echoed off the office walls.

Clary turned to face the older man. "Can you see through that window into the main office, sir?"

"I work there every day, Miss Ruthven."

"Yes, but do take a look now and indulge me."

With a huff of frustration, the diminutive man got to his feet, leaned over the table, and peered through the magnifying lenses of his pince-nez spectacles. "I can attest that it is indeed the workroom, Miss Ruthven."

"Would you kindly count the number of females you see in the workroom, Mr. Daughtry?"

Like an accordion folding slowly in on itself, his brow furrowed into deep lines. "There are no young ladies at work in the Ruthven Publishing office."

"So you see, sir, excluding gentlemen from my project won't create an inequality as much as rectify one." She winked at him, and he blushed a furious pink. "Even the score, so to speak."

A feminine chuckle emerged from Sophia at the opposite end of the table. When Clary glanced down, a slow grin tipped the edge of Kit's mouth.

Beside her, Adamson cleared his throat. "While the concept of employing numerous young women to right society's wrongs may appeal to you, I am charged with seeing to the financial health of Ruthven Publishing."

"And you've done a fine job, Adamson." Kit's declaration caught Clary off guard. The two were overdoing the mutual masculine respect a bit.

"Thank you, Mr. Ruthven." Even as he thanked her brother, Adamson continued to stare at her, as if he'd posed a question and waited on her to answer.

Clary crossed her arms. She hadn't yet revealed the best part of her proposal.

"Your idea must be financially viable, Miss Ruthven," Adamson added. "Who will buy copies of your ladies' magazine?"

Clary leaned toward him, though not close enough for him to turn her into an overheated ninny as he had in the carriage. "The answer you seek is in the name. *Ladies'* magazine."

"So, a publication written by women to be purchased by women," Sophia explained helpfully.

"Exactly." Clary cast her sister a grin of gratitude. She lifted a clipped rectangle of newsprint from her folder. "This article and others I've collected indicate that women drive consumption of magazines and reading material in their households."

"Why?" Adamson queried. He was like a buzzing fly, determined to dive in and spoil her soup.

"Why what?" The two words emerged on a frustrated growl. The man truly did have the worst effect on her.

"Why will women wish to purchase your particular publication? New ladies' magazines spring up every year. Many fail. What will yours offer that's unique? Why should a lady buy yours rather than the dozens of others sitting at newsagents' as we speak?"

"Fashion is a fine lure," Mr. Daughtry suggested. "My wife can never get enough of frippery magazines."

Clary held very still and fought the urge to roll her eyes. Eye rolling wouldn't do when she was trying to convince everyone she could manage a publication project on her own. "Fashion won't be the focus. This magazine will be appealing to the eye, of course, with color art and illustrations, but the main impetus will be to inform ladies of social and political news of the day. Provide insight on ways they might contribute and organize to support causes they care about."

She didn't have to look at Gabriel Adamson to note his disdain. He'd begun tapping his fountain pen like an insistent drumbeat against the tabletop.

"Perhaps we should discuss this matter further at home," Kit suggested from the far end of the table. He was using his soft, brotherly voice.

"This is a business proposal, Kit. I wish for the board to consider my proposal as a business matter."

Kit released a sigh and focused his gaze on Adamson, who was bubbling like a boiling pot at Clary's side, eager to release a cloud of steam.

"How many young women do you plan to employ?" he asked her.

"Ten. Perhaps more." Clary hoped to offer work to as many young women as she could, with special consideration to be given to those graduating from the Fisk Academy.

Mr. Adamson uncapped his fountain pen and began scratching notes onto the paper under his hand, finally drawing a slash at the bottom of a list of figures. "I can only estimate costs and guess at potential sales, but I fear investment in such a venture would not be repaid for years. If at all."

"I only expect to utilize the printing facilities. The new chromolithograph press sounds perfect for our purposes. Otherwise, the project will fund itself." They couldn't object. She'd keep the project self-sustaining. A surge of victory filled Clary. If she'd been a balloon, she would have floated up among the clouds. "The income from the journal will be used to pay the young women employed in its production and produce new issues. Any overage, we can count as a profit. We'll only need an initial outlay of funds, and I shall take on the project of finding that money."

Something was amiss.

Her explanation should have satisfied everyone, yet no one at the table looked pleased. Mr. Daughtry stared at her as if she'd lost her head, Sophia nibbled her bottom lip nervously, and Kit looked completely befuddled. She didn't bother looking at Gabriel Adamson. It was bad enough that his black hair had dried into the most distracting waves and that his clean scent was tickling her nose.

"How do you plan to find those funds, my dear?" Sophia's voice was a welcome interruption in the tense silence.

"With a charity ball." Clary had initially hated the idea, but Helen convinced her. The wealthy loved balls, she insisted, and they'd need the wealthy to collect donations for both Fisk Academy and *The Ladies' Clarion*, as Clary had decided to title the periodical.

Sophia looked at Kit. Kit cast a gaze at Mr. Daughtry, and Adamson stood, hovering at her side. The broad length of him blocked the light from the room's single window.

"I can leave this discussion, if you prefer, Mr. Ruthven," he said to her brother, ignoring her completely, as if her proposal wasn't the current matter up for discussion. "This sounds like a charity endeavor rather than a business matter."

"Why can't it be both? And of course you can't depart," Clary snapped. "This project will involve the use of paper, printers, and supplies that fall under your management."

"Very well." He didn't take a chair but strode to the window, positioning himself to recline against the sill. All the better to glare directly at her.

"I'm afraid Adamson is right." Kit ran a hand through his hair and stared at her in confusion. "We cannot use charity donations to run an enterprise from which we hope to turn a profit. That would be unethical."

Clary's throat closed, as if her collar had been cinched too tightly around her neck. Then the tightness spread, as if someone was twisting the laces of her corset like a vice. "Unethical is the state in which many girls live, while others flourish a few miles away. If we cannot do both, then I shall view this as a charitable endeavor entirely. Not a project to earn a profit. Why can't Ruthven's undertake a philanthropic effort? Father never gave a dime to anyone he didn't owe."

"Not even then, at times," Kit groused.

"Initially, we can employ young ladies from Fisk Academy to run the magazine. Perhaps Helen could arrange for their work to earn them credit toward graduation. This could reduce the cost of salaries initially."

Adamson moved in her periphery, sweeping a hand across his mouth. "Running the presses costs money, so unless we wish to take a loss, some funds will need to be repaid to Ruthven's."

Sophia pushed away from the table and crossed her arms before lifting a hand to fiddle with the broach at her neck. Clary recognized her sister's pondering stance. "Perhaps a scheme could be worked out to donate use of the lithograph machine for the magazine project. Clary does have a point. Ruthven's has never engaged in any sort of philanthropy."

"Because we are a business and wish to earn a profit," Kit insisted. He stood too, as if to emphasize his point.

Only Mr. Daughtry remained seated, and he seemed supremely entertained by the tense debate.

"We are turning a profit," Clary noted. "And a healthy one, according to Mr. Adamson." She risked a glance at him, and he narrowed his gaze, as if irritated to have his report used in support of her idea. A moment later, he strode toward her and scooped up his folio from the table.

"I'm not sure we can accommodate the project, Clary." Kit sounded disappointed, but his voice was firm. "We plan to add new titles each month for the rest of the year, not to mention the literary journal we plan to produce. When would the presses be used for your charity venture?"

"More etiquette books?" She couldn't keep the derision from her tone.

"Updated etiquette books," Sophia said defensively. "A few years ago, you assisted us to update the ladies' *Ruthven Rules*."

Frustration twisted Clary's stomach in knots. "What is the point of teaching gentleman to be more gentlemanly or ladies to be more ladylike?" She swiped a stray hair behind her ear and dislodged a hairpin, which plinked onto the table.

A massive hand burst into her line of vision, collecting the bent metal.

A moment later, Adamson engulfed her hand in his, turned her palm up, and deposited the hairpin in the center. Just as suddenly, he let her go, and Clary clenched her fingers around the pin.

His eyes had taken on a shuttered aspect, but she could detect emotion beneath the surface of cool blue. Pity lurked in that bright gaze of his, and seeing it was far worse than Kit's treating her idea like a child's improbable fancy.

Collecting her notes, she stuffed them into her folder and clutched the whole to her chest. "I'll figure out a way to do this, with or without Ruthven's." Pivoting on her heel, she stomped to the door, then turned back. "And if we're going to produce more etiquette books, at least let them be useful."

"Such as?" Adamson asked, with more interest than she would have expected.

"How to succeed in business." She glowered at her brother. "How to remain healthy into one's dotage." Mr. Daughtry perked up at that suggestion. *How not to be affected by an insufferably handsome man.* Or better yet, how to make such a man realize a brilliant idea when he hears one. "How to woo a wallflower," she sputtered and marched from the room.

Chapter Seven

———————————————————

"Clary, don't rush off." Kit was on her heels as she made her way through the workroom. "Hear me out, would you?"

"Is there anything more to say?" Still vibrating with frustrated energy, she spun to face him and found half the clerks gaping their way.

"Yes, quite a lot, actually. I have a proposal to speak to you about." He said *proposal* without a hint of irony, somehow failing to realize she'd just presented one that mattered to her and had been soundly rejected.

He gestured toward a long storage space at the edge of the workroom. Apparently, Mr. Adamson was the only one at Ruthven's who merited an office.

Clary followed Kit into the tidy, well-lit space, and she was surprised to find a long table and chairs tucked inside. A perfect place for a group of young women to sort out a ladies' magazine project.

"Will you sit?" he asked, gesturing toward a chair.

"I prefer to stand." At least then she could move, pace. Her blood was fizzing in her veins, and sitting primly had never been her style.

"Very well." Kit chafed his hands together. "You wish to seek employment?"

"You know I do." She began to pace, wary of what he'd suggest next. "If you're going to attempt to prevent me—"

"Why not work at Ruthven's?"

Gabriel Adamson.

There were other reasons, surely, but he was the first thought that came to mind. "I would prefer to make my own way. Find a position on my own merits."

"You have no experience." He stepped in front of her to stop her pacing, as if keeping her still would forestall the retorts brewing in her mind. "A fine education, I'll grant you that, but why not gain a bit of experience here? You said you wish to know more about how Ruthven's is run. I saw you banging at the typewriter when we came in." His amused grin was maddening.

"I was not banging. I was practicing. Learning to hit the keys in the right order takes time. Plus, I lack speed."

"You could learn with more practice. And if you spent more time at Ruthven's, you could practice all you like."

"No." She hated it when he made sense. Impulsive, she might be, but she found logical arguments hard to resist.

Clary sidestepped past him and resumed pacing, biting her nail as she considered her options. She'd visited two employment agencies, and neither had responded with much eagerness. They had mentioned her lack of experience too. But working for her own family's business was a half measure.

Stepping forward but with leading strings still attached. "How would it work? Since I'm now on the board, how could I be employed by the business?"

"I'll speak to Whitaker about that," Kit said, looking far too pleased with himself. Far too ready to claim victory. "But I thought, at least at first, we could consider your role a mentorship. I'm sure we can arrange a stipend. Enough to pay rent, if you're still determined to secure your own lodgings."

"I am." A mentorship? Which meant she would have a mentor. She looked out toward Adamson's office, and her heart kicked into a wild hammering in her chest. *No.* She shook her head. "I don't wish to be mentored by Mr. Adamson."

"Who else would know as much about Ruthven's?" Once again, he had a point she could not refute. "Clary, I think your ladies' magazine might have merit if you can secure initial financing with your charity ball. Bring the matter to the next board meeting in three months, and we all can reassess the costs and what Ruthven's could donate."

Clary slid her brother a rueful glance. As much as Kit raged against their father's manipulative ways, he was not above adopting Papa's habit of wielding leverage to get his way.

But both of them had learned negotiation from their father. Clary wasn't willing to give in and get nothing in return. "I'd prefer to call a special board meeting to consider the magazine project again in one month's time." Why wait to begin helping the girls of Fisk Academy?

"You'll devote yourself to this endeavor?" Kit assessed her. "You'll put your focus and energies here, rather than at your charities and ladies' unions?"

Goodness, he really did intend to cage her. "If I'm here for a full workday, that will curtail my time for volunteer work. I expected as much once I found a position."

He clenched his jaw, his throat working as if he wished to say more. But he was wise enough to know she would not concede everything. "I'll agree to a month. In the meantime, consult with Adamson to come up with a workable plan for financing your magazine venture beyond the charity ball."

A grin twitched at the corners of her mouth, despite her best intentions. A few years earlier, her brother had been a playwright and a rogue with a dreadful reputation. Now he spoke of business with almost as much knowledge as Mr. Adamson. Perhaps he'd learned something from their surly manager.

The man himself had come out into the workroom. She could feel him, hear his heavy footsteps, smell his scent in the air.

Kit stepped toward Clary and stuck out his hand. She hesitated, still uncertain of his plan. Adamson lording over her for weeks? The prospect held no appeal, yet she knew there were far worse employers in London. The girls at Fisk weighed on her mind too. How eager they'd be when they heard about her plans for employing some of them. And Helen was already making preparations for the fundraising ball.

Clary reached for Kit's hand to seal the bargain they'd struck.

"Adamson." Kit's call brought the man closer.

He stood inches from her elbow, a dark blur in her periphery. He still smelled of rain.

"I've convinced her," Kit declared proudly.

Clary quirked her brow. "You two conspired to come up with this plan?"

"You make it sound dastardly." Kit ruined his mock offense with a guilty guffaw.

"Not everyone has a temperament for mentoring," Adamson declared, without a hint of amusement.

"Not sure you're up to the task, Mr. Adamson?"

"I was referring to you, Miss Ruthven. The receiving of instruction, not the giving." He bit off each word, his full lips barely parting, as if he didn't wish to express a syllable more than was required.

"I've always been an excellent student, Mr. Adamson."

"We shall see," he said ominously.

She found herself staring at Mr. Adamson's mouth, wondering if he'd let any more syllables escape.

But Kit spoke next, and she forced herself to stop staring at her soon-to-be mentor and listen to her brother.

"Can you start today?" her brother asked. "You could continue on the typewriter." He gestured toward the one she'd been using, and Mr. Daughtry glanced up in wide-eyed horror, his nose twitching like a rabbit's.

Adamson gestured toward the older man. "Daughtry, Miss Ruthven will be working in the office for a while. We'll need to find her a desk. In the meantime, teach her everything you know about typewriters." With that, he dipped his chin in the merest of acknowledgments and strode back to his office.

Mr. Daughtry waved her over, and Kit patted her arm, offering a pleased smile, before she followed the old man back to his desk. A moment later Kit joined Adamson at the threshold of the management office. They spoke in low tones, and Clary strained to listen in on their exchange as Mr. Daughtry launched into a recitation of the various parts of a typewriter.

One word carried across the room because Kit pronounced it with extra emphasis. *Whitechapel.*

So this *was* about containing her.

Kit judged East End by its reputation for crime and skullduggery, refusing to consider that most of its habitants only wished for a day's work, food in their bellies, and a home to keep them warm. Not so different from his well-off businessmen neighbors in Bloomsbury Square.

She wasn't oblivious to the city's dangers, but she wouldn't allow fear to hem her in.

After Kit departed, Adamson rooted himself at his office doorway, taking up the whole width of the frame. Arms crossed, he observed her interactions with Daughtry and the other clerks. Even with her back to him, she sensed the press of Gabriel Adamson's gaze, the intensity with which he noted her every move.

Allow him to teach her about her family's business? Yes, she could do that. But if Kit thought Adamson would serve as her watcher, he was utterly mistaken.

End-of-day sounds filtered into Gabe's office, and chatter rose in the workroom as clerks prepared to depart for the evening.

Between worry for Sara, rage at the notion of Malcolm Rigg invading their lives again, and the distracting presence of Clarissa Ruthven, he'd accomplished little. She'd avoided him, as he expected her to do. But he'd never forgotten she was a few feet away. Like a buzzing in his ears, she electrified the air.

He'd noted that Daughtry had warmed to her as the afternoon progressed. An hour ago he'd peered into the workroom to find the pair laughing, as if they'd known each other for an age. In the years Gabe had worked with the man, Daughtry had rarely laughed and never had said anything even remotely amusing. One day in *her* presence and the old clerk had discovered a sense of humor.

Gabe had debated storming into the workroom to put an end to their frivolity, but they'd both looked up as if sensing his displeasure. Soon after, Miss Ruthven resumed her spot in Daughtry's chair, her hands poised over the typewriter keys.

Her presence exhausted Gabe, if only from the effort of trying to ignore her.

"Good night, sir." A clerk strode past on his way toward the building's exit.

Gabe nodded at the young man and stood to roll his shoulders, a useless attempt to ease the tension that had built in his neck and back. The outer office emptied, and Gabe watched his doorway, expecting Daughtry's arrival. Each day he summarized attendance and productivity for the clerks under his supervision. On cue, the older man ambled in and placed his daily report on the edge of Gabe's desk.

"She's gone, then?" Gabe took up his assistant's report, keeping his gaze trained on the words and numbers.

"Aye, sir. Just stepped out the front door." Daughtry didn't leave after delivering his report. He mumbled to himself, shuffling his feet, as he always did when he had news he did not wish to convey.

"What is it?"

"Not sure I should say." His eyes went wistful behind his spectacles. "Wouldn't want to get the lass into any sort of trouble."

"She's not a child, Daughtry." Gabe rolled his hand in the air. "Out with it, man."

After a maddening period of indecision, he blurted, "Say she's going to the East End this evening, sir. Some charity school there she's keen on supporting."

Bloody rotting hell. He lifted the master key from his desk and tossed the bit of metal at his assistant. "Lock up." Bursting out of Ruthven's front door, he stopped and scanned the pavement to the east and west. Half a mile away, he spotted her striding toward a lane of hansom cabs. Racing toward her, he sidestepped around a gaggle of ladies fussing over a pram and nearly knocked a top-hatted gentleman to the ground.

"Miss Ruthven!" The shout emerged so loud he captured the attention of half the Londoners making their evening journey home.

"You're not thinking of stopping me, are you, Mr. Adamson?" Her eyes glowed with determination, and her shoulders quivered like a bird on the verge of taking flight.

"Your brother is concerned about your ventures to the East End. And I take it you don't plan to heed my advice not to return to Whitechapel."

"I'm aware of Kit's worries, and I do recall your warning, but I can see after myself." She turned away from him and lifted a hand to catch the notice of a cabbie.

"Only fools are fearless, Miss Ruthven." The lady was so bloody blithe, so sure of herself when she had no real notion of the city's dangers. Beyond her youth, there was a freshness about her, an innocence that irked him. She was optimistic and full of possibility.

She was everything he'd never been.

And she was undeniably a fool. She wore her impulsivity and recklessness like a badge of honor. He'd thought perhaps her years away at a ladies' college would have curbed her fool-hardy tendencies and taught her a bit of poise and polish. If anything, her education had emboldened her. She carried herself with confidence now, as if she relished her uniqueness and would never bow to anyone's expectations or to society's rules.

"You're naïve," he told her.

Shards of violet stabbed at him when she turned her gaze his way. "I've been to Fisk Academy dozens of times."

It only took once. One attack, one strike of a knife, one man determined to cause a woman misery.

"No harm has ever befallen me in Whitechapel."

Gabe arched a brow.

"Mr. Keene was emboldened by drink. He'd never caused any real trouble before, and I'm sure he won't again."

Ah, yes, because angry, frustrated men rarely turned to the bottle twice. If he was a gambler, Gabe would put money on the rotter returning and doing much worse. Wounded male pride led to every brand of malfeasance.

The cab she'd hailed took on a passenger and rolled away. She moved farther down the pavement to seek another.

Letting her go was the easiest option. But Gabe was caught, as he'd been so many times, between self-interest and doing a noble deed. For most of his life he'd chosen selfish-ness and survival, and he yearned to do so now. He needed to get home and check on Sara. Clarissa Ruthven was a grown woman and damnably determined to make her own choices. No matter how reckless.

He started back toward the corner where he caught the omnibus each night. Let the little fool go to her char-ity school. What she did with her free time was none of his concern. Yet even as he reasoned with himself, some dam-nable magnetic force drew him back. Turning on his heel, he covered the pavement he'd just traversed with long, burning strides.

Gabe sized her up as he would an opponent in the ring, considering how she would defend herself, what danger she might pose to an assailant. She was petite, many inches shorter than his six feet, and amply curved. Overpowering her would not be difficult for any fiend wishing to do her harm, but with speed and skill, her size could become an asset.

"Come with me," he said when he reached her side.

"I'm not going anywhere with you, Mr. Adamson."

"Over there." Gabe pointed to a narrow alley that led to a mews behind the row of buildings.

She planted a hand on one hip. "You want me to follow you into a dark lane?"

"Just for a moment. Trust me." He started toward the mouth of the alley, doubting she'd follow. But then he heard her boot heels clicking a path toward him.

Positioning herself a few feet away, she crossed her arms and sighed. She was still too far away, too visible to pedestri-ans passing by, for Gabe's taste. But it would have to do.

"Hit me," he told her.

She tipped her head and stared at him as if debating whether madness had overtaken him. Then laughter bubbled up, a lush throaty sound, far deeper than the titter she'd treated Daughtry to earlier. Hearing her amusement made his chest tickle. Other parts of him responded to the sound too.

"Come, Miss Ruthven. I don't have all night. Make as if you're going to strike."

All at once, she seemed to recognize his intention. She squared her shoulders, loosened her stance, and balled her hand.

"Your thumb is sticking up," he instructed. "Let it rest on your clenched fingers."

Following his direction, she bent her thumb and lunged toward him. But before she swung out to strike, she wound back too far. Gabe arched away, and she stumbled forward. He caught her arm to steady her.

"Rounding back gives your opponent more time to avoid your swing. A closer jab is more effective."

Quick as a flash, she raised her free arm and jerked a fist toward his face. Gabe caught the force of her punch against his palm.

"Good speed," he praised. "But you lack control."

At that she emitted a little growl of frustration and stepped away from him. After rubbing a hand over the spot where he'd caught her arm, she unbuttoned her cuffs and rolled up the sleeves of her shirtwaist. "What else?" Hands on her hips, she blew a strand of hair from her face. "Teach me."

"Come closer and I will."

She closed most of the distance between them. "Did my brother put you up to this?"

"No." If her brother knew he'd put his hands on her, Ruthven would have his head on a spike.

"Knowing how to defend yourself and having the opportunity to do so are two different things." And a Whitechapel thug would never give a lady time to get her fists up.

"My goodness, you're as pessimistic as my brother."

"Realistic." He lifted a hand to her. "A little closer."

She obeyed but warily, her steps short and hesitant. "Why?"

"As you demonstrated with Keene, certain parts of the body are vulnerable. But there are other spots. Higher. Easier to reach." He raised his thumb, folding the rest of his fingers back. "The eyes." He reached up and made a hooking motion near her eye.

She blinked, a quick fan of thick lashes, but she didn't pull away. In fact, she studied him closely, her breath feathering heat against his face as he dropped his gaze to her neck. She'd undone the top buttons of her shirtwaist, and the long stretch of smooth skin beyond made his mouth water. He knew how she'd taste. Like the flowery scent he could smell wafting off her skin. He reminded himself that he hated flowers.

"The throat," he said huskily.

"How would I strike a man's throat?" She lifted a loosely clenched fist, pushing it to the knot of his tie. "You gentleman have the protection of your haberdasheries." Gaze fixed on his necktie, she bit her lip. "Unless I got a good hold." She slipped a warm finger between the fabric of his shirt collar and the skin of his throat.

The contact sent a ribbon of heat down his body, straight to the base of his spine. Warmth spilled through his blood.

"No." Gabe grabbed her wrist and pulled her hand free. "Never get snagged on your assailant. Your objective is to get free."

She stared at the place where he held her. Without realizing, he'd begun stroking his thumb across her soft skin. Her gaze locked on his. Her lips parted, breath quickening. Inch by inch, the even curves of her mouth tilted in a grin.

The little hellion was enjoying this. But it wasn't a game. The skills he could teach her might mean the difference between life and death.

One lunging step, and he drew close to her. Gripping her shoulders, he spun her away from him, then lashed an arm across her chest. He held her lightly but far too close.

"Try to free yourself." He could feel her hair against his cheek. Feel her heartbeat under his arm. Feel the energy— that wild, frenetic voltage she exuded—pulsing through her.

"Truly?" She turned her head, and her mouth came dangerously close to his. "I don't wish to injure you."

Her words almost pulled a chuckle from him. With her backside riding his groin, and her hair tickling his chin, he was fairly certain whatever came next would be a relief. "Do your worst."

She tipped her head farther, until she could look him in the eye. "Remember you said that." In two swift moves, she jerked her right arm up, bent at the elbow, and thrust back against his midriff.

He grunted at the impact. But he'd already tensed his stomach muscles, anticipating her blow. "You've forgotten what I told you," he whispered near her ear. "Vulnerable. Soft."

Reaching the same arm up, she pressed a palm to the scruffy edge of his cheek, then slid her hand up until she reached his temple. Striking out a thumb, she tried for his eye. Gabe arched back but didn't release her.

"Good," he said when she lowered her arm and settled back against him.

He should have released her. But now that she was in his arms, he found himself stubbornly unwilling to let go.

"I could bite." She placed both hands on his arm where he'd wrapped it across her upper chest, tucking her chin down as if looking for a tasty spot.

"Unless your attacker is bare, or you're capable of chewing through layers of fabric, you wouldn't do much damage." He tapped his thumb against her arm where he held her. "Fingers are useful."

"Are they?" She turned to look at him again, a frown pinching the skin between her brows. "Ah!" she exclaimed as she gripped his thumb and wrenched it backward at a painfully odd angle.

Proving his point, he edged away from her to break her hold. Despite the inches of distance he'd created, her heat and scent still clung to him.

She faced him, bouncing on her toes, smiling as if her horse had just won the Derby. "I did it," she crowed.

If by "did it" she meant stirring him in ways he hadn't been affected in years, yes. He was damnably aroused. And by the one woman he could never touch. So, of course, being the wrongheaded fool he was, he'd touched her. And he'd bloody enjoyed every minute.

"Lesson over." He backed two steps away. Hiding himself in the alley's darkness, he flicked a hand toward the cab stand. "Go and secure a hansom, Miss Ruthven."

She marched up to him instead. "Thank you. That was a truly valuable lesson. I feel safer already."

With the sliver of self-restraint he had left, Gabe managed not to roll his eyes. He'd taught her a fraction of what he knew. He'd meant to equip her, not make her feel more oblivious to danger.

"Watch your back in Whitechapel, Miss Ruthven. And if someone approaches, cross to the opposite pavement."

"Even if they don't look dangerous?" Her cheeks were flush with color, her eyes glowing in the dusk light. She was breathtakingly lovely and shockingly innocent.

Women, children, the elderly. Rigg had run them all, assigning them to do all manner of mischief at his direction. Clarissa Ruthven saw the potential in the girls at Fisk Academy. Gabe hoped she'd never see the uglier parts of the East End.

"Trust no one." He revealed his cardinal rule.

Rather than acknowledge his advice, she seemed to take pity on him. Her gaze turned desperate, full of yearning. No doubt she planned to combat his pessimism and win him over to her bright-eyed view of the world.

"Nonsense," she said softly. "I trusted you this evening, and you taught me how to defend myself."

Here, in the dark, he wondered pointlessly if anyone had ever taught her how to kiss. Suddenly, it was all he could think of.

"Well, good night, Mr. Adamson." She began to stride away, then turned back. "If I ask you to call me Clary, will you let me call you by your given name?"

He almost agreed, just to hear her say his name. But a remnant of rational thought broke through the haze of ridiculous longing she sparked in him. "I would prefer you didn't." Daughtry's and every other clerk's brows would merge with their hairlines, never mind her brother's reaction, if they heard her referring to him so casually.

"Very well, *Mr.* Adamson. I'll bid you a very good evening." She pivoted on her heel and continued away from him.

He fought the urge to call her back. He hated how much he'd enjoyed her nearness. Her heat and energy.

Clarissa Ruthven wasn't for him, and he sure as hell wasn't for her.

So he waited in the shadows, yearning and frustrated, until she secured a cab and climbed inside. Then he started toward the corner to catch an omnibus home.

Nothing would serve better to remind him how far he was from an innocent like Clarissa than going home to deal with the specter of Malcolm Rigg.

CHAPTER EIGHT

"Learning a great deal at the office.
Typewriting, how our books are distributed
to various shops, and how a single touch can
feel warm enough to spark an inferno."

—JOURNAL OF CLARY RUTHVEN

Four days after the strange twilight encounter with Gabriel Adamson, the man persisted in taking up far too much space in Clary's thoughts.

She arrived at Ruthven's early, letting herself in with the key Kit had given her, and wondered if Adamson was already in his office. At least he couldn't glower at her for arriving early to use Daughtry's typewriter anymore. He seemed content to let the old man personally oversee all her mentoring. Since there was a great deal more to learn than typewriting, Daughtry had encouraged her to come before the other clerks arrived for additional practice on the machine.

Despite her initial misgivings, she found herself eager to get to Ruthven's each day. There was a unique satisfaction in working for her first bit of income. Publishing was a fascinating enterprise, and though Ruthven's was a relatively small operation, each day presented new challenges and lessons to be learned.

Gabriel Adamson seemed loathe to teach her any of them. Only defensive maneuvers, apparently. Since that evening when he'd touched her, trained her, they'd barely spoken. Most days, he locked himself away in his office and barked at anyone who dared enter.

Yet she was always aware of him.

Vivid memories vexed her—the firm, warm wall of his body at her back, his fingers caressing her skin, the searing heat of his breath as he'd whispered in her ear. She tried not to think of that night. Of how he unsettled her and how oddly appealing his nearness had been.

Yet the experience presented a mystery she found hard to ignore.

She struggled to reconcile the man who'd held her with the one who was respected and feared by his employees in equal measure. The man who never smiled and ruled Ruthven's with ruthless efficiency. The man whose white-knuckled hold on etiquette prevented him from calling her by her given name.

Clary did her best not to let the conundrum of Gabriel Adamson consume her thoughts. She worked hard at Ruthven's each day, visited Fisk Academy every evening, and had managed to attend one lecture at her ladies' union during the midday lunch respite. Whether the man ever spoke to her again or not, her days were filled with purpose, and at the end of the week, she'd have funds of her own.

Heading straight for Daughtry's typewriter, she laid the satchel she carried to work aside and planted herself in his chair. In just a few days, she'd learned to type with improved speed and accuracy. Pulling out her practice page, she inserted the paper and rolled up to the next available line.

Her keystrokes filled the empty office, echoing in the high-ceilinged workroom. She tipped a glance toward Adamson's office, wondering if the noise would draw the angry bear from his cave, but he didn't appear.

A few more letters, and she built a rhythm as she typed lines from favorite novels and poems she'd memorized over the years. Once she settled in, the keystrokes created a music that quieted her mind. Before she knew it, she'd run out of paper and yanked her type-covered sheet from the platen.

There was no blank paper on any of the clerks' desks, and when she checked Daughtry's drawer, she found none there either. Heading toward the storage room, she discovered her key to the front entrance didn't fit the lock. She felt odd about searching any of the clerks' drawers. Despite being co-owner of Ruthven's and commandeering Daughtry's typewriter, she'd come to know the young men who kept the business going, and they treated her as one of their own.

She knew one hid a penny dreadful in his drawer that he read surreptitiously during quiet periods. Another was a stargazer and kept an astronomic map in his desk. Rifling through their belongings seemed out of order.

Which meant—she looked toward Adamson's office again—she'd have to risk being barked at by the ruler of Ruthven's.

A soft knock brought no response. Still nothing when she tried a more strident rap. He could be running late, which seemed completely out of character, or he could be avoiding her. She drew her fingers over the letters of his name, printed on the frosted glass of his door, then slid her hand down to the latch. It gave way against her fingers, and the door creaked open.

She skittered backward. If investigating the contents of the clerks' desks was wrong, invading Adamson's domain was out of the question.

Yet his clean scent wafted enticingly through the open door, and a fresh pile of foolscap beckoned from a tray atop his desk.

A quick in and out. One sheet of paper. He'd be none the wiser.

Sucking in a breath, she pushed the door open, vaulted for the desk, snatched up a clean sheet of paper, and turned to go. Except the desk held her. She'd snagged her cuff on the edge of the metal tray, and when she jerked away, the tray came too, sending a torrent of paper fluttering to the floor. Dropping to her knees, she collected them quickly, cursing when she found several bent sheets under her skirt. She folded two and stuck them inside the neck of her shirt-waist, smoothed the rest, and placed them at the bottom of the pile.

Settling the tray back on his desk, she tried to square it precisely. That's how Adamson maintained his desk. A place for everything, and everything in its place.

But as she straightened the tray, her hand bumped the brass stand that held his ink and pen. His fountain pen teetered off-kilter. Taking the cylinder between her fingers, she aligned the pen's body perfectly in the center.

Scooting around his desk, careful not to touch anything else, she surveyed the whole from a distance and decided it all looked as settled as when she'd entered. Aside from his rubbish receptacle, the room was spotless. Glancing down into the bin as she made her way out, she noticed two crumpled sheets of paper. One word caught her eye. *Resignation.*

Retrieving the paper, she stretched the sheet between her fingers and skimmed the words quickly. The letter was addressed to Kit, informing him of Adamson's decision to leave Ruthven's and take a position with a rival publisher.

"What are you doing?"

His bark made Clary jump. Her heart plummeted into her boots. Before facing him, she drew in a long, bracing breath. "Looking for a clean sheet of paper." Crumpling his letter, she stepped forward and flung the wad behind her toward the bin. Out of the corner of her eye, she could see she'd missed by several inches.

"In the rubbish?" Stomping into the room, he brushed past her and retrieved the letter from the floor. "My discarded correspondence is none of your concern, Miss Ruthven."

For the most part, Clary agreed, though the letter she'd found seemed an important topic to explore. "If you're unhappy with your role here at Ruthven's—"

Before she could say more, he moved past her again and closed his office door. "The matter has been resolved, and I would prefer you speak of this letter to no one."

"Of course." Her cheeks were burning, as they always did when she was embarrassed. "I'm sorry. I shouldn't have entered your office when you weren't here. I thought you'd have been in earlier."

He narrowed one pale blue eye at her. "I arrive before the others of my own accord. My workday does not start until"— he yanked a watch from his waistcoat pocket—"now. If you'll excuse me, Miss Ruthven."

"Were you busy saving another young woman from a drunken brute?" Clary found it impossible not to tease him. Especially when he wore such a fearsome scowl. "Or perhaps you found some damsel in need of training in the defensive arts."

He gripped the back of his chair and closed his eyes. She watched his broad chest expand and contract as he drew in half a dozen long breaths and let them out. When he looked at her again, his gaze was as frosty as a winter breeze. "If you must know, I was seeing to a personal matter. My sister and I are moving lodgings. A location closer to the office."

"I didn't know you had a sister."

"Why would you?" Today he was every inch the cold, snappish manager. No warmth in his gaze or tone. Not a single glimpse of the man who'd held her in the dark of an alleyway.

"You know all of *my* siblings." She knew the faultiness of the comparison, but she loathed the sharp edge of his retort. Hated that he worked so hard to put distance between them. She preferred that other man who'd put his hands on her and allowed her to pretend she was jabbing him in the throat. Was he only capable of being kind to her in the shadows? Softening her tone, she added, "I should like to meet her. What's her name?"

"I know your sister writes of detectives, but perhaps you should consider the profession itself. You never seem to lack for questions, Miss Ruthven, and you're clearly incapable of repressing the impulse to investigate." He tipped his gaze down at his rubbish bin and arched an ebony eyebrow.

"I've already apologized for that, and do call me Clary."

"No." He shook his head, managing to avoid displacing a single strand of hair. "First names are not appropriate for the workplace."

Clary chuckled. "That's ridiculous. What does it matter what we call each other?"

He stared at her, dumbfounded. "Have you truly never read a word of your father's books?"

"Every word. He insisted. But it doesn't mean I agree with any of them."

"Of course. Ever the rebel."

"And what's wrong with rebellion? Sometimes one must, if the cause is just." Clary laughed. "That rhymed."

His full mouth twitched, his lean cheeks quivered, and she willed him to smile at her. Just once. Instead, he knitted his brow and deepened his glower.

She threw up her hands in frustration. "Calling people by the name they prefer would make the workroom a kinder place. More congenial."

"Now you're telling me how to manage the workroom? After three days on the job?" He let out another long breath and folded his arms. "I don't refer to anyone here by his given name. Surnames or job titles. You'll find the same in every office in London."

"And what's my title?"

He squinted at her as if she'd just asked the silliest question he'd ever heard, unbuttoned his suit coat, and slumped into the chair behind his desk. "Employer," he said, flicking his hand her way, "co-owner, mentee." He squared his gaze on her. "Heiress."

Clary snorted. "You make it sound as if I should be covered in silk and velvet and dripping with jewels."

"Shouldn't you be?" He swept his gaze down the insubstantial length of her, from her brows to the toes of her boots, as if struggling to imagine her bejeweled and wrapped in a sumptuous gown.

She struggled to imagine the scenario too. But his gaze unsettled her. Clary pressed a fist to her hip to stop her hand from trembling. "You manage the finances of Ruthven's. You know we don't possess that kind of wealth."

"Your sister married an earl."

"They fell in love. Besides, Sophia is beautiful, proper, elegant. She's the perfect candidate to be a countess."

"And you?" He braced his hands on his blotter and leaned forward, his mouth softening, gaze fixed on her, as if something about her finally interested him.

An unladylike guffaw burst from her lips. "I'm not that sort of woman." The words were surprisingly hard to get out. She'd accepted that she'd never be a beauty like Sophia. "I don't snag men's notice in a crowd." Speaking the fact aloud—to him—scalded her throat.

"Now *that* is nonsense." He spoke emphatically, forcefully enough to stifle the retort that rose to the tip of her tongue. "I've never met a lady who's harder to ignore."

"Because I talk too much?"

"No." He pursed his mouth, and there was a glint of humor in his eyes. "Though you do have a good deal to say."

"Then it's because I wear beads on my shirtwaist and garishly colored clothes?" Clary found it hard to meet his gaze. He watched her intently, studying her face, glancing down at the pink shirtwaist she'd adorned with lace and a few jet beads along the collar.

"I'm not interested in ladies' fashion." He left the rest unexplained, the reason he found her difficult to ignore. Though he didn't seem to regret the admission. He stared at her boldly, only stopping when someone knocked at his office door.

One of the clerks stuck his head in.

"Daughtry says I'm to take Miss Ruthven up and show her the workings of the chromolithograph."

"Yes, by all means." Adamson stood and waved them off.

On the threshold, Clary paused and let the clerk proceed without her. Turning back, she said quietly, "I still want to know your sister's name, Gabriel, and I still think you should call me Clary."

Uttering his name seemed to affect him mightily. He flinched and swallowed hard as he stared at her. Heatedly. Almost hungrily. Very akin to the look a wallflower craved from the handsomest man in a ballroom.

She grinned and pulled the door closed behind her.

"**M**essenger for you, Mr. Adamson." The clerk handed Gabe a note, the reply he'd been awaiting from Sara.

In a few words, she let him know she was settling into their new lodgings, and all was well. "Grass beyond the front window," she added with a few upward, sloping pencil strokes to indicate spears of lawn.

For a reasonable rent, bearing his new salary and the twenty-five pounds Ruthven paid him immediately, he'd found rooms with a kindly old widow in a tidy three-story brick home, just a few steps away from a respectable pub. He and Sara could take their meals without traveling far, and they were miles closer to Ruthven's. Within walking distance. If he could bear the fog and rain, he'd never have to take an omnibus again.

The thundering noise above his head set his teeth on edge. They'd rarely put the chromolithograph to work since purchasing the expensive machinery. The original plan had been to add more colored plates in some of the novels they sold, and, of course, Kit Ruthven had grand designs for his literary journal.

The intricate beast of a press ran on steam and took up much of the second floor. Only a few of the young men were trained in its use, and they'd hired one man who was a true master at transferring original art onto the lithographic plates. The process of applying the various layers of ink was messy and could be dangerous once the machine was set in motion. He hoped they were insisting Clary—er, Miss Ruthven—kept a safe distance.

With Sara settled, Miss Ruthven occupied, and the workroom humming with productivity, he settled behind his desk to finally get some work done. He started with vendor correspondence, finished that, and progressed to working on billing statements. Just as he was preparing the second, a ruckus erupted. Clerks in the workroom rose from their chairs, and two of them sprinted toward the stairwell. A moment later, a scream echoed down from upstairs.

Gabe shot up from his chair and rushed toward the stairwell. She was coming down with two clerks at her heels. Gabe's heart stopped. Blood stained her shirtwaist, her fingers, even her face. He lunged up the steps between them, hands shaking as he reached for her.

"What the bloody hell happened?" he roared at the clerks behind her. "Clarissa, Clary," he said softly, "where are you injured?"

She turned a miserable gaze his way. "Wherever my pride is located."

"Pardon?"

The clerks snickered behind her, and Gabe barely resisted throttling them both. Then she started in, a little gurgle of mirth at first and then full-blown laughter. An infectious sound, throaty and enticing. And when his heart started again, he thought he might be amused too, if someone explained what the rotting hell was going on.

One of the lithograph operators skidded to the edge of the landing above. "She got into the paints, sir. We tried to clean the mess, but it doesn't come off easily."

She held her breath, trying to control her laughter. Gabe reached for a part of her arm that wasn't stained and led her to his office.

"It wasn't her fault, Mr. Adamson," a clerk shouted in her defense.

Daughtry beelined toward them, fatherly worry etching lines across his wrinkled brow. "Is the lass all right, sir?"

"Find me some rags, water, soap, maybe a bit of turpentine, and bring them to my office."

Clary allowed him to lead her and had almost calmed by the time he pointed her toward a chair. She refused to sit.

"What if I stain it?"

He didn't care. All that mattered was that she was in one paint-splotched piece.

She scooted the tray of paper aside on his desk. Even that didn't irk him. After tipping her head back to inspect the rear of her skirt, she settled her bottom warily against the edge.

Gabe rolled up his shirt-sleeves. "Tell me what happened."

"Isn't it obvious?" She held up her hands and paint dripped down her wrists. Now that he looked closer, it wasn't just red. A bit of blue too. At her cuff, they blended into a vibrant purple, a darker version of her eye color.

Daughtry shuffled through the door with a small folding table, his arms brimming with all the other items Gabe had requested. "Can I help, sir?"

"Thank you for your concern, Wilbur," she answered reassuringly. "I'll be all right."

Wilbur? Daughtry cast her a quick grin and ducked out of the room.

"You've won him over quickly." Gabe didn't want to think about why it irked him so.

She pointed a red-tinted finger at him. "You only think so because I used his given name. See how much friendlier it sounds?"

Gabe started with a damp cloth against her wrist and found much of the paint came off, except for a faint pink stain. He hated to use harsh turpentine on her skin. Returning to the basin to wring out his cloth, he dabbed it against the bar of soap before returning to her. He took her hand in his, and she pulled up her sleeve to give him access. The soap worked better at removing the coloring.

"I could manage this myself," she said softly as he worked, though she made no move to pull away.

Gabe looked into her eyes a moment, and her breath seemed to catch. "This won't take long." He turned her hand over to clean the underside of her arm. "I can see what happened. Why don't you tell me how."

She glanced up at the ceiling, down at his hands where he held and washed her, anywhere but into his eyes. "I was curious," she mumbled. "And I wanted to be useful."

A few splotches of paint had managed to get on her face, and Gabe pressed two fingers to the edge of her jaw, tipping her head up. "Go on."

She was warm and soft under his fingertips, and he stretched out his hand to cup her cheek as he rubbed at a spot near her chin.

"The red paint spilled. I didn't realize how full the container was. And then I accidentally brushed the blue plate while trying to clean up the red." Her eyes slid closed for a moment, and he missed her violet gaze. "It was a disaster."

"Hardly. I thought you were injured."

She opened her eyes, and her mouth fell open as if she'd say more. Her breath came in warm, tickling wisps against his face.

Gabe turned to retrieve a clean rag. He willed away his response to her. She was a Ruthven. He was from the gutters of Whitechapel.

"Were you worried about me?" The thread of hopefulness in her voice kindled heat in his chest. Right in the spot where his heart would be, if he still believed he possessed a working one. His whole body warmed, and he was buzzing with that devilishly appealing energy she exuded.

He swiped a wrist across his brow before turning back to her. She gasped and lifted a hand to her mouth.

"What?"

"You've…" She waved toward him and pressed her lips together. "I'm afraid you've gotten a bit of paint on you too."

Wonderful. "Where?"

Dropping to her feet, she approached and tugged the clean rag from his hand. "Your turn on the desk, Mr. Adamson."

"Not necessary. Just tell me where."

"Too hard to describe," she insisted, though there was a mischievous glint in her eyes. "You'll at least have to lean down so I can reach."

He rested his arse on his desk's edge and tried to pretend having her fuss over him was a nuisance. He even worked up an irritated sigh, but it turned to a gasp when her fingers swept through his hairline.

"Hold still," she said breathily.

She was a pretty young woman any day of the week, but when applying herself to a task, her eyes widened, her lower lip plumped, and her soft round chin jutted forward. Her touch came gently, forcing her to smooth the rag over the spot several times.

"Almost done," she whispered and pressed an inch closer, right between the V of his thighs.

He gripped the edge of his desk because he remembered how it felt to hold her this near, and every instinct told him to tuck his hand to her waist. One dip of his head, and he could take her determined mouth. Slide his hand into her hair and free those curly waves trapped in pins at her nape.

"There." She smiled at him and took a step back. "Now just make sure you don't touch me again, and you'll remain spotless."

"That's not as easy as it sounds." He meant being spotless. After the things he'd done, he would never be clean. But the other was true too. Keeping his hands off her was an increasingly impossible challenge.

"Isn't it?" The rasp in her voice shot shivers down his back. She moved closer again, her skirt pressing against his legs. "Then you'll touch me again?"

Before he could answer, she pressed her clean hand to his. He gripped the desk so hard his knuckles ached.

"Gabriel," she whispered.

His name sounded perfect on her tongue. So good he could almost forget the times he'd heard it shouted like a curse.

The front doorbell echoed through the workroom, and Gabe edged off the desk, sidestepping away from her. "I have no appointments scheduled," he told her pointlessly. His tongue felt as thick as the sluggish haze in his mind, and he struggled to remind himself that this was work. She was his employer's sister. Hell, she was his employer.

Daughtry's signature double knock sounded at his door before the man pushed inside. "Visitors to see you, sir."

"I don't entertain visitors." No one knew that better than Daughtry, who maintained his appointment calendar.

"Say they're friends. Say you invited them to stop in to see the office. A Miss Morgan and her cousin, Miss Banks."

One of Clary's gilded brows winged high.

"I'll come out to greet them in a moment." He turned to face her and was shocked to find the same regret in her expression that he felt in spades.

"Go. I'll tidy this up so that you can visit with them in your office."

"Yes," he said. Yet he couldn't force his feet to go. He preferred to stay here, with her. Even when she ignored him and began collecting the crimson-stained rags, he liked being near her. He couldn't lie to himself about that anymore. The impulse was too strong to deny.

Miss Morgan's voice filtered in from the workroom. She was just the sort of woman he'd always told himself he wanted. Demure, well mannered, agreeable.

But she didn't fire his blood. Or cause him to stand stock-still, clenching his fists so that he didn't reach for her. He didn't think of Jane Morgan from the beginning of one day to the start of the next.

The only woman who lingered in his thoughts was Clarissa Ruthven.

CHAPTER NINE

"**H**ow many more?" Clary shook out her hand and glanced at the wall clock, adorned on either side by watercolors completed by her students at Fisk Academy. After addressing twenty invitations in a swirling round hand style, her wrist throbbed from the tension of striving not to make a single error.

"Are you tired already?" Helen teased. She'd already thanked Clary for leaving Ruthven's and coming straight to the school for more work. "Luckily, this is the last of the lot. We've already sent dozens of invitations ahead of these. Sally has a lovely looping hand, if not nearly as neat and precise as yours."

"How is Sally?" Since she made her visits in the evenings, Clary missed seeing many of the girls. The few who lodged at the school were sent to bed at seven, though as one of the oldest, Sally was allowed an extra hour to read before turning down her lamp. Of late, Helen reported that Sally had been quiet and depressed, often choosing to retire when the younger girls did.

"We've had no more visits from her unwanted suitor, if that's what you're asking." Helen wouldn't even speak the man's name around the girls. She'd also gone straight to H Division police station and informed them of his antics.

"Good." Clary clenched her fingers and stretched them out, noting that nearly every nail was stained with black ink. It made an interesting contrast to the pink still coloring much of her hand. Clenching a fist again, she recalled the moment she'd placed her hand on Gabriel's. How he'd tensed in response. Perhaps he'd simply been wishing she'd take her paint-splattered self and leave him alone.

"Would you mind ticking off the ones you've finished?" Helen laid a handwritten list in front of Clary.

"You've invited so many people." The list covered both sides of the paper, written in Helen's tight, neat script, and the numbered names included thirty-five invitees.

"Your sister said her ballroom could accommodate forty easily. A few on the list were invited to bring guests."

After Clary's mention of the charity ball, Sophia had sent a note offering the use of her Mayfair townhouse's ballroom. At the prospect of spending an evening with her sister and Grey, Clary was almost looking forward to the event. Almost. She still wasn't thrilled about the notion of a ball, but the money raised would be put to good use. Even if Kit never agreed to her ladies' magazine project, they could pour every penny into Fisk Academy. Perhaps even rent a larger space and admit more girls.

Helen pasted penny stamps at the corner of each envelope before passing them back to Clary to tick off the list. As she skimmed names looking for a Lord and Lady Avery, her finger stalled on another. *Adamson.*

"You sent Mr. Adamson an invitation?"

"It seemed the least I could do." Helen gazed at Clary over the rim of her spectacles. "He did help you fend off an attack."

"My croquet mallet would have done quite nicely." Clary could still see him striding up. A perfectly attired Galahad coming to her rescue. After years at Rothley, she'd almost forgotten how much his excessive masculine beauty irked her. Now another emotion sparked when he was near. A reaction that had little to do with his looks and everything to do with what she felt when he touched her. "I doubt he'll donate any funds."

"I didn't realize you disliked him so." Helen settled back in her chair and cast Clary one of her bloodhound expressions. "I invited him as a kindness. Do you loathe him so much that you can't bear to spend an evening in a crowded ballroom with him?"

"I spend every day with him." And still found herself thinking about him at night. "Maybe he won't come." She swept her finger over his name before proceeding down to the lord and lady she sought.

"Well, I hope he does. He seemed dubious about the value of the school. Maybe hearing more about our programs will change his mind." Helen planned to present information about the school's successes. She'd even invited the oldest girls to attend and speak of their experiences at Fisk. So far, only Sally had accepted, and she'd been giddily working on sewing herself a ball gown ever since.

"He doesn't seem to care for charity." Clary recalled how he'd snapped at her during their cramped carriage ride.

"Well, he should, if he's pulled himself up from the East End."

Clary chuckled. "What makes you think that?"

"His accent." Helen reached for the last few envelopes and carefully applied stamps to each.

"His accent is perfect."

"Isn't it though? Too perfect. A bit like mine, wouldn't you say?" Helen grinned wryly. "I spent years shedding my Cockney dialect. I'm sure he has too, but I could hear it underneath all the polish, yearning to get out."

Clary took the stamped envelopes and ticked off the final names from the list. "But he speaks of this place as if it's loathsome, a kind of hell from which no one escapes unscathed."

"Many of the girls upstairs would agree." Helen shrugged her slim shoulders. "This corner of London contains some of the worst elements of the city and some of the best people I've ever known. It's why my father insisted on remaining, even after he'd earned his wealth." She cast her gaze toward the window, but her eyes glazed as if she was staring into the past. "Unfortunately, staying in the East End meant all his vices were near at hand too. Gambling, opium, and all the rest. The poverty of his last days are so vivid in my mind that I can hardly remember the years of plenty."

Helen's father had risen up from meager beginnings to become one of the most successful businessmen in the East End. He'd bought up, renovated, and resold numerous properties for a sizable profit. But by the time of his death, he'd lost all his wealth, forcing Helen to seek a scholarship to fund her education.

All at once, Helen burst up from the table, reached across, and clasped Clary's arm. She pulled her toward the wall and twisted the knob of the single gaslight sconce to cut off the light, casting the front schoolroom into darkness.

"What is it?" Clary clutched Helen's hand and found her skin clammy and cool.

"Is that him?" Helen whispered. "Is it Keene?"

As her eyes adjusted to the light, Clary could see the shape of a man in the shadows of a shop awning across the lane. He seemed to be watching them, but she couldn't tell if it was Keene. As pedestrians passed on the pavement in front of their window, Clary blinked, and he was gone.

"I had a nightmare that he came back," Helen whispered. "I was staying over at the school, and he broke in." When one of the matron volunteers was ill or couldn't monitor the girls at night, Helen stayed to keep watch. "In the dream, I'd fallen asleep, and he took us all by surprise."

"It was just a dream, Helen." She'd never known her friend to give in to fancy or fright. At Rothley, Clary had been the one up late, reading penny dreadfuls, painting macabre scenes, and attempting to write her own scary stories, while Helen read Euclid and Pythagoras.

"You're right, of course. But I've considered whether we're doing enough to protect the girls. Nathaniel suggested we hire a guard, at least for evenings."

"Wouldn't that make the girls more frightened?" Clary appreciated that Dr. Landau wished to protect Helen and the girls at Fisk Academy, but, thanks to Kit, she also knew how stifling overly protective instincts could be. "Where would we even find someone willing to serve as a guard?"

"Is your Mr. Adamson available?" Helen asked, her voice lilting mischievously. "The girls seemed to like him all right."

"The same could be said of *your* Dr. Landau. Mr. Adamson is not *my* anything."

"Not true." Helen released Clary's hand and crossed the room to retrieve matches from a drawer. When she returned to light the gas sconce again, she added, "He's your employee, and now, oddly, your manager and mentor."

"He leaves the mentoring to Mr. Daughtry."

"You sound disappointed."

"Why would I be?" Damn Helen's bloodhound instincts. "You saw how domineering he can be. How dismissive."

"I'm sure there's more to him."

There was. He could turn gentle in a heartbeat, touching her as if she was delicate and precious. He could be helpful, instructing her with patience and praise on how to defend herself. And, apparently, he'd come from a part of London he spoke of with loathing.

As if she'd read her mind, Helen added, "Best not to bring up what I said about him coming from the East End. If it's nothing he's volunteered, then he may have his reasons for keeping mum."

"He's mum about everything. I know nothing about the man." And she wanted to know. Desperately. "He admitted he has a sister, but he won't tell me her name. Oh, and he has two friends, a Miss Morgan and her cousin."

"I hope he brings one of them to the ball. The invitation does include a guest."

"Perhaps." Would he bring the young woman who'd visited him at the office and blushed every time he looked her way?

If nothing else, Clary would have a good view. She and Helen had already decided where to place their chairs in the back of the Stanhope ballroom to oversee the festivities.

"**S**he'll be eager to see you, of that I've no doubt." Sara blew into her cupped hands to warm them. While the sun had managed to break through the clouds midday, the evening had turned cold, and London's hansom cabs offered meager shelter from the elements.

"You've forgotten your gloves again." Gabe removed his own and passed them to his sister. A lifetime of counting gloves as a luxury meant that Sara often left hers behind. But they were good for hiding the scars on his knuckles, so Gabe rarely forgot his pair.

"Miss Morgan, I mean."

"I know who you meant." His sister was tenacious but rarely subtle.

"You don't mention her much."

Unfortunately, Sara took his failure to speak of Miss Morgan as a sign of his determination to avoid marriage. In fact, it was that Jane Morgan didn't interest him in that way. Though he had no interest in admitting to his sister which woman did.

"Perhaps we should stop accepting every invitation we receive from Jane Morgan."

She pivoted to face him in the carriage's close confines. "She's one of few friends we have. Thomas's family is scattered around the countryside. Jane Morgan may very well turn out to be the only guest at our wedding."

"You're right, of course." Mercy, he was a selfish bastard. Because of the past, the secrets he needed to keep, he'd narrowed their lives to a few select interactions with people he believed he could trust. And it was a very short list. Miss Morgan and her father, when he was alive, and perhaps the Ruthvens and Thomas Tidwell, Sara's betrothed. And, of course, Daughtry and his wife. Gabe and Sara joined the couple for supper at the pub around the corner from Ruthven's once in a while.

She nudged him with her elbow and grinned. "Wish I had a sixpence for every time you tell me I'm right." Shifting to reach into the pocket of her coat, she gazed over at him, wide-eyed, and added, "Seeing as how you've decided to accept all of Miss Morgan's invitations, perhaps you should extend one to her in return."

The envelope she placed in his hand had been sliced open, and the thick paper was covered with a ridiculously fancy script, full of useless loops and swirls. Among the decorative handwriting, he noted his name and their old address.

"You didn't go back, did you?" They'd agreed to leave without notice, though they paid their landlord an additional sum to tell no one where they'd gone. So far, there'd been no more sightings of Rigg, and Sara was increasingly convinced she may have been mistaken in her identification of the man she saw.

"Not at all. Remember our neighbor, Mrs. Honeychurch? She dropped it by." Her voice rose in excitement. "She apologized for opening the envelope. Said she didn't notice your name until after. Soon as I saw that fancy hand, I thought perhaps you'd been summoned by the queen."

Gabe pressed a thumb to the spot where tiny fists were pummeling behind his brow. "You told Mrs. Honeychurch our new address?"

Sara quieted for a moment. "You have to trust some folks, Gabe. Not everyone is a threat."

His bitter chuckle echoed off the hansom's interior. "And on that count, we'll never agree."

"It's an invitation to a ball." Her tone dipped low as a whisper. "I thought perhaps you could ask Miss Morgan to accompany you."

"I don't go to balls." Gabe slid the invite free of its envelope and nearly dropped the creamy square. It was the charity ball Clary Ruthven had mentioned. Which meant she'd be in attendance. He pressed the paper so hard, it began to ripple in his fingers.

"No, but this could be your first ball."

"I don't own proper clothes, nor do I know how to dance."

"You can rent proper togs, and dancing isn't difficult." Sara nudged his shoulder. "It would be an excellent opportunity to become better acquainted with the young lady."

"Not a good idea." The ache in his forehead sharpened. He was quickly losing patience with his sister's determination to pair him off with Jane Morgan. Unfortunately, she wasn't the young lady dominating his thoughts.

"You're not giving the girl a chance." She folded her arms. A move that, as a child, had often spurred him to relent. Because Sara had been his only ally. The only one who cared whether he lived or died.

Gabe still hated disappointing his sister.

"If I invite her, she'll expect more than I'm willing to offer." According to the *Ruthven Rules* etiquette books, an invitation to a ball was a sure sign of courtship. He'd read every word of the damned book when he'd taken his role at Ruthven's. The rules had seemed comical, but they'd taught him where the boundary lines were. What was expected of honorable men.

He'd absorbed enough to know there was no honor in giving false hope to a baronet's daughter.

"Now, yes, but perhaps soon—"

"No, Sara. I will never wish to marry Jane Morgan." He'd always known the fact and wasn't sure why he'd held back from confessing the truth to Sara so bluntly. "She and I wouldn't suit." Every time he looked at the girl, she became a blushing bundle of nerves. Hardly the makings of a happy marriage.

Of course, imagining Clarissa Ruthven reacting to him in the same overheated way held a disturbing appeal.

"Then I fear she will never marry." Sara turned her head to watch the other carriages passing, pedestrians making their way along the gaslit streets. "She's the sort of girl men don't notice. Quiet and shy. I doubt she receives many invitations to accompany gentlemen to balls."

Miss Morgan was far too well bred and connected to turn spinster. From what he knew of her, she was kind and gently mannered. Some man would find that appealing.

Gabe already spent his days playing a role, controlling his impulses, attempting to be a proper, buttoned-down man of business. Marrying Jane Morgan would complete the picture. Gain him valuable social connections. He knew all the reasons he *should* marry the young woman. But he craved something in his life that was real. The woman he married would damn well spark something in him beyond practical impulses and put-on manners.

"Why don't you attend the ball with me? You've never been to one."

"Don't be barmy." Sara cuffed him on the leg. "I wouldn't know which foot to put where, but I'll wager Miss Morgan does. Ask her, Gabe. I'm not insisting you marry the girl, but give her an evening out and a turn or two around the dance floor."

He wasn't going to win. He rarely did when his sister set her mind on something.

While he mulled all his possible rejoinders and all Sara's arguments to knock them down, the carriage stopped along the pavement in front of the Morgan's modest red-brick home in Hampstead.

"I'll ask her," he finally said.

Sara beamed beside him.

"*But* I will make clear the invitation is extended out of friendship, nothing more." Which sounded much easier said than done. Hell, he didn't like disappointing anyone.

After jumping from the carriage, he held out a hand to assist Sara down.

"Of course you will," she said, in a way that made him doubt she believed him about his lack of interest in Jane Morgan.

"Sara," he said in a warning tone, "she is not the young lady I wish to marry."

"Oh?" Halfway to the Morgans' front door, she tugged his arm to pull him to a stop. "Then there's another young lady?" She wore one of the knowing smiles he remembered from their youth. Her smiles had been in short supply of late, and he liked seeing her eyes alight with mischief.

"I never said anything of the kind." There was an odd catch in his throat that his cunning sister wouldn't fail to notice. He knew better than to hide anything from her.

"No, Gabe, you didn't say," she said as they continued to the Morgans' front stoop. "You didn't have to."

CHAPTER TEN

"You're ready for your meeting, lass?" Daughtry approached and peeked over Clary's shoulder.

"I am." She typed the last word of the letter she'd prepared, pulled the sheet from the typewriter roller, and added it to the pile. "Would you hand me those?" She pointed to a large stack of papers she'd placed on a side worktable near his elbow.

"Boss isn't shy of giving you work, is he?" Daughtry collected the stack and placed the whole in Clary's arms.

With both arms lashed underneath, the pile nearly reached her chin. "I had no idea we received this number of submissions."

"Oh, aye. Never a lack of those who wish to see their stories in print."

"I hope we can give a few more that chance," she said over her shoulder as she weaved between desks toward Adamson's office.

"Don't know about that, miss." Daughtry cast her a dubious frown. "They have to get past Mr. Adamson first."

Ah, yes, Ruthven's gatekeeper. And he could be a ferocious one, judging by the manuscripts he'd marked *Rejected* and she'd decided to reread. Some of the stories had merit, and Clary hoped that she could make Gabriel acknowledge the potential she'd seen.

"Is it noon already?" he asked as she knocked on his door with her elbow before stepping inside. "Please have a seat, Miss Ruthven."

Always a seat. Clary suspected a good deal more might be accomplished if people were allowed to stand and move and stretch their legs once in a while. Instead of taking the chair he indicated, she strode toward his desk, edged his pen stand out of the way, and plopped her enormous pile in front him.

To say he did not look pleased would be akin to saying Da Vinci's *Mona Lisa* did not look giddy.

"What's all this?" He pushed the pile toward her with two fingers.

She pushed back with her hip to keep the whole from falling off the edge of his desk. With a hand planted on top, she explained, "These are the recent submissions, including those you've rejected. I'd like to speak to you about a few of them." She slid a folder atop the pile and offered it to him. "Also, the letters you asked me to type up."

He narrowed one eye at her, grimaced at the sight of his pen pushed off-kilter, and flipped open the folder. A grunt came, following by a disgusted sniff, as he scanned her work. "Appears there's been a mix-up. These aren't the letters I asked you to type."

Clary frowned and leaned forward to see which one he was looking at. "Yes, addressed to Miss C. Bently, who submitted *Lady Catriona's Liberation*. She was on the list you gave me."

"Indeed, but the list I gave you requested that you reject her drivel and send her manuscript back to her." He shook out the sheet before him as if hoping to rid himself of fleas. "Here, you urge her to 'persevere' in her fiction endeavors, to improve the plot, and to resubmit her story as soon as she's able."

Clary crossed her arms, picking at a zigzag of beads she'd sown on the arm of her blouse. "Yes, that is an accurate reading of the letter I prepared."

He flung the typed sheet away from him and settled against the back of his chair, mimicking her gesture by folding his arms across his chest. "And yet the diametric opposite of what I asked you to convey. Her story is atrocious. Her writing juvenile. Have you read the letter she included with her submission?"

"I have." Clary recalled that the lady's language was overly stilted, and the writing did lack finesse. "But everyone can improve."

He let out a trapped breath and made a noise that sounded suspiciously like a strangled chuckle. "Why doesn't your rose-colored view surprise me?" Taking her letter in hand again, he set it aside, flattening his palm on top. "Please revise this note and tell Miss Bently to submit her story elsewhere."

"That's too harsh. Everyone deserves a second chance."

Adamson stilled in the act of reaching for the next letter in the folder. "Do you truly believe that?" He turned his gaze on her, and the brightness of his eyes was like a beacon, searching her out, seeking something more than whatever answer might fall from her lips.

"Yes, of course I do."

The fervency of her answer kindled a dangerous pleasure in his chest.

Such hopefulness was folly. Clary's philosophy wasn't what most people experienced in life.

Men who died in the boxing ring, or after, never recovering from their injuries. They never got a second chance. Most of his fellow child pickpockets hadn't gotten a second chance either, especially once they'd fallen into Rigg's clutches.

But a tantalizing possibility kept his gaze fixed on hers. If she believed in giving others a chance to improve themselves, could she forgive a man like him for his sins?

"So may I send my letter to Miss Bently?"

He directed his attention to the next letter. "Let her resubmit. Though I reserve the right to re-reject."

When he glanced up at her, she pressed her lips together in an expressionless line, though her eyes were dancing.

Her next letter was even worse. A gentleman had submitted a book on horses. Their physiology, biology, scatology. Far more than anyone would wish to know about equines. Gabe had skimmed the initial chapters and known instantly that the book was better off delivered to a scientific publisher.

Apparently, Clary Ruthven had read every word of the horse lover's manuscript. She'd replied with detailed eagerness about his work.

" 'I never dreamed horses' teeth were four inches long,' " Gabe read before gazing up at her again. "Really? You now have an interest in horse anatomy?"

She inched up one ruffle-covered shoulder. "To be honest, I never gave horses much thought."

"Nor I. Which is why I soundly rejected his submission. You're too late on this one. I've already sent him a letter."

"I'd like to send him another," she said in that determined way of hers, her pretty chin set firmly in the air. "Everyone can use a note of encouragement now and then."

Gabe pressed his thumb to the space between his brows and willed his head to stop throbbing. "If we're to be about the business of encouragement, shouldn't we start with our own authors? I can provide you with a list. Send a cheery note to each of them."

She chuckled as if he'd said something amusing. "But they already have a publisher." With one slim finger, she drew her nail along the edge of papers stacked in front of him, creating a strange shuffling tune. "These people submitted their words, their works, with such hope. No doubt fearful that they'd be rejected and that would be the end of their creative endeavors."

"Some of them deserved to be rejected. Not everyone can succeed."

"Whyever not? Is there not enough success to go around?"

Not where he came from. Everything was a competition for a place to lodge, food to eat, liquor to warm one's belly. Only the strong and the dastardly survived. Resilient ones like his sister. Brutes like him, with fists big enough to beat everyone else away.

Gabe huffed as he read the next letter she'd typed. He shoved the sheet toward her. "Read that aloud, if you will."

After skimming her gaze over the contents, she cleared her throat daintily and began, " 'I adore that your story started with a murder, but I would humbly suggest that you add a good deal more blood.' "

"You actually typed that?"

She nodded readily. "As you see. What's wrong with it? She wrote a penny dreadful. They benefit from blood."

"We don't publish penny dreadfuls."

"Perhaps we should." Walking toward the window, she unsettled his mostly closed curtains to peer outside onto the rainy gray day.

Gabe took a deep, steadying breath and reminded himself that she wasn't familiar with publishing. That she was here to learn, and as much as he might wish to avoid her and the reactions she sparked in him, he had been tasked with teaching her.

Standing, he rolled his head to ease the tightness between his shoulders. Then he approached her at the window. "The market for penny tales of horror is saturated."

She whirled to face him, except that a pin in her hair had snagged the edge of the curtain, and she brought half the fabric along with her. As she reached up to dislodge herself, the curtain popped free of one of its rings, and her cheeks begin to flame as pink as her mouth.

"Let me," he said as he found the misshapen pin and freed her from the fabric. As soon as he touched the crooked metal, the pin slipped from her thick tresses, and he swept the strands back behind her ear. Mercy, she was warm; the softness of the skin behind her nape kept his fingers lingering. And when she gazed up at him, cheeks flushed, lips parted, he learned the agony of maintaining control.

Her gaze fixed on his lips, and then her hand found his. She worked the misshapen pin away from him, but she kept her fingers against his far too long.

"Thank you," she said on a breathy whisper. "If I had a ribbon in my hair, I'd lend it to you to tie this curtain back."

Her grin did odd things to him. A lightness filled his chest. The knots in his shoulders unfurled. He remembered the first time he'd met her, years ago. When she'd shed her pristine white ribbon and tied his office curtain back, offending him by insisting he needed a bit of beauty in his world.

Little did he know she'd come back when she was a lush, desirable woman and torment him.

"Watching the world pass by is a distraction." What he truly wished to tell her was that *she* was a distraction. His world had been ordered, manageable, respectable before she walked into Ruthven's as its new co-owner. Now he found himself longing for the kind of intimacy he'd spent his life avoiding. One touch. One glance from her, and he was on tenterhooks. Eager for more. Each moment in her presence had him thinking ridiculous thoughts. Wishing for what could never be. He'd never been one to waste his energy on daydreams.

What had to be done. What he needed to do to survive. That was all that mattered.

"Shall we finish these?" He moved back toward his desk, and after a moment she followed. "Are there any you *seriously* believe we should consider for publication?"

Leaning toward him, she flicked through the pile and tugged out one manuscript. He recognized the title. A short story about a waif who'd risen from his humble beginnings to become a successful barrister, eventually prosecuting the vile crime lord who'd forced him into thievery as a child.

"I'm quite fond of this one." She squared the manuscript in front of him.

"Sentimental nonsense," he pronounced.

At her sharp inhale, he looked up to find her sharp violet glare on him.

Yes, that was better. Let her loathe him. Her disdain was precisely what he deserved.

"Don't you have a heart, Mr. Adamson?"

"Not that I am aware of." He knew it wasn't true. She'd put a lie to the claim. Since Clary strutted into his life wielding a croquet mallet, he'd been reminded of the nuisance of his heart every damned day. The rusty organ responded to her, crashing against his ribs every time she was near, as if she was a magnet and his heart nothing but a twisted bit of metal.

"The story is well written," she insisted while he got lost studying her lips. "You cannot deny the merits of the author's style. So you must object to the content." She started pacing around his office, in front of his desk at first and then circling around behind him.

Which he loathed. He hated anyone at his back. Especially her. She was the most dangerous of all.

"I can't help but wonder why the tale disturbs you."

"As I said, it's ridiculously sentimental. There is a glut of such stories on the market. London doesn't need another."

Leaning toward him, she flicked through the pile and tugged out one manuscript. He recognized the title. A short story about a waif who'd risen from his humble beginnings to become a successful barrister, eventually prosecuting the vile crime lord who'd forced him into thievery as a child.

"I'm quite fond of this one." She squared the manuscript in front of him.

"Sentimental nonsense," he pronounced.

At her sharp inhale, he looked up to find her sharp violet glare on him.

Yes, that was better. Let her loathe him. Her disdain was precisely what he deserved.

"Don't you have a heart, Mr. Adamson?"

"Not that I am aware of." He knew it wasn't true. She'd put a lie to the claim. Since Clary strutted into his life wielding a croquet mallet, he'd been reminded of the nuisance of his heart every damned day. The rusty organ responded to her, crashing against his ribs every time she was near, as if she was a magnet and his heart nothing but a twisted bit of metal.

"The story is well written," she insisted while he got lost studying her lips. "You cannot deny the merits of the author's style. So you must object to the content." She started pacing around his office, in front of his desk at first and then circling around behind him.

Which he loathed. He hated anyone at his back. Especially her. She was the most dangerous of all.

"I can't help but wonder why the tale disturbs you."

"As I said, it's ridiculously sentimental. There is a glut of such stories on the market. London doesn't need another."

" 'I never dreamed horses' teeth were four inches long,' " Gabe read before gazing up at her again. "Really? You now have an interest in horse anatomy?"

She inched up one ruffle-covered shoulder. "To be honest, I never gave horses much thought."

"Nor I. Which is why I soundly rejected his submission. You're too late on this one. I've already sent him a letter."

"I'd like to send him another," she said in that determined way of hers, her pretty chin set firmly in the air. "Everyone can use a note of encouragement now and then."

Gabe pressed his thumb to the space between his brows and willed his head to stop throbbing. "If we're to be about the business of encouragement, shouldn't we start with our own authors? I can provide you with a list. Send a cheery note to each of them."

She chuckled as if he'd said something amusing. "But they already have a publisher." With one slim finger, she drew her nail along the edge of papers stacked in front of him, creating a strange shuffling tune. "These people submitted their words, their works, with such hope. No doubt fearful that they'd be rejected and that would be the end of their creative endeavors."

"Some of them deserved to be rejected. Not everyone can succeed."

"Whyever not? Is there not enough success to go around?"

Not where he came from. Everything was a competition for a place to lodge, food to eat, liquor to warm one's belly. Only the strong and the dastardly survived. Resilient ones like his sister. Brutes like him, with fists big enough to beat everyone else away.

Hovering at the edge of his desk, she stared down at him, which caused him to focus furiously on the next letter.

"The boy in the story is from the East End," she said as she traced shapes with her finger on the surface of his desk. "Obviously, you've visited the area."

"Not as often as you, apparently."

"You still haven't told me why you were in Whitechapel that day." She tiptoed around the topic he was determined to avoid.

"The day I stopped you from attacking a drunken man with a mallet?" he threw back at her.

"Here I thought you'd stepped in to save me," she said in a small voice.

And he'd happily do so again. Just the thought of Keene stoked violent impulses Gabe had spent years attempting to bury under layers of propriety.

"Do you often rush in to assist others? Perhaps you're a bit like the hero in the story."

"I'm not a hero. I don't rush in." He stood up from his chair, determined to end this mentoring session. She was too appealing, too near, too damned curious about his past. "Luckily, I know very few ladies foolish enough to put themselves in harm's way." Lifting the manuscript she seemed determined to champion, he shoved the sheaves back at her. "Contact the author. Ask if she has additional stories. Preferably less overwrought. We could consider a small collection of her tales."

She beamed at him, and he tried not to get caught in the glow of her smile. Bending to retrieve a folder from the small cabinet he kept in the corner, he pulled out an original of a letter that he often replicated when responding to dreadful submissions.

"This is the letter I sent to the horse gentleman. It's the wording I suggest you use when rejecting the others. A personalized note to everyone will take far too long."

Taking the paper, she read, her eyes darting from line to line as her expression crumpled into a grimace. "This is ghastly. Cold and unkind. There's not a single line of praise or a shred of gratitude that an author would entrust their work for our consideration."

After casting him an angry glance, she lifted the foolscap and tore the sheet in two, then again, and again, until she'd gathered eight uneven squares between her fingers.

"Ruthven's can do much better than this." Stepping toward him, she slid the fragments into his top waistcoat pocket, patting her palm against the lump she'd created. Suddenly, she stilled, her hand a soft weight against his chest. "Oh, Mr. Adamson, I've found it." A delicious smile lit up her face, her eyes, the entire room. "Apparently, you do have a heart after all."

Chapter Eleven

---

*"I never truly understood the allure of
ballroom dancing. Until tonight."*

—Journal of Clary Ruthven

"They're here!" Clary waved through the long sash window
of Stanhope House before picking up her skirts and sprinting
toward the front door. Slippers skidding on marble, she passed
the appalled housekeeper and cheerily called back, "I'll get the
door, Mrs. Simms. It's my friend Helen and her student."

Sophia and Grey's new housekeeper, a steel-haired lady
with a back as straight as a fire poker, looked supremely
unimpressed. "Very well, Miss Ruthven."

Clary yanked the door open before they had a chance to
knock, and Helen let out a gasp.

"My goodness, you look like a fairy-tale princess."

"Stop talking nonsense and come inside." Clary smiled
as Sally and Helen, their eyes aglow, took in the dusk-gilded

facade of Sophia and Grey's London home. "You both look magnificent."

Helen wore a simple, elegant gown of dark green velvet. Sally had chosen a riotous pink from among the fabrics donated to Fisk Academy. She'd added ribbons and neatly stitched rows of seed beads around the bodice. Clary thoroughly approved of the girl's style.

"I'm sorry we're late," Helen said as Clary led them both to the ballroom. "London traffic is always full of surprises."

"You're early enough. Though a few guests have begun to arrive, dancing won't start for a good half hour." Clary realized Helen was no longer following her and turned back to find her friend had stalled on the ballroom threshold, examining the ceiling and walls and spacious polished floor. Musicians had already assembled in a corner, and Helen tapped her foot in time as they warmed their instruments with a lively allegro. Sally swept toward the center of the room and pinwheeled around, giggling with glee.

"It's magnificent," Helen pronounced. "Truly the most beautiful room I've ever seen."

The pale dove walls were opalescent on closer inspection, as flecks of mica had been added to the paint, according to Grey. And the ceiling had been decorated with a glorious fresco—fat cherubs and svelte angels frolicking against a bright blue sky filled with wispy clouds. The wainscoting had been gilded, as had every fixture in the room. Though gaslight had been installed throughout the house, candle sconces burned on the ballroom walls to give the space a warm glow.

"I'll have to thank your sister again for loaning us use of her home." Helen began tapping her lip, no doubt plotting where to position herself to give the speech she planned to make to the assembled guests.

"She was glad to do so, and she's promised a generous donation too." Clary hoped Kit and the many others they'd invited would share Grey and Sophia's philanthropic impulses.

"And I did mean what I said. You're downright princess-like tonight," Helen mused.

"Stop." Clary patted the coiffure Sophia's maid had spent far too long fussing over. "Do you want to take a bet on how long it will be like this before it all comes tumbling down?"

"Your dress is too pretty for anyone to notice."

"Thank you." Unwilling to spend more money at the modiste, Clary had altered and embellished her favorite purple gown, taking the tight-sleeved bodice apart to create one that left her arms and shoulders bare, except for a dark purple cluster of velvet rosettes that served as straps. "These are the worst part." Clary tugged at the long white gloves Sophia had loaned her. On Sophia's slim arms, they sat precisely as intended, but Clary found them gathering at her elbows and feared she'd spend the entire night yanking them up.

"Ladies, you look stunning." Grey appeared at the ballroom threshold, utterly dashing in white tie, though his coppery locks were as disheveled as ever. "Clary, do you wish to help greet guests? The carriages are beginning to line up out front."

Clary nodded at her brother-in-law and told Helen, "Mrs. Simms will show you to the drawing room after you've had your fill of the ballroom. You'll have a chance to mingle with donors before the dancing begins." She gave Helen's hand an encouraging squeeze and followed Grey into the entryway.

"Don't be afraid to speak of money tonight," he said as he led her to the door. "We aristocrats can be odd about lucre. I suspect your father's etiquette books claim the topic is unfit for polite society, but name a sum that Lord and Lady So-and-So donated, and the others will be desperate to outdo them."

Clary grinned up at him. "I'll keep that in mind."

"I'll help, of course." He sniffed in mock haughtiness. "I can be very persuasive. Just ask your sister."

On the verge of nudging him playfully with her elbow, Clary's breath snagged in her throat.

Gabriel Adamson stood on the threshold, waiting as a footman took his companion's wrap. The lady was the same who'd visited him at the offices—Miss Morgan—and she gazed at Gabriel as if he were Prince Charming in the flesh.

When he noticed Clary, his body jerked as if he'd been shocked by an electric current. Their gazes locked.

"He's the one from the office, isn't he?" Grey asked as they paused halfway down the hall.

"The ruler of Ruthven's," Clary said when she caught her breath. "That's what the clerks call him."

"Is he as awful as everyone says?" Grey teased.

"Worse," Clary rasped as Gabriel approached with Miss Morgan on his arm.

"Welcome to Stanhope House," Grey boomed in his gregarious way. "You're Adamson, the ruler of Ruthven's, so I hear." He winked at Clary, who concentrated all her energy on keeping her cheeks from turning as pink as the roses overflowing in tall vases near the door.

After formal introductions, Clary offered her hand to the young lady. She looked rather bereft, clinging to Gabriel's arm as if she didn't wish to get lost. "Miss Morgan, we've yet to meet, though I saw you when you visited Ruthven's."

"Miss Ruthven, of course. Gabriel mentioned you during the carriage ride over," Miss Morgan said softly.

"Did he indeed?" Clary cast him a quick glance. Oh, to be a fly on the wall of that carriage and know how he'd described her.

"How enterprising you are to wish to work for your family's publishing business," Miss Morgan said, though she emphasized *enterprising* as if she didn't intend the word as a compliment. "I cannot imagine throwing myself into employment or attending to the workaday world as gentlemen do."

She was perfectly polite. Soft and gentle in manner and speech. And whether by intention or accident, she'd neatly emphasized that she was everything Clary was not and didn't wish to be.

"May I lead you to the drawing room?" Clary struggled to sound cheerful, but even she could hear how her pitch had turned brittle. As she strode ahead to lead them, there was no relief in having Gabriel at her back. Thoughts of the other time he'd been behind her came to mind. He wasn't close enough for her to feel his breath against her nape, but some ridiculous part of her wished he was.

Inside the drawing room, Sophia held court, receiving new guests and chatting with those who'd already arrived. At the threshold, Clary stopped, and Gabriel swept past her, his coat sleeve brushing her arm. He glanced back, and his clear gaze seemed to see straight inside her. Right to the spot where she'd hidden her wayward, jumbled feelings for him.

"Thank you," he said quietly, his gaze never wavering from hers.

"Enjoy the evening," Clary bid him and then turned to start down the hall.

The farther she went, the faster her gait, until she was virtually running for the library. On the other side of its heavy door, she bent at the waist to catch her breath, calming herself on the scent of book leather and beeswax polish. There was one enormous window in the room, but Grey and Sophia left it covered to keep the book spines from fading. She rushed to the window, shoved back the drape, jerked up the wide pane, and sucked in deep gulps of the night's cool breeze.

She'd known all of this might happen. That if he came this evening, he would likely bring that shy young lady who'd visited him at Ruthven's. Clary had prepared herself. And why should it matter whom he escorted? She wasn't even sure what she felt for the man—only that seeing him with another young lady on his arm had her stomach twisted in knots and the center of her chest burning as if she'd swallowed a hot coal.

He was the same humorless, arrogant, joyless man she'd met five years ago. She told herself that over and over, yet the damnable part was that now she knew her characterization wasn't quite true. She'd seen flashes of more. And that was the man she truly wished to know.

Someone tried the knob on the library door, and Clary sank back into the shadows, loath to be seen. She didn't want to speak to anyone, and she definitely didn't want to sit in the back of a ballroom watching others glide merrily across the dance floor.

"Miss Ruthven?"

Clary pressed a fist to her chest where her heart thumped wildly. "I'm here," she answered. The two words were shockingly hard to get out.

Gabriel stepped in and closed the door behind him as the gaslight sconce near the door devoted itself to gilding the side of his face.

"I thought this was the door you hid yourself behind."

"I'm not hiding. Just enjoying a bit of solitude."

"The window's open. Were you thinking of escape?"

"Maybe." *If only getting away from him was that simple.* Even if she fled the house tonight, she'd have to face him on Monday morning. And he'd no doubt crowd her thoughts every day in between. "Where's Miss Morgan?"

"Mingling, as your sister insisted she do. Lady Stanhope has taken Jane under her wing."

"Jane?" Clary let out a rusty chuckle. "Finally, someone you'll call by her given name."

"She's a family friend." He flicked his coat back to place a hand on each hip. "I've known her for years."

"You've known *me* for years." Clary swallowed, hating the petulance in her tone. More softly, she said, "She seems kind and completely enamored with you."

"She shouldn't be. Her father was a friend. My sister encouraged me to invite her." He drew in a deep breath before continuing. "I've come to ask something of you."

For a stupid, folly-filled moment, she thought he'd come to ask for a dance. But that didn't make sense. He'd come with another, and etiquette dictated he show her special deference. Seeing as he took etiquette far more seriously than she did, Clary doubted he'd breach the rules.

"What is it, Mr. Adamson?"

"Reciprocity." After swallowing hard, he squared his shoulders and said, "I taught you how to jab a man in the throat. Would you teach me how to dance?"

"You came to a ball without any notion how to dance?" She tried hard to temper her surprise. But not hard enough, judging by the tightening of his jaw.

"Never mind," he bit out before turning back toward the door.

"Wait." Clary started forward, tripped on her gown, picked up her skirt, and stumbled the rest of the way. She reached out to keep herself from slamming into him, and he pivoted just in time for her to plant her palm against the hard wall of his chest. "I'll teach you," she said breathlessly. Not because of her bumbling journey to reach him but because she could feel his heart thrashing as riotously as her own.

"The first dance is the quadrille," he said, pronouncing the word as if it pained him. "According to your sister."

"Ah." Clary pulled away from him and clenched her fingers to trap his heat against her hand. "That's a dance with multiple partners but fairly simple. Come this way." She strode to the center of the library, a large open space between settees on one side and a massive desk on the other. "First, you must bow while I curtsy."

Clary dipped, and he bent at the waist, but unlike the times her brother or dance instructor had partnered her when she was young, Gabriel kept his gaze fixed on her as he lowered and straightened again. Clary licked her lips and tried to remember what came next.

"Now you'll come toward your partner as she approaches you. We'll join hands, and then you'll pass me to the next gentleman as you take the hand of the next lady." Clary started forward slowly. "Like this."

He approached and took her hand, but rather than continue on, he stopped as she swept forward, pulling him along behind her.

Clary laughed. "You have to let go of me and move on to the next lady."

Like the first time he'd touched her, he didn't wish to let go.

Her laughter warmed his chest, loosening the tension that had been building about this evening. He'd dreaded the moment he would face her with Jane Morgan at his side. Though he didn't owe her an explanation for his actions, he longed to offer one.

When she'd fled after greeting them, every bit of etiquette he'd learned, everything he knew about behaving like a proper gentleman, dictated that he should remain with his guest rather than follow Clarissa.

But he had.

Jane seemed content to speak to Lady Stanhope, and he'd given in to impulse. The desire to be near Clarissa Ruthven was beginning to outweigh reason and all the careful control he'd clung to for years.

"When we come back around, there's a silly bit where we dance toward each other and then back." She circled around him, the train of her gown lashing his ankles, and then positioned herself in front of him. "Like this." She gripped the edges of her gown, lifting her skirt slightly, and pranced toward him, then ducked back. Her scent hit him in a mouth-watering wave, vanilla and a profusion of flowers. "Now you come toward me."

Gabe stepped forward and was rewarded with a little grin. Stepping away from her was much less appealing.

"Good," she praised. "Do that twice. Then join hands with your partner and circle around with her." She came forward and pressed her gloved hands against his bare palms. "Now we move together." She started moving, and Gabe followed.

He twirled in a circle with her and then again, until she stumbled forward and began laughing again. Catching her around the waist, he pulled her closer than he needed to do. Closer than he should.

"Only one revolution is required, but I find twirling to be the most enjoyable part," she said as she pressed both palms against his chest. One hand wandered to his lapel. "This is a very fine suit. Do you attend many balls?" She swept a finger down the line of buttons to the tip of his waistcoat. "Very pretty buttons too, Mr. Adamson."

She was torturing him. Never mind the innocent look in her eyes or the laughter lightening her tone, she was a vixen. Touching him, taunting him by repeating his surname, making him ache to hear her call him—

"Gabriel?" She seemed to read something in his eyes.

He lifted a hand to her nape because he needed to feel her bare skin. Needed to thread his fingers into the silken waves bound in an elaborate pile of braids and curls. He ached to know if her hair was as soft as he imagined. Softer.

Her eyes burned with a fire he felt in his chest, kindling low in his belly. If he she kept looking at him with that hunger, he'd rebel against every damned rule, throw over every bit of etiquette, and rush headlong into a pursuit that would ruin them both.

Mercy, how he wanted her.

He hovered his lips near her forehead and whispered against her skin. "I should go. Tell me to go."

He needed her to redraw the line that had blurred for him—what he should do and could never have when it came to her.

She stilled in his arms. A terrible empty tensing of her body, a cessation of her bright vibrating energy. "Then go, Mr. Adamson."

"Clary..." He wanted to—needed to—make her understand why whatever was between them couldn't be.

Before he could find a single word, she lifted onto her toes, braced a hand on his shoulder, and pressed her mouth to his. A soft tentative brush of her soft, plush lips. "Gabriel," she whispered as she edged away.

He couldn't let her go. With his hand at the small of her back, he tugged her closer. He stared into her eyes a moment, willing her to stop him. To tell him they'd gone too far. Instead, her mouth fell open as her breath quickened, and he bent to take her mouth.

Soft. Hot. Her lips, her breath tangling with his, the little moans humming between them. Clary undid him. He deepened the kiss, pulled her tight against him, needing to feel her, taste more of her sweetness. She arched against him, slid her fingers into his hair, slid her tongue into his mouth. Still, he wanted more. He'd never get enough.

When her hand came up between them, Gabe tensed and reared back, fearing he'd gone too far. That she was pushing him away. Instead, she reached for the buttons of her glove. "I want them off," she said huskily.

Together, they tugged and pulled at the fabric, and as soon as she was free, he pressed a kiss to the center of her palm. Higher, he laved the petal-soft flesh of her wrist and drew a delicious gasp from her.

"Clary?" A woman's voice sounded through the closed door.

"It's Sophia," Clary whispered. "She'll try the door." She pressed a palm to his cheek, stroking along his jaw as if they had all the time in the world. "I needed to touch you with my bare hands."

Every stroke drove him closer to the edge. Nearer to the mad impulse to lock the bloody door and escape with her through the open window. To take her someplace where it didn't matter who she was or what he wasn't.

"We should go before my sister bursts in." She retrieved her gloves, collecting them into one hand while she swept the other down her gown and tucked a loose strand of hair behind her ear. "I'll go first, and then you can follow in a moment."

He was on fire, his brain melted and useless, his body aching and hard, but she was cool and blithe and without an ounce of shame for what they'd done. On the threshold, she turned back and gave him a look that spiked heat down his spine. A look full of hunger. He suspected she could see the same mirrored in his gaze.

And then she was gone. Slipping through the door without allowing the countess a peek inside.

Gabe stumbled to one of the settees, slumping onto the worn leather. He raked a hand through his hair, balled his fist, and still couldn't make the tremors rippling through his body cease. He pressed a fist to his mouth. He could still taste her kiss. More than anything, he wanted to find her, haul her into his arms, and taste her again.

What was happening to him? Weeks ago he'd planned to leave Ruthven's. Now he rushed to work each day because she was there.

This is madness. Swiping a hand across his mouth, he struggled to focus on what needed to be done. He made a list in his mind, as he did each day at Ruthven's. Dance the bloody quadrille with Jane. Endure an evening of trying to keep his eyes off Clary. Forget all of that had passed between them. Behave like a damned gentleman, not a raving fool.

For years he'd practiced control, learning to bury his impulses deep. Apparently, not deep enough. She'd excavated his heart in less than a month.

Clary was the last woman he should pursue. The last woman he had a right to touch or kiss or hold in his arms.

If she knew his secrets, she'd agree.

CHAPTER TWELVE

Clary reached the ballroom just in time to hear the tail end of Helen's speech. She was compelling, as she always was when speaking of a cause she cared for passionately. One gentleman near the front of the gathered guests applauded with particular vigor. Tall, slim frame, wavy chocolate hair. When he turned to smile up at Helen, Clary recognized his chiseled jaw in profile.

Dr. Nathaniel Landau.

Clary pressed through the guests and drew up next to him. "I'm glad to see you this evening, Dr. Landau."

"Miss Ruthven, I had no idea you were the sister of an earl." Even as he spoke to her, he kept his gaze fixed on Helen. Like any besotted man should.

"I never expected to be, but my sister lost her heart to him and he to her." Clary waved as Helen stepped from the small dais that had been placed at the ballroom's edge for her to stand on while she spoke. "Perhaps you know how that feels, Doctor."

The man finally cast his light brown gaze her way. "Perhaps I do," he admitted, the faintest wash of color infusing his cheeks.

"Good." Clary liked him, and any anxiety she'd felt about losing her best friend and comrade to marriage faded as she saw how the man's gaze kept finding Helen in the crowd. He was well and truly smitten, and Helen deserved nothing less. "Be sure to dance the waltz with her."

"Believe me, I intend to."

Helen finally reached them, with Sally in tow. "How was my speech? Too strident? Too wordy? Did I mention everything I should have?"

"Perfect," Clary and Nathan Landau assured at nearly the same time.

When the musicians began playing, the young doctor turned immediately to Helen. "Miss Fisk, thank you again for inviting me this evening. Would you do me the very great honor of dancing the quadrille with me?"

Helen swept a stray hair from her cheek and looked from Dr. Landau to Clary to Sally. "Perhaps you should partner Sally for this first dance."

Beside her, Clary sensed Sally beginning to vibrate like a leaf in a strong breeze.

"Very well," he said politely. "Shall we, Miss Sally?" He offered the girl his arm, but the disappointed look in his eyes was as clear as Sally's giddy grin. He started toward the center of the ballroom where couples were taking their places for the dance, then paused to gaze at Helen over his shoulder. "The waltz, then, Miss Fisk?"

Clary nudged her friend's arm.

"The waltz, Dr. Landau," Helen said in a whispery tone.

When he'd departed with their student prancing behind him, Clary and Helen burst out in nervous laughter.

"I may actually get to dance this evening." Helen folded the page of notes from her talk and began fanning herself. "And what about you? Where did you disappear to?"

"The library."

"Were you so convinced we'd sit out this dance along the back wall that you actually went in search of reading material?" Helen peered quizzically at Clary. "The library couldn't have been very exciting, so what happened to put that flush in your cheeks?" After glancing at couples performing the quadrille, Helen narrowed her gaze on one tall, bulky, black-haired dancer. "Did Mr. Adamson, by any chance, stumble into the library too?"

"I was the one who stumbled, straight into him, as luck would have it." Clary licked her lips as she watched him, recalling the feel of his mouth on her skin. "I gave him a dancing lesson."

Helen squinted at her and pushed up her glasses. "Is that a euphemism I'm not aware of?"

"No." Clary chuckled and took Helen's folded notes to fan her cheeks. "He followed me to the library and asked me to teach him to dance. That is all."

"That is decidedly not all. I've known you too long to mistake that tremor in your lips. There's something you're not confessing."

Clary bit her lip and forced her gaze anywhere but at Gabriel. She gestured toward the dance floor. "He brought Miss Morgan with him this evening."

"I see." Helen assessed the young lady. "She dances well. Blushes freely. Smiles at him a great deal. And yet he's looking at you."

He was. In between revolutions around the dance floor, and every time his body was positioned toward Clary, he looked toward where she stood at the side of the ballroom. Each time their gazes met, a tremor of awareness rippled through her, as if he'd reached out and touched her.

When the quadrille ended, the guests applauded before drifting to the edges of the ballroom to await the next set.

"You should ask him to dance," Helen whispered.

"That's not proper etiquette, Miss Fisk. You know as well as I do that gentlemen ask ladies, not the other way around." Clary pointed to where Nathaniel Landau was wending through the guests with Sally at his side, coming to claim his waltz. "As Dr. Landau so admirably demonstrated earlier."

"I've always loathed that part," Helen admitted. "If ladies could invite gentlemen to dance, there would be no more wallflowers."

"I thought we'd decided there were advantages to being a wallflower."

"True," Helen mused, "though I'm too tired for plotting this evening, and I'm afraid I couldn't concentrate on Euclid if I tried." Her eyes fixed on Dr. Landau as he drew up beside her.

It was abundantly clear what Helen *was* focused on, and Clary couldn't blame her. A moment later, the handsome doctor swept her away to prepare for the waltz. Sally swayed, unable to keep herself still, at Clary's side.

"I wish I could dance every day." Sally grinned at her. "Won't you partner with anyone this evening, Miss Ruthven?"

"No one has asked me yet."

The girl cast her gaze around the room and stopped at the only other man she'd met before. "Why not that gentleman who came to the school and stopped Mr. Keene? He did us both a good deed that day." Sally shivered, as she often did when referring to the man who refused to let her be, despite her repeated rebuff of his advances.

"I happen to know that Mr. Adamson is not skilled at dancing. He may not know how to waltz."

"But it's the easiest dance ever. It's just a lot of twirling and stepping." She demonstrated by dancing the waltz box pattern and spinning at Clary's side. "You could teach him."

Clary pressed the back of her hand to her overheated cheeks. "I needn't dance tonight, Sally."

"Miss Ruthven." A soft voice came from behind.

Clary stood and turned toward the sound. Miss Morgan approached. Alone.

"I came to offer you a word of thanks, Miss Ruthven."

"Oh? For what?" Clary's pulse began fluttering in her throat, and her nervousness did nothing to cool the heat in her cheeks. She scanned the room, but Gabriel Adamson was nowhere to be seen.

"For teaching Mr. Adamson to dance the quadrille."

"He told you that?"

"Indeed. He spoke of little else as we danced." Miss Morgan looked toward the corner of the room.

Gabriel had returned to the ballroom. Clary tried not to stare.

"Mr. Adamson and I are longtime friends, Miss Ruthven. He knew my father, who considered him the son he never had. When Papa died, it was only natural that Gabriel and I continue as acquaintances. I'm very fond of his sister too."

If the lady had come to tell her details about Gabriel's history, Clary was all too eager to listen. But if Miss Morgan had come to brag of their connection, Clary wasn't sure how much more she wished to hear.

"What I mean to say is that I sense how much he wishes to dance with you, and I hope you will accept his invitation." She peered down at the program folded in her hand. "Another waltz comes soon. That is a rather facile dance."

Also the one requiring partners to stand the closest. Clary shifted on her slippers. "Thank you for coming to speak to me, Miss Morgan. However, Mr. Adamson hasn't asked me to dance. Until he does, I shall await another partner." Not that she expected one to appear. Though she suspected Helen would urge Dr. Landau to take the same pity on her as he'd shown Sally.

"For his sake," Jane Morgan leaned in and whispered near Clary's ear, "I shall offer him a bit of encouragement."

G abe escaped the heat of the ballroom and strode into the Stanhope's high-ceilinged main hall. The air smelled of roses, and he spun around, expecting to find Clary nearby.

Disappointment welled up when he saw only footmen preparing to dispense refreshments and a cluster of maids watching at the threshold as the guests danced.

Striding forward, he swiped a champagne flute from a footman's tray and downed the fizzy sweetness in one swallow. Sweet and fizzy. Champagne and Clary Ruthven had a good deal in common. He reached for another glass, tipping it back so quickly, a bit dribbled onto his rented suit.

"Are you trying to drown yourself in it or just get soused?" The feminine voice emanated from near a potted palm in the long hall.

He knew that voice, and he knew he shouldn't seek her in a spot where others couldn't see them. Not that he wanted anyone to see what he wished to do with her, but he had no desire to risk her reputation or his job.

"Come here," she insisted. "I need to speak to you."

His hesitation was so momentary it could hardly be called hesitation at all. "Yes, Miss Ruthven? What did you wish to speak to me about?"

A hand shot out and gripped the lapel of his jacket. She pulled him toward her, behind the leafy foliage.

"Miss Morgan says you spoke to her of me."

He frowned. He expected Jane Morgan to be a bit more discreet and a bit less eager to play matchmaker. "I told her that you instructed me in dancing the quadrille."

"Nice of you to acknowledge my assistance."

"No, it wasn't." Nice. He didn't wish her to think him nice. Nothing he'd done in his life was nice, and nothing he wanted to do when she was near was nice either. "Perhaps I simply wanted you to get the blame if I stepped on her toes."

"Did you?"

"Step on her toes? Thankfully, no." He looked down, where her fingers were still curved around his lapel, and then at her mouth. He licked his lips, longing to taste her again. He lifted his glass between them. "Do you like champagne?"

"I do." Without any hesitation, she took his flute and downed the rest. She shivered and smiled up at him. "I love the bubbles."

He loved her smiles and how freely she gave them.

"I would ask you to dance, but I don't know how to perform any of the other sets."

"Ah," she said, tugging at his lapel. "That is the matter I wished to speak to you about." Releasing his jacket and scooting out from behind the palm, she crooked a finger and said, "Come with me."

He'd never received a more innocent, erotic, enticing invitation in his life. And he knew with bone-deep certainty that if he took the next step and followed her, there would be no going back. Not just tonight. But every night after. He wanted her. If he followed her, he'd snap his thread of self-restraint and touch her again. Taste her again.

"I thought I'd show you how to waltz, and then wait to see if you ask me to dance the next one with you." Her laughter had a musical quality that echoed in his chest.

He followed as she led him into the drawing room he'd entered with Jane when they arrived. Empty now but for the detritus of discarded cordial glasses and teacups.

"I think we'll have enough room here." In the space between the fireplace and the settee, she spun in a circle, causing the hem of her gown to flutter up, much as it had that day he'd seen her storming out of Fisk Academy with a mallet in her hand. She lifted a hand out to him. "Dancers get a little closer for the waltz."

Striding toward her, Gabe shouted at himself to go slow. To behave like the gentleman he'd trained himself to be.

Gloveless fingers on him, she slid a hand down his arm until their palms were flat against each other. Their fingers threaded together. She came closer, guiding his arm around her waist.

Gabe hissed at the feel of her body against him. The quadrille hadn't felt like this, and he was grateful he'd chosen that dance rather than this one to partner Jane. "What comes next?" He gazed at her mouth and wished more kissing was on the agenda.

"We move in a box pattern." She moved closer, her left hand braced on his arm. "Just follow my lead. At least for now." She slid one foot over and then other, then the same foot back, followed by the other. Then over again, back again. A box shape, just as she'd described. "Excellent," she praised, and he hated the thrill of pleasure the single word spun through him. "Except once you've gotten the steps down, you should keep your head up, eyes on me."

"That won't be difficult."

She tripped, her lips parted, shock widening her eyes. Mercy, did the lady truly not know how appealing she was?

"The real trick," she said in a quavering voice, "is weaving along with the other couples."

But there weren't any other couples in the drawing room. Only him. Only her. The settee in the periphery of his vision taunted him. How easy it would be to lead her back, lay her back, and continue what they'd started in the library.

He stumbled, and she squeezed his arm tightly.

"You're distracted," she chastised. "Perhaps we should stop and rejoin the others."

"I was thinking of you." He glanced at their joined hands. She hadn't put her gloves back on, and he loved that her heat was warming his palm. "Remembering your hands on me." He licked his lips when hers parted, her breath rushing out to tickle his face. "Remembering our kiss. Wishing we could pick up where we'd left off."

He brought their joined hands to his mouth, pressed a kiss to the back of her fingers. Warning bells raged in his head. He'd silenced his conscience all those years in Rigg's employ, but the voice was stronger now. Yet he couldn't stop kissing her, pressing his lips to her hand, her wrist. She responded, lifting a finger to trace the shape of his mouth. When she slid gently along the seam, he took her fingertip between his teeth. She tasted of vanilla and cinnamon, as if she'd just pulled her hand from a biscuit jar.

Running her finger across a jagged line near his mouth, she traced an old scar. "Tell me how you got this."

The spell was broken. Even the slight buzz of champagne couldn't keep reality at bay. He was a scarred, twisted man, and she was lovely and good and everything he could never deserve.

He looked around him to ground himself. Gazing into her eyes, holding her in his arms, he'd forgotten who he was. Who she was. That he stood sucking her finger in her own brother's home. The brother who paid his wages and could decide to sack him without a second thought.

"We should go back to the ballroom," he said, though each word was painful to get out, as if he didn't have enough breath for any of them.

She stilled as she had in the library. Frozen in frustration and disappointment. "Very well, Mr. Adamson." Without waiting for him, she rushed for the door. "Tell Miss Morgan there's no need to thank me this time."

"For what?"

"For the moment when you take her into your arms for the next dance."

"And if I ask you instead?" He shouldn't. He couldn't. But he wanted to. Desperately.

"I'd say no."

CHAPTER THIRTEEN

On the Monday following the charity ball, Clary beat her usual arrival time at Ruthven's by an hour.

She'd slept fitfully, risen before the sun came up to dress in the dark, and left the house with a bag filled with a drawing pad, pencils, brushes, and a portable watercolor set. She'd walked the short distance to the British Museum to sketch, attempting to catch the pinks and golds and peaches of dawn in quick washes of watercolor as morning glow lit up the Portland stone facade.

The hour was still early when she finished. She'd walked the park for an hour, ambling along the row of costermongers' carts before finally making her way to the office.

After unlocking the front door, she settled her bag on the desk she'd been given, directly across from Daughtry's, and carefully pulled out the cluster of blooms she'd purchased from a flower seller. This, she realized, was the danger of having one's own money. Coins in one's pocket were too easily spent.

A rustle of movement set her senses tingling, and she turned to find Gabriel in the doorway of his office, shoulder against the frame, arms crossed, as if he'd been settled there awhile. Watching her.

"Good morning," she offered cheerily, attempting to be as professional and unaffected by him as she'd promised herself she'd be. At least during working hours. She was prepared to allow herself to think whatever thoughts she wished about him after leaving the office.

"Flowers aren't allowed at Ruthven's," he barked from across the room.

"That's outrageous." Clary whirled on him, nearly dropping the cluster of tulips and daffodils. "Flowers should be allowed everywhere. If I ruled the world, they'd be required." She stomped over, holding the bouquet out under his nose. "How can you ban such beauty from any space?"

He glared down at the perfect pink tulip heads and frilled daffodil trumpets and sniffed. "Very nice," he said in a smoky voice. His lips eased into a mischievous grin.

Clary's mouth fell open. "You're teasing me. *You* are actually attempting to be jovial."

"And doing a terrible job, apparently." He returned his mouth to the stony expression he usually wore. "I shan't try again."

Clary started to insist he must, and he grinned once more, sending her belly into a flip-flopping tumble. She leaned closer, and he bowed his head. When he reached up, her heartbeat skipped several beats. But instead of touching her, he swept a finger along the edge of a daffodil petal.

"They're prettier than most flowers," he acknowledged.

"Tulips and daffodils." Clary pointed from the pink blooms to the yellow. "They're harbingers of spring and always welcome after the winter doldrums. Don't you like flowers?"

"If I admit that I don't, are you going to tell me again how you'll require them everywhere once you're queen?"

"Perhaps." Clary breathed deep, relishing the combination of the flower's green scent mixed with his. "But first tell me why you don't like them."

He stared at her intensely before turning away, moving into his office. "Flowers remind me of death. A friend of my mother's was a flower seller. She'd gift us the old ones, mostly roses whose petals had begun to wilt. They smelled sour and sickly."

"But these don't." Clary smelled them again and wished she'd purchased pungent lilies or hyacinths, scents sure to win over the staunchest flower doubter.

"No," he said, turning to face her as he leaned against the front edge of his desk. "They smell fresh and sweet. Like you."

For a long breathless moment, they stared at each other. His gaze dropped to her mouth, and heat flared there and in her cheeks and then her chest. He didn't have to touch her to affect her because she remembered, with searing detail, every time he had.

Then the bubble burst, and he stood up sharply from his desk, buttoning his suit coat and casting his gaze over her shoulder. "Good morning, Daughtry. Thank you for coming in early."

Clary had been so focused on Gabriel she hadn't heard the older man shuffle up quietly behind her.

"The missus says spring blooms always bring cheer," Daughtry said approvingly as he joined them in the office. "Well done, Miss Ruthven." Passing a folder to Gabriel, he said, "Here is the information you requested, sir. Everything is in order for the vendor appointments this morning. The first arrives at nine."

After flipping through several of the sheets in the folder, Gabriel glanced at Clary. "Would you like to sit in on one or two of the meetings, Miss Ruthven?"

"I'd like to sit in on all of them, if you don't mind."

He lifted a hand and gripped the back of his neck, staring at the floor with a concentrated frown as if doing complex mathematical calculations in his head. Finally, he shot her one his cool all-business looks. "Very well. I'll see you in my office in a couple of hours."

The man was like a faulty tap that couldn't decide whether to run hot or cold. Clary told herself to take the dismissal in stride, nodded once in agreement, and offered Daughtry a friendly smile before returning to her desk. As she went, she heard the old man rise to her defense.

"Can't but admire the girl's eagerness, sir."

Mr. Adamson offered no reply.

The problem for Gabe was that he admired a great deal more than Clarissa Ruthven's eagerness.

The lady got under his every defense. This morning he'd arrived early, vowing to take a new tack, to remember when he caught sight of her that this was a place of business. Her brother had entrusted her mentoring to his care.

But she'd come in humming merrily and drawing that damned cluster of pretty flowers from her bag. The minute their gazes clashed across the office, every vow he'd made shattered, and he'd only wished to see her smile.

In the ring, he'd quickly learned that taking every opening to throw a punch took too much energy. He'd learned the power of feint, flight, defense. How to keep light on his feet, to anticipate his opponents' moves, ducking and weaving to tire them out.

But there was no ducking away from what Clary stirred in him. Nor was there any escape from the disaster that would result if he gave up his defenses and let her in. He would hurt her, and she would end up loathing the very sight of him.

"Thank you for these, Daughtry," he said, dismissing his assistant. After lowering himself into his chair, he planted his elbows on his desk and steepled his fingers in front of him. How had a plan with such promise—minding his employer's youngest sister for an increase in pay—come to this?

She and her cheery blooms had gone, but he was still drowning in her scent, ruminating on her smile, wishing she was buzzing around his office again.

Work. That had been his salvation years ago. He'd been awful at managing Ruthven's at the start. Only by applying discipline had he been able to succeed. Surely he could do the same now.

Turning his attention to Daughtry's reports, he found details missing, especially particulars about inventory. He took the folder and a fountain pen and headed for the storage room, managing to avoid a glance Clary's way. Time passed quickly as he recounted ink supplies and began comparing the various brands they'd purchased against Daughtry's reports. He'd left out one entirely, and Gabe began doubting the accuracy of the rest of his numbers. He examined the rolls of paper and other stock. By the time he'd finished, his first appointment with an ink vendor was just minutes away.

The workroom was quiet, clerks bent over their work, as he made his way back to his office. Precisely the kind of diligence and productivity he liked to see.

A few feet from his door, he caught Clary's scent in the air. Before he could stop himself, he pulled in a deep breath. Then, on the threshold, irritation began bubbling in his veins like boiling water.

Despite three empty chairs in the office, she'd perched her perfect round bottom on the edge of his desk, pushing his blotter aside and moving the brass stand that usually held his fountain pen. One booted foot swung near the side of the desk, buffeting the battered wood.

She had her back to him and scanned a newspaper stretched between her hands. His newspaper. To keep abreast of publishing news and nationwide events that might affect the business, he read the *Times* every day. One copy, which he purchased, neatly folded, and placed at the upper corner of his desk each morning.

A corner now adorned with a petite blonde hellion.

He wasn't sure which was more maddening—her complete lack of respect for his space or the sensual lines of her curves. The lady was made for embracing, for shaping one's hands above the camber of her hips. Too bad he'd never have the chance again, since he'd vowed not to touch her or think of her as anything other than his mentee and Ruthven's co-owner.

"Would you mind taking a chair, Miss Ruthven?"

Her spine stiffened, and he could have sworn her neck lengthened an inch. Which only drew his eye to the knot of flaxen hair above the downy skin of her nape.

Finally, she sprang into action. After dropping his newspaper, she swiveled on his desk and hopped down. Then she made an enormous production of lowering herself into a chair, fussing with her skirt, settling the fabric just so. Finally, she perched her clasped hands in her lap, the picture of feminine propriety. Except for the tattoo of her boot heel against the floor and a glint of rebellion in her eyes.

"Happy now?" she asked archly.

Not in the least. He hated himself for it; he liked her better on top of his desk. "Only pleased that you're using furniture as it was intended."

She grinned, revealing dimples in each cheek and a tantalizing divot at the edge of her chin that he'd somehow failed to notice. "Tell me," she said. "Were you always so ridiculously rule bound, or did my father convert you?"

Mention of her father sounded a warning bell in Gabe's head. That was not a path he wished to tread, nor one he wanted her to explore.

"A man who works for an etiquette-book publisher should believe in his product, should he not?"

"You can't truly like the *Ruthven Rules* books. They're dry as stale toast, outmoded in the extreme. No one behaves like that anymore"—she lifted a hand and swiped through the air to indicate the row of hardbound *Ruthven Rules* books on a shelf behind his desk—"and if they did, everyone would consider them a frightful bore." She smirked, and the tilt of her voluptuous mouth felt a bit like a dare.

"Perhaps you're correct, Miss Ruthven." He didn't mind ceding her this skirmish. The battle to resist her would be a long one.

"Of course I am." Her pale brows knitted together, and her mouth slackened. A bit of fire banked in her amethyst eyes.

"What would you suggest?" Gabe laid his folder on the desk and settled his fountain pen in its place, putting his tray and brass pen stand back where they belonged. "You clearly have opinions on this and every other topic. How should people behave? If not according to long-accepted rules of etiquette, then how?"

"I…" Her lips continued to move, shaping words that never emerged.

"Impulsively?" Gabe would frighten her if he gave in to his impulses. If he ever let her see just what she did to him. He lifted a fresh piece of foolscap from his desk to take notes for the upcoming meeting, but the thin paper skittered across the surface, almost escaping over the edge. She reached out at the same moment he did, and their hands met, hers landing atop his.

He should have pulled away. She should have retracted her hand. Neither of them moved. The office heated, and the air became charged.

"You're playing with fire," he warned her, though the admonition was truly for himself.

"I'm not afraid of you," she whispered.

"You should be." This near, her scent surrounded him. If he closed his eyes, he could convince himself he'd wandered into an English country garden, far away from the city's smoke and soot. But he wasn't a man given to fancies, and he'd learned long ago the mistake of closing one's eyes, even for a moment, when an opponent might strike.

Clary was the loveliest opponent he'd ever faced in his life.

At the sound of movement in the outer office, they pulled away from each other. He missed her warmth, her soft skin, immediately.

"The ink vendor is first," he said, clearing his throat and trying desperately to care about the price of supplies.

"Right." She opened a notebook on her lap and removed a pencil she'd tucked between the buttons of her shirtwaist. Oh, to be that damned pencil.

Yet it wasn't the ink vendor who crossed the threshold but Daughtry, rolling in a wheeled cart like a bloody footman.

"You got the cart," Clary enthused, springing up from her chair. "It's perfect."

Atop said cart was a steaming teapot, several cups, a plate of digestive biscuits, and a tiny clear glass vase containing a bit of water and a few of her spring blooms. All sat centered on a dainty doily. Gabe squinted around his office to ensure that, in the fog of yearning she provoked, he hadn't wandered into a London townhouse for tea.

He pointed toward the tray. "I'm sure there's an explanation." He wasn't sure he'd like it, but he suspected she had one.

"I think meetings should be as pleasant as possible. Flowers"—she grinned at him—"because they are required everywhere. Tea because it makes everything better, and biscuits in case anyone's peckish."

"We're conducting business meetings, Miss Ruthven, not a ladies' afternoon social."

"Being hospitable to others and enjoying the simple pleasures of life shouldn't be women's exclusive domain."

"They shouldn't be part of a business gathering either." He was beginning to overheat. He longed to wrench the tie from his neck and fling the strip of fabric at the teapot. "Where the hell did you even get a teapot?"

She scrunched her brow. "From the tea shop two doors down."

"Take it out, Daughtry." He waved the damned frilly feminine lot of nonsense away. A part of him, the rational man of business, wanted her to go too. Yet the rest of him, the man who had suddenly become addicted to the scent of spring flowers, longed for her to stay.

"No!" She braced a hand on the tray. "Please, Mr. Adamson."

Gabe narrowed his gaze at her. That name was like a twist of the knife now. He hated to hear her call him by his surname when he knew the devilish pleasure of hearing his given name on her lips.

He was defeated. Like those rare moments when an opponent bested him in the ring. He relented. "Leave the damned thing, Daughtry. Pour yourself a cup, if you like."

The old man chuckled. "We'll see if the vendor wants some first, shall we? I'll send him in as soon as he arrives." He ducked out after offering Clary a conspiratorial wink.

"Thank you," she said softly to Gabe. She beamed at him, a dazzling smile that turned to spirals of pleasure in his chest.

No, this didn't feel like a defeat at all. When she smiled at him that way, he felt like a victor. As if he'd vanquished the dragon and every other foe. It was the headiest satisfaction he'd ever felt in his life.

But another emotion came too. Terror. Every bit as powerful as the pleasure. She possessed power over him, as easily wielded as a smile, and he had no earthly idea how to resist her.

CHAPTER FOURTEEN

*"I'm learning how much can be conveyed,
without words, with a single glance."*

—JOURNAL OF CLARY RUTHVEN

After the second vendor meeting, Clary was astounded at how much Gabriel knew about the inner workings of her family's business. Down to specific numbers of inventory. He was conversant with binderies, printers, distributors, which bookstores favored their stock and which did not. He also seemed apprised of their competitor's businesses, not to mention the various features and costs of every product each vendor offered. One discussion with an ink distributor had lasted ten minutes on the topic of the translucency and viscosity of their various brands.

By the fifth meeting, she had no idea how he remained seated in one spot for such a long stretch at a time. Between each visitor, she paced around his office or went out onto the pavement for a breath of air. During meetings, she found herself tapping her pencil, her fingers, her heels. And then he'd look at her, not in the chastising way of a man charged as her mentor, but a shadow of the way he had in the library. An intense look, as if she was the only other person in the room. He had a knack for choosing the moments when their visitor had his head down, making notes.

His looks were almost as powerful as his touch, warming her from across the room. She spent a good deal of time sipping tea, which only made her warmer and more eager to move.

The last vendor ate every last biscuit and complimented her on the tea. Daughtry had fetched them a second pot midday, and the flavor was deeper and richer than the first.

"This was very nice," Mr. Bast said as he stood to depart, handing Clary his empty teacup. "I never get treated with half this much thoughtfulness when calling on your competitors, Miss Ruthven."

"Then you should remember us, Mr. Bast." Clary grinned at the slim young man. "And give us a discount."

He chuckled so heartily that the two wings of his mustache danced above his lips. "Perhaps I shall do just that, Miss Ruthven. You'll be receiving a proposal from me via post based on our discussion, Mr. Adamson. Thank you both." He tipped his hat before ramming it onto his pomaded blond hair and striding from the office.

"Is that the last one?" Clary paced, swinging her arms and stretching her back to ease the knots from sitting too long.

"For today," Gabe said as he watched her. "Though as charmed as they all were by you, I suspect most would be willing to return tomorrow if you like."

"Were they charmed?" She pivoted to make her way back toward him and deliberately passed behind him. He'd shed his coat midday, and the shiny material of his dark gray waistcoat fit snuggly, emphasizing his narrow waist and broad back.

He twisted his head to watch her pass. "You know they were."

"You almost sound jealous, Mr. Adamson." Returning to her chair, she retrieved her notebook and clutched it to her chest.

Ignoring her comment, he pointed. "What did you write in there? You were scribbling madly during every meeting."

"Just notes." Clary slid the small notebook behind her. "Nothing important."

He grinned, and she sucked in a breath. How long had she wished he'd smile at her? Now she knew why he dispensed them so rarely. His grins were potent.

"Well, now I'm desperate to see," he said as he came out from behind his desk and stalked toward her.

"Honestly, there's nothing here you don't know." Clary gulped as he drew nearer. "In fact, I meant to say that I am very impressed with your..." Her mind filled, and she forced herself to narrow in on today. "Your knowledge of the publishing industry and Ruthven's."

"That *is* my job, you know." He came close enough for his boots to shift the hem of her skirt.

Clary nodded and stared at the knot of his necktie. "And you're clearly very good at your job."

"What's in your notebook?"

"Words."

He crossed his arms, and his shirt-sleeves brushed her bodice. "Is there anything I can do to persuade you to show me?"

So many things.

The shuffle of feet indicated the workroom was emptying. He glanced up as if he could see through the frosted glass of his door.

"We should both be headed off." He backed away.

She hated when he walked away from her. When he turned his back on what was between them. Clary shoved her notebook at him. "Here."

His eyes lit as if she'd offered a present wrapped in shiny paper and trimmed with bows. He parted the binding gently.

Clary winced and held her breath.

"Good grief." He flipped pages. "You decorate every inch of every page."

She did have a tendency to scribble in the margins. Often the drawings around the edge had nothing to do with the main composition. At one time, bunnies had been a favorite embellishment, but she'd grown out of that.

He continued flipping, and when he swallowed hard, she knew he'd found today's pages. "You...watch me very closely."

"There are words too," she insisted, pointing to the notes about ink vendors and paper mills in the middle and ignoring the sketches of his face, his eyes, his jaw, the waves of his hair.

"You left off the scars." He offered her a tight grin. "Not artistic, are they?"

"Actually, I didn't." Clary flipped to the next page, where she'd focused on his brow and his lips, and to the next, where she'd sketched his hands. No one could miss the crisscross of scars on his right hand. "How did you get them?"

He closed her book, took her hand, and pressed the leather binding against her palm. "Not a story worth your time. Nor a page of your notebook."

He wouldn't tell her. He'd shut himself away as easily as he'd closed the pages of her book. All the spark had gone from his eyes, and his jaw tightened. "Thank you for sitting in on the meetings today."

She wasn't sure if she'd offended him with her question or frightened him with her excessive drawing studies of his face. But before she knew it, he had donned his overcoat and was halfway to the door.

"Shall we walk out together?"

Clary followed him, racking her mind for anything she could say to take them back to the teasing way the day had begun. She didn't wish to part with such awkwardness between them. "Would you like to accompany me to Fisk Academy?"

He tensed, much as Kit did when she mentioned her trips to the East End.

"Sally has the girls obsessed with dancing, and they're teaching each other in the evenings. You could take a lesson too."

"Not tonight. Good evening, Miss Ruthven."

Her look of disappointment gutted him.

Proceeding up the street toward a cab stand, Clary cast peeks back over her shoulder. Those glances stilled him in place. There was no question of accompanying her to the East End, but he couldn't bring himself to leave his spot on the pavement until he'd seen her safely on her way.

Finally, she climbed up, and the hansom rolled away, but he remained rooted. Recalling her sketches, how she'd recorded his scars boldly. Marveling that she thought him a worthwhile subject for her clever hand at all.

"Plan to stand there all night, guv?"

Gabe cast his gaze into the shadows where the child stood.

"Adamson, ain't ye?" The thin boy strutted forward and stuck out a hand. "Got a message for ye, guv." Hidden in his cupped hand was a folded note. "Wouldn't mind a bit o' blunt for me trouble."

"Niven didn't pay you?" The note was from the old woman. Five words. *Peg found. Come at once.*

The boy tipped a grin and held out his grubby little hand.

"Did she say anything more?" Gabe flipped a coin in the air, and the boy caught the shilling in his palm.

"A message to ye quick, guv. Nothin' more."

In the flash it took for Gabe to flip the square of worn paper, searching for any other details, the boy was gone.

A twinge in his gut told him trouble lay ahead. He'd sought out their mother for Sara's sake, but the woman had rarely brought either of them anything but misery. The notion of being dragged into her web of intrigue again turned his stomach.

Still, he stomped toward the cab stand and hired a hansom, barking his childhood address to the driver. Sara and her betrothed were attending a musical evening at Jane Morgan's.

Gabe had insisted he'd be working too late to attend but would join them for supper. A short trip to Whitechapel and back would allow him to keep his promise.

Traffic through the city proved unexpectedly light, and the cab man dropped him in the dark lane within an hour.

No light illuminated Niven's window, though with the layer of muck clinging to the building, he couldn't be sure from the street. In the pitch-black stairwell, he placed his feet warily on the rotting wood. The entire house groaned and creaked at him with every step.

"That you, Ragin' Boy?" the wily old woman called down, her scratchy voice accompanied by the cock of a pistol's hammer.

"You invited me, Mrs. Niven. Try not to shoot me."

Her cackling laughter echoed down the stairs, and after several thumps, she appeared at the top. "Come on with ye, boy. 'Aven't got all night."

Gabe held back when he reached the top of the stairs, scanning the room behind her. Something wasn't right. Nothing he could see or touch. Just a sense. Intuition. The twist of his gut.

"Come in, boy, come." She hunched over her cane and shuffled away from the threshold. "Got a tale you'll wish to 'ear."

Gabe stepped into the lodgings warily. Without a single candle or gas lamp lit, the room was cast in shadows but for a slice of moonlight splashing in through a bare window.

"Is my mother here?" He didn't sense her. Couldn't smell the cheap rosewater scent she favored in the air. He sniffed, and his blood turned to ice.

Another smell. Slightly sweet. Almost pleasant. A herald of evil.

Gabe pivoted to bolt, but before he could take a single step, a gun muzzle slammed into his cheek.

"Best not to go quite yet, my son." Rigg spoke around the edge of a smoking cheroot, his dark eyes dancing with glee. "My how you've polished yourself. Barely recognize the creature I dragged up from the gutter."

Gabe clenched his fists, calculated, then made his move. He jerked one hand up to push away the gun's barrel, jabbed Rigg in the gut, then hooked a fist up to knock him back.

As the old bastard stumbled, behemoths charged Gabe from the shadows. The full weight of two men barreled into his side. Turning against the force, he raised his fists, thrashing one of the men on the shoulders and head in quick, scissoring strikes.

The other man straightened, whipping back his arm to strike. Gabe ducked, tucked his head, and charged at the man's middle.

The second thug tumbled back, crashing down on his backside.

"Enough!" Rigg pointed his gun at Gabe again. "Sit down, my son."

"I'll stand." Gabe swiped at the blood dribbling from the cut on his cheek. He glared at Niven, who'd scurried off to a far corner of the room. "Nice ruse." No such thing as loyalty in Whitechapel.

" 'Course it was, boy." She shot him an ugly smirk. "Peg's been dead for ages. Know it for yerself, you would, if you'd given a damn."

Gabe swallowed down the fact of his mother's death. He considered how Sara would take the news, then pushed the thought away. He couldn't be distracted now.

"Never mind that, boy. Rigg 'as got a proposition for you, 'e does." The old rotter loved to speak of himself by name, as if he was both the body and some wicked marionette pulling his own nefarious strings. Along with everyone else's.

"Not interested." Gabe raised his fist and grinned when Rigg shrunk back. He pointed a finger at the puppet master. "I'm done with you, old man."

Rigg sucked on his cheroot, a fiery point of light in the room's overwhelming murk. He blew out a cloud of smoke without removing the cigar. Bending his head to stare at the dust-covered floor, he tsked. "Stubborn as ever, are ye? Damned pity, my son." Like a whip, his head snapped up toward the corner near his back. He nudged his chin up. "Soften 'im up a bit, boys."

Another thug had been crouching in the darkness, but he jumped to his feet at Rigg's signal, lunging for Gabe.

Gabe put up a forearm to fend off the man's grab, slamming his fist into the rotter's face with a left hook. Then a vice encircled him from behind. One of the first set of behemoths squeezed him like a twist of tobacco, nearly lifting Gabe out of his boots.

"I'll be seeing ye, my son." Rigg tipped his ratty top hat Gabe's way.

"Go to hell." After he spat the words, the man in front began pummeling his stomach in rhythmic, punishing jabs. Right fist. Left fist. Gabe kicked the beast at his back, stomping his heels on the man's massive jack boots. Then the thug in front of him wound back and landed a blow to Gabe's temple.

He shook off dizziness. Pushed away the blurry blackness, brought his fists down again and again on Behemoth's hold. Then another blow came to the side of his head. And another. Then darkness. Silence.

When he opened his eyes again, Gabe struck his arms out, lashing at his attackers, but there was nothing but air in front of him and a brick wall at his back. He'd been dumped in the alley behind the lodging house. A rat skittered along the wall as he got to his feet.

After shaking the muck from his coat, he removed a handkerchief from his pocket to swipe at his bloody face. Dizziness made him stumble, but he forced himself to straighten, willed himself to keep going, one boot after another toward the main crossroad. He glanced at the corner, toward Fisk Academy.

If Rigg knew to send a messenger to Ruthven's . . .

Around the corner, the windows of Fisk Academy and a shop nearby were the brightest along the row of buildings. Gabe picked up speed, but kept to the opposite side of the street. He couldn't allow Clary to see him like this, but he needed to know she was all right.

He approached a closed-up shop across the street, tucking himself under its awning. Through the windows of the school, he saw several girls gathered in the main room, huddling together, but no sign of Clary.

A few yards down the street, a man burst from the narrow lane between buildings, shifting his gaze nervously up and down the pavement. When a pedestrian passed, he ducked into the shadows. Gabe didn't need gut instinct to tell him the man was up to no good.

Tucking his head down and his collar up, Gabe ambled toward the man.

The man shifted nervously, sinking farther back into the darkened lane.

"Oy," Gabe called to him.

"Didn't mean to do it," he said miserably.

"Do what?"

At a constable's high-pitched whistle, Gabe winced, and the shifty man's eyes ballooned. He began backing away. Gabe reached out to snag his jacket lapel, but the man ducked out of his hold and sprinted down the dark passage.

"Wot are you lingerin' 'ere for?" the constable called to Gabe.

"A man's run off." He pointed toward the diminishing shadow.

" 'As he now? And wot about you? We've 'ad a report of a young woman attacked hereabouts." The constable gazed up at the sign above the school. "Right 'ere at Fisk Academy."

"Who?"

Helen emerged from the front door of the school and approached the copper. "Thank goodness you're here, Constable. You'll want to go around back. He ran off from there."

Rather than wait for the policeman to act, Gabe started toward the narrow passage the man had bolted down and broke into a run. As he splashed through a puddle of rainwater, broken glass crunched under his boot heels. Every footfall was like a fire poker to the pain in his temple, but he kept on. He told himself he could catch the bastard.

The passageway emptied into an alley behind several buildings. Gabe scanned the dimly lit lane, but the man was nowhere in sight. Then he saw a flash of movement. A boot sticking out behind a cluster of barrels near the alleyway's mouth.

He raced for the spot, grabbed the man's boot, and dragged him into moonlight. "Keene. Isn't that what they call you?"

The same blighter who'd confronted Clary that first day he'd seen her in Whitechapel. Gabe had wanted to thrash the man that day, but he'd held himself back because she was standing nearby. Nothing restrained him now. His blood was up, his body ached, and after years of fighting, he knew nothing was better for pain than battling through it.

He hauled the man to his feet.

"I didn't mean to," Keene sniveled, tears and blood and mucus collecting on his lips. "I'd never 'urt the girl. I love 'er."

"Tell it to the rozzers." Gabe got a good hold of the back of the man's coat and shoved him forward. "Walk. Quickly. Before I change my mind and pummel you into the pavement."

Gabe pushed the man along toward the back side of Fisk Academy. A gaggle had assembled. The constable had been joined by another uniformed copper, Helen, and a few older students. Clary stood just outside the rear door.

"Gabriel."

His name on her lips was like a balm, making him forget everywhere he hurt. Clearing the hatred of Rigg that boiled inside him.

"That's the man," Helen said, her voice firm and decisive as she pointed to Keene. "Girls, go back inside."

"Where is she?" Keene called.

Gabe gave the man a hard shove, then jerked him back. "Speak only to the rozzers. Leave the ladies alone."

The fool didn't listen. He did what he'd done the first day Gabe saw him. He made a terrible choice. Twisting back, he began swiping blindly, attempting to strike. Gabe arched back, avoiding his blows.

Releasing the fabric of Keene's coat, Gabe let the man wheel around to strike. When Keene came at him with a roundhouse swing, Gabe ducked the blow, landing his own on the man's jaw. Another to his midriff, and then Gabe took Keene down with a swipe of his boot behind the man's ankles. Keene didn't move from where he landed, moaning and crying, mumbling his defense for whatever heinous acts he'd committed.

"That was magnificent." Clary rushed up and stopped short when she drew near, raising a hand to her mouth. "What did he do to you?"

"Wasn't him." Gabe grasped her wrist when she reached for him to keep her from getting blood on her fingers. He glanced toward the school as the constables came forward to collect Keene. "You're all right? He didn't harm you?"

"I'm fine." She looked away for a moment before lifting her gaze to his. "He lured Sally out to meet him and turned violent when she wouldn't…respond as he wished." She shivered, and Gabe could feel the tremor in her wrist. "She fought him. Scratched him. I should have taught her to punch him in the throat." Her voice quavered, and her eyes shone in the moonlight.

Gabe drew her into his arms. She fitted herself against him, and he rested his chin atop her head. Underneath his overcoat, she wrapped her arms around his waist.

Bruised and bloodied as he was, he let out a ragged sigh. She was warm, soft, sweet-scented bliss, and her trust in him was a gift he didn't deserve. Too soon, she lifted her head and squinted at him in the darkness.

"You dispatched Mr. Keene quickly." She slid her hand down to his, caressed his knuckles, where his scars were stinging like in the old days. "You were a fighter once?"

"Once. Tonight. Does a man ever really change?" Gabe unlatched her arms from around his waist and set her away from him.

He hadn't changed. Not truly. Fighting Rigg's thugs, taking Keene to the ground, striking out, fist to flesh, had sparked those bone-deep instincts he'd honed for years on Whitechapel's streets. Some awful part of him had enjoyed every second of besting Keene. And he'd loved the flash of fear he'd seen in Rigg's coal-black eyes.

"Come inside. Let me at least clean your cut." She'd taken his hand, tugging at him, despite his determination not to follow her. He didn't wish to involve her with this part of his life.

"I need to get home to my sister."

She didn't release his hand, and he couldn't bring himself to let her go. "Do you wish for her to see you like that? You can tidy up inside."

Sara had seen much worse. She'd been the one to stitch him up after many of his fighting ring injuries.

There was such determination in Clary's face, mixed with real concern. When he was near her, she reminded him of the man he wished to be, the one he pretended to be, not the one he'd left behind.

"Just for a moment," he said, relenting and stepping toward her.

She gave him one of those smiles, and he feared they'd be his undoing. When she looked at him like that, he was apt to follow her anywhere.

CHAPTER FIFTEEN

"We can use Helen's office." Clary led him by the hand because she liked how the strength of his grip grounded her after the night's events. Also, she suspected if she let him go, he'd bolt in the opposite direction.

He took in the small, meticulously organized room with an appreciative glance. He and Helen shared fastidiousness in common when it came to their work space.

"I'll go and fetch some water and a cloth." At the door, she turned back. "You'll still be here when I return?"

He gave her a single nod, and she took the gesture as his promise he wouldn't duck out the back door.

When she'd asked him about violence, he'd shuttered, closing himself off from her. Clearly, he wasn't a man who liked speaking of his past. But the more time she spent with him, the more she needed to know. What haunted him? Why did he guard his secrets so tenaciously?

After filling a basin in the kitchen and retrieving a few clean rags, she returned to find him settled on the stool, his head tilted back against the wall, eyes closed. But he didn't look peaceful. Lines pinched his brow under a fall of glossy black waves. His mouth had firmed in a tense grimace.

She breathed deeply, steeled her nerves, and focused on the injury to the side of his head. He'd been bashed, perhaps more than once, and his cheek bore an abrasion too. Blood had dried on his face, near his ear, and trickled down his neck, completely saturating his crisp white shirt.

"You must be in a great deal of pain," she said softly, causing his eyes to flicker open.

"I'm fine." When he saw her approach with a damp rag, he reached for the cloth. "I can do this. You needn't get blood on your hands."

"Let me." A tug-of-war ensued, though he didn't fight her with much might. "I'll be quicker."

He let his shoulders slump and turned his head so that she had a clear view of the area in need of cleaning. Without a single wince or flinch, he allowed her to wash the area, casting his gaze toward the floor as she worked. The abrasion on his cheek wasn't bad, but he'd have a fearsome bruise.

"How bad?" he asked, once she'd started wiping at the injury at his temple. "Will the cut require stitches?"

"I don't think so. It's more of a large abrasion than a cut." She applied the cloth gently, desperate not to cause him more pain.

"The sight of blood doesn't bother you?" He glanced up at her. "Most young ladies would be appalled. Or faint dead away."

Clary bit her lip before replying, weighing how much she should reveal about her childhood preoccupation with tales of horror and garish drawings. "When I was a girl, I spent a good deal of time up in the nursery, drawing and painting."

"Based on what I've seen, you're very skilled."

She waved away his compliment. "I tended to draw bloody scenes."

He tilted his head back to narrow an eye at her.

"I read a lot of penny dreadfuls," she confessed with a shrug. "Every single issue I could I get my hands on. And Kit taught me to love Shakespeare's plays, which are brimming with violence."

"So you're a lady with cutthroat tastes." He stared at the floor again. "Who loves flowers."

For a man who'd suffered real, painful injuries this evening and used his fists on another man, her interest in fictional violence must have seemed childish to him. Frivolous. Naïve.

"Why are you in Whitechapel tonight?" she asked quietly. "Who did this to you?"

He ignored her questions as if she hadn't spoken.

"What are those?" he finally asked, pointing to long rectangles of butcher paper hanging on the wall.

"Sketches for the ladies' magazine. We're trying to design a masthead." Clary had worked up a few ideas for *The Ladies' Clarion*. They needed a symbol that represented women and knowledge and inspiration, all at the same time. A few of the students whom Clary tutored in art had worked on sketches too.

"You're still determined to make a go of your project?" He flicked her a rueful grin. "I thought perhaps a few weeks in the office would put you off Ruthven's altogether."

"Not at all." She reached for another clean rag, returning his grin. "I'm more interested in the business than ever before."

"There's a bit more to publishing than charming vendors and dousing yourself with printing ink."

She let out a wry laugh and nudged his shoulder. "I've always loved the smell of books and paper and ink, but to see so many people working together to create books is truly impressive. To watch the presses steaming away and know all the work that's gone into printing a single page. It's breathtaking. Inspiring. I'm excited to come to work each day."

"Daughtry must be a good teacher to have such an enthusiastic student."

"You've taught me a few things too." Her breath tangled in her throat, and he looked up, his gaze glittering and intense.

"What are you doing?" He caught her hand in his when she reached up to untie his neckcloth.

"Your collar is ruined. There must be blood underneath."

He allowed her to remove the paper collar and unbutton the top button of his shirt. Against the backs of her fingers, the skin of his throat was hot and smoothly shaved. He swallowed, and she felt the movement against her skin. After cleaning a bit of the dried blood, she reached for his second button gingerly, fearing that once she began undressing him, she wouldn't wish to stop.

"Leave it," he said, as he clasped her hand and stroked his thumb in dizzying circles against her palm. "I'll wash when I get home."

"Home, where you live with your sister, whose name you still won't tell me."

He released her hand and started up from the stool.

Clary flattened a palm against his shoulder. "I'm not done yet."

Settling back, he trained his gaze on her, watching her every move. With a clean damp rag, she removed the last bits of blood near his ear, then above his temple. She lifted the fall of hair over his brow to ensure there were no injuries on his forehead and found herself stroking the strands back, running her fingers through the thick waves.

Dropping her hand lower, she pressed two fingers under his jaw and tipped his head up. Bending close to swipe at a spot below his chin, she felt his breath coming in quick, hot gusts against her face. Her own breath quickened. When she finally looked into his eyes, the heat in his gaze warmed her from her chest to her toes.

"Won't you tell me what happened?" she whispered, their mouths inches apart.

"No," he whispered back.

"Because you refuse to confess anything about yourself." When she began to pull away, he took her waist between his hands to hold her near.

"I won't let my past touch you." He lifted his hands from her body. "*I* shouldn't touch you."

Clary pressed one hand to his shoulder, the other to his cheek. "What if I want you to?"

He shuttered his gaze. "What would your brother say, Miss Ruthven?"

"Don't call me that." She gripped the fabric of his coat in her fist and pressed between his spread thighs until her chest was flush with his. "Here, tonight, I'm Clary to you. Just a woman. Like any other."

He let out a ragged chuckle. "You're not like any other."

No, Clary knew she never would be. Not beautiful like Sophia, or an organized mathematics goddess like Helen, or domestically inclined, as her mother had been. But she did know what mattered to her, and when she cared about a cause or a person, she did so fiercely. With her whole heart.

She cared about Gabriel Adamson.

He wrapped an arm around her waist and rose from the stool, nearly lifting her off her boots. "I need to go." Rather than keep her close, he released her, setting her away from him and starting for the door. "Thank you for tending to my wounds." Glancing up, he pinned her with a look that singed her straight through. A gaze filled with yearning. "Good night, Clary."

Frustration bubbled up, a trapped shout to call him back. All that yearning she'd seen in his gaze? She felt the same. Yet he possessed what she lacked. Skill at hiding himself away, pretending to feel nothing.

"Good night," she told him, looking into his eyes. Trying desperately for the cool facade he'd mastered. "Sleep well, Mr. Adamson."

A muscle jumped in his cheek, and fire sparked in his winter-blue eyes. He wrenched the door open, and Clary turned so she wouldn't have to watch him walk away. The door slammed shut behind her.

Don't cry. Don't you dare cry.

His boot heels sounded at her back, and she whirled to face him. Gabe pulled her into his arms, bent his head, and took her lips. A hard, hungry kiss that had her clutching at his shoulders, curling her fingers around his nape to draw up onto her toes. Then he gentled, drawing his mouth over hers slowly, nipping gently at her lower lip before dipping his head to kiss her neck. "I want to hear you say my name," he whispered against her skin.

"Gabriel," she moaned when he swept his tongue across her skin.

With a flick of his thumb, he undid the first button of her shirtwaist, kissing every swath of skin he exposed. Clary immediately reached up to help him, unfastening the next two buttons.

If she had her way, she'd remove every stitch of clothing between them. All the secrets too. Anything that kept her from getting close to him.

When he kissed the swell of breast, just above her corset, her body caught fire. Heat rushed down her chest, her belly, pooling at the apex of her thighs. He pushed her chemise aside and ran his teeth along the edge of her corset, and her knees buckled. She gripped the warm, muscled swell of his shoulder to stay on her feet.

He traced the line of her corset seam with his finger, right above the spot where she was hard and taut and aching.

"Please," Clary whispered against his hair. She pulled her chemise lower, tugging at the edge of her corset. "I want you to touch me."

She lowered her hands to push the front of her corset together and free a few of the hooks, but he stopped her.

"If we don't stop now," he rasped, "we won't stop at all."

"Then let's carry on." Clary pressed her lips to his, drew a finger lightly along his stubbled jaw as she kissed him.

He broke their kiss and cradled her face in his hands. "Say it one more time."

"Gabriel."

He rewarded her with another kiss, and when he lifted his head, Clary was breathless. But she still wanted more.

"All this just to hear me say your name?"

He smiled, a genuine, face-creasing, devastating smile. "Because I couldn't resist you anymore."

Clary gave a muffled laugh. "No one's ever found me irresistible."

"Then they're idiots." He stroked a finger down her cheek, and she bent toward his touch. "As difficult as walking away from you will be, I must go. Sara will be worried."

"Sara? Your sister."

He nodded, sliding a hand down her neck, "I wish I didn't have to go."

"Me too." Wrapping her fingers around the warm wool of his coat lapels, she teased, "Perhaps now you'll stop resisting me."

"I must." His demeanor changed, all the heat and desire cooling bit by bit, until his face fell into an expression of pure misery. He drew back, dropping his hand. "I wish circumstances were different, but nothing's changed."

"Everything's changed."

"When we enter Ruthven's tomorrow, you'll still be an owner, and I'll still be an employee. Your brother looks to me to mentor you, and he'd merrily murder me if he knew I'd laid a finger on you."

Clary threw up her hands and spun away from him, pacing the narrow stretch of bare wood floor in front of Helen's desk. "Why are you more concerned with my brother's opinion than I am?"

"Because Ruthven's pays my wages," he barked. "And he's right to wish to protect you," he added more gently. "If you had any sense of your own safety, you wouldn't spend your time in this part of London." He ducked his head, as if he couldn't quite face her to say the rest. "And if you had any discernment, you wouldn't want a man like me to touch you."

Clary's throat burned. Her chest, which had been so full and warm and fizzing with bliss, went hollow. "You kiss me, and now you're trying to make me despise you?"

"Is it working?"

"Maybe."

He stared at her a moment, keeping all his thoughts and emotions hidden behind the icy surface of his gaze. Then he left her alone.

Don't cry. She swiped at a tear. *Don't you dare cry.*

CHAPTER SIXTEEN

*"Nothing puts an ocean of distance
between two people like a secret."*

—JOURNAL OF CLARY RUTHVEN

On Tuesday after the incident at Fisk Academy, Clary stood on the pavement outside Ruthven's awhile before going inside. The gas lamps suspended above clerks in the workroom blazed through the glass.

She'd come late today, her eagerness to get inside vying with uncertainty about facing Gabriel.

As she stepped inside, she smiled at the buzzing activity of the place. Book stock had been delivered from the bindery and would soon be sorted for distribution to various shops around the city. The scents of Ruthven's were familiar now—paper, binding glue, ink, and the peppermint sweets Daughtry kept in a bowl atop his desk.

"The wife insisted I bring them in to share," he'd always say before popping another in his mouth.

Winding its way through them all, Gabriel's scent set off an unbidden fluttering in her chest. Movement beyond the frosted glass of his office door caught her eye. He was here, and eventually she'd have to face him.

The kiss changed nothing, he'd said. But it had changed her. Now she was more determined than ever to discover the man behind his controlled facade. Whoever he truly was, he was a man she wished to know better.

One of the young clerks greeted her as she stepped toward her desk. "Good morning, Miss Ruthven."

After smiling at the boy and greeting Daughtry, she scooped up a folder she'd prepared, pressed a hand to her cartwheeling stomach, and strode toward Gabriel's office. She rapped twice and let herself in without giving him a chance to reply.

"Kit?"

"Clary. Good morning." Her brother sat behind Gabriel's desk, consternation crimping his features. "Where the hell is everything? Have you ever seen a desk this tidy in your life?"

Ruthvens weren't known for their tidiness, except perhaps Sophia.

"He's extremely organized. What are you looking for?" And why was he behind Gabriel's desk?

"The report he provided last week."

Clary pointed to a short wooden cabinet in the corner where Gabriel maintained documents and correspondence by topic, organized alphabetically. He'd shown her the filing system only briefly, giving the impression he did not trust anyone to rifle through its contents.

Kit opened the top drawer and began thumbing through the papers inside. A moment later, he'd retrieved the report and squared the sheet before him on the desk.

"Where is he?"

"Adamson? He'll be in later," Kit mumbled, his gaze fixed on the document on the blotter.

"Did he provide a reason?" A kiss he regretted, perhaps. A desire to avoid his mentee.

"Read the message if you like." He retrieved a folded piece of paper from his breast pocket and slid the note toward her.

The contents were as straightforward and devoid of detail as Kit's explanation. Though Gabriel did at least mention a reason. *Absence necessitated by a family matter.*

"Odd, isn't it?" Kit mused. "The man's never requested a single hour away since Father died."

Clary stared out the office's single window and fought the heat flooding her cheeks.

"How's the mentorship proceeding?" Kit chose precisely the wrong time to fold his hands on the desk and give her his full attention. "Is he teaching you everything you ever wished to know about Ruthven's?"

Almost. And not nearly enough about himself.

"Do you know why Papa hired him, or when?"

"Business didn't interest me back then." Kit smiled and glanced down at Gabriel's report. "To be honest, there are days when the details bore me now. We're lucky to have Adamson at the helm."

His words sparked an image in Clary's mind. Gabriel at the helm, not of Ruthven's but a ship. His black hair long, wild, and flowing around his shoulders. With his knack for management and physical strength, he'd make a fearsome pirate.

When the image faded, she found Kit scrutinizing her with a single dark brow winged high.

"You weren't fond of him at first," she said, recalling how the men had initially clashed.

"I didn't know what to expect when I stepped into Ruthven's after Father's death. The West End theater world may be only a few miles away, but while I was living that life, it felt like a different world. Nothing could have persuaded me to set foot inside this place. When I met Adamson, I thought he was…" Kit looked bemused, as if doubting whether he should continue.

"You found him what?"

"Insufferable. Arrogant, proud, and far too bloody young." He chuckled and settled back in Gabriel's chair. "Perhaps I envied an upstart managing Father's enterprise so well when I hadn't managed to stage a decent play in four years."

"He must have been young when Papa hired him? Eighteen?"

"Younger than when I first pursued employment."

"What convinced Papa to give him the opportunity?" Clary hadn't known her father to be a particularly generous man, but she also had no real notion of how he'd run Ruthven's. Business was a topic he'd never discussed with her.

Kit shrugged. "I suppose the old man saw potential in him. As I told Adamson recently, his hire may be the only decision Father ever made that I have reason to commend."

Clary offered him a tight grin. After spending time with the girls at Fisk Academy, she knew that Leopold Ruthven, however controlling and cold and miserly, had been a good father compared to the horrors some of the girls experienced at their caretakers' hands.

"What's that?" Kit indicated the folder she pressed to her chest.

"Notes regarding my magazine project. I'd hoped to discuss them with"—Clary caught herself before calling Gabriel by his given name—"Mr. Adamson."

"Let me have a look."

She was happy to pass him the documents, including a few of the images she'd considered for the cover. At least he was showing more interest than he had when she'd first broached the concept at the company board meeting.

"You've put a good deal of thought into this."

"Helen and I both have. We're determined to move forward, even if we can't use Ruthven's presses. We're going to take some of the funds we raised at the charity ball and pay two upcoming graduates of Fisk to work on an initial issue. They'll produce articles. I'll work on art and illustrations."

"So you've been going to Whitechapel?"

"I teach the girls art and science." Clary sat in a chair near Gabriel's desk and leaned forward as far as her corset would allow. "After hearing about our plans, that's your only question?"

"Does Adamson know you continue to venture to the East End?"

Clary bit her tongue. Gabriel wasn't her keeper, and she wasn't at all certain he'd want his own visits to the area divulged. She definitely didn't wish Kit to hear a word about the matter with Keene. He'd lock her in the guest room in Bloomsbury Square and never let her see sunlight again.

"Why don't you come to visit the school? See the good we're doing. Bring Phee along."

"I won't expose Phee to danger."

She wouldn't win the debate. They could continue like this all afternoon, and Clary suspected she'd get no further in convincing her brother that working at a school in the East End was a worthy cause. Keene's attack had left Sally shaken but, thankfully, unharmed. Now that he'd been arrested, the tension that had been hanging over Helen and the students had begun to ease.

"I'm sorry, Clary. I know you care about your causes." He stood, his frown softening into the shadow of a brotherly grin as he looked at her. "I can't stay. Sophia and I are meeting with one of the writers we hope will join the literary journal as a regular contributor." He lifted the copy of Gabriel's report. "I just wanted another look at these numbers."

There was still something amiss between them. Not in tone or expression but an unsettledness she could feel like static in the air before a storm.

"I trust you'll bring the plans for your magazine to the board meeting in a few days. If your project will keep you here at Ruthven's more often, and I could make the decision myself, I'd send you up to use the lithographic press right now." He dipped his head and swallowed hard. "Commanding you not to go back to Whitechapel holds enormous appeal, but you'd find a way, wouldn't you?"

Clary gave a firm nod.

Kit pursed his lips and narrowed his gaze at her. "We Ruthvens can't keep a desk clean to save our lives, but we're stubborn as hell, aren't we?"

Stubborn, tenacious—words of praise or reproof, depending on how they were wielded. Kit was enough of a wordsmith to know it was a compliment with a cut, and Clary bristled at the characterization.

She didn't go to Fisk Academy because she was stubborn. She went because it was a place she was needed, a place where she could do good. And the sense of belonging was a thousand times what she felt anywhere else. Except perhaps here, at Ruthven's. At least when Gabriel was sitting in the chair across from her.

"I only want you to be safe, Clary." He approached and pecked a kiss on her cheek. "Can't blame me for that. You are my baby sister."

"And now a grown woman."

"Indeed," he said as he straightened his necktie and started toward the door. "I suppose you're in charge until Adamson returns."

"Do you ever plan on speaking to me again?" Sara placed a hand on Gabe's sleeve as they approached their lodgings.

"I'm speaking to you now." He reached out to steady her when she stumbled, not noticing a stone on the pavement. "Have a care." Never one to be fussed over, she brushed away his hand, but Gabe reached for her again, hooking her arm in his. He noticed how pale she was. Now that he knew she was with child, he couldn't help but be protective.

After days of sickness, he'd insisted on accompanying her to a doctor. She'd been shocked by the diagnosis. And from that day, she'd refused to believe that he did not judge her or think any less of Thomas Tidwell. All he truly felt was the pressure of gifting the man her dowry and seeing them married as soon as a wedding could be arranged. But first, Sara needed to inform her beau of how their future had changed.

"You're ashamed of me. I know you are."

"I'm not." Gabe led his sister in through the front door and upstairs to their rooms. He didn't wish to have a discussion where their landlady might overhear.

"What will Thomas say?" She wrung her hands and started pacing the length of their narrow sitting room.

"If you wish, I'll accompany you when you tell him." He couldn't imagine Tidwell responding badly. The boy was utterly smitten with Sara. But if he did reject her, Gabe couldn't bear for her to face it alone.

And, of course, as her older brother, it would be his duty to throttle the bounder.

"No." She shook her head in that firm brook-no-argument way he knew so well. "This child is ours, and we will do what's right by him." She cast Gabe a soft smile. "Or her."

"Best not to say a word to—"

"To anyone other than Thomas. I know." Lifting a hand, she nibbled at a nail. "Can you imagine how Jane Morgan would react? Even if you're not ashamed of me, she would be horrified. Jane is so proper, she'd probably never speak to me again." Her lower lip began to tremble, and she swiped her hand across her mouth as if she could wipe the emotion away.

"It doesn't matter. Thomas and I will be married soon. I'm to meet his aunt and uncle this evening. I must go to him now. I'll tell him we must set a date to be married. What's taking him so long?"

Gabe couldn't bear her inquisitive gaze and turned to glance out the window into the tidy back garden. He spotted one of those yellow flowers Clarissa had shoved under his nose and wished he could smell its scent.

He knew exactly why his sister's beau hadn't set a date for their wedding. Tidwell was waiting on him. The young man worked hard and saved as much as he was able, but marriage and securing a home required the dowry Gabe had promised to provide.

What Gabe hadn't planned on was Sara spotting Rigg near their Cheapside lodgings. Part of the twenty-five pounds Ruthven had paid out for mentoring Clarissa had gone to their new landlady, and Gabe awaited his next wages to add to the sum he'd give Tidwell. He'd planned to keep adding to the pot for months, but now they'd need the money quickly. He had no idea where he'd acquire the funds.

"Thank you, Gabe, for taking me to the doctor this morning."

He shot her a grin. "Thank me by getting rest, as he suggested."

"I can't." She shook her head determinedly. "I must go and speak to Thomas."

"Is he not at work?"

"He promised to leave early today. As I said, we're going to visit his aunt and uncle in Walthamstow."

Gabe knew the town was miles north of the city, but he had no idea how far. Like his sister, he'd never ventured outside of London.

"Don't you need to be returning to Ruthven's?"

"I do." He did need to get back. Wondering how Daughtry was managing the place had weighed on his mind all morning. No, that wasn't true. Clarissa had been on his mind since the moment he'd stepped away from her, the taste of her kiss still lingering on his tongue. Thoughts of returning to Ruthven's tormented him. It was the one place he felt as if he belonged. The one place where he was in control. The one place others treated him with deference and respect.

Now it was also the place where the presence of Clarissa Ruthven had upended his control.

He couldn't resist her, couldn't govern his feelings where she was concerned. And more terrifying, he no longer wished to.

"You'll be all right?" He glanced back at his sister as he started for the door. "Both of you?"

She placed a hand on her belly and smiled. "We'll be fine. And Thomas too."

"You know I'll happily pummel him if he doesn't do right by you." Gabe opened the door and stepped into the hall. "Give him my regards, and ask him to call on me as soon as he's able." He'd need to visit the bank and withdraw what funds he could to ensure Sara and Tidwell had the best start they could in their life together.

As he made the short walk to Ruthven's, his mind wandered. He'd told Clarissa nothing had changed, yet he felt the lie in his very bones. The moment he saw her again, he'd want to kiss her. He couldn't imagine a day going by now when that desire, and others, would not be paramount.

Wrestling with what lay ahead, he could think of only one option. The question was whether he had the brass to do it. Consequences be damned.

He frowned as he started down Southampton Row toward Ruthven's. The sky had filled with dark clouds, and the air was dense with moisture. Along the row, gaslight beyond office windows cast a buttery glow onto the pavement. But not Ruthven's. Its windows were dark. Had they shut up shop because he hadn't come to work?

Quickening his pace, he reached the door and found the latch unlocked. Stepping inside, he took in the empty workroom. Clerks' desks were irritatingly untidy, as if they'd all stepped away in the middle of their duties and abandoned the office in a rush. A ripple of fear shook him. Had some mischief chased them all away?

Ahead, his office door stood ajar. Through the opening he could see a candle glimmering at the edge of his desk. In the flickering light stood the most enticing woman he'd ever met. Candle glow lit up the rich burnished gold of Clary's hair. She heard his footsteps and turned, blew out the candle, and burst through the door.

"It's you," she said, offering him a smile that chased the day's worries from his mind. "I can explain." She lifted a hand, and he longed to catch it in his and feel the soft warmth of her skin.

He glanced at the suspended gaslights dotting the workroom. "You wished to save on the cost of gas?"

"You'd probably commend me for that, wouldn't you?" Another smile. Another shot of warmth through his chest. "Actually, there's some trouble with our gas line. We're not the only business affected on the row. The solicitor behind us and a tobacconist next to him are without lights too. The clerks waited an hour in the darkness, and I finally told them to go home for the day." Clasping her hands in front of her, she bit her lip before asking. "That's what you would've done, isn't it?"

"Indeed." By rights, she could have told the men to take the rest of the week off if she'd liked. "But why did you stay?"

"To wait for you." She licked her lips, and Gabe swallowed hard, remembering the heat of her mouth against his. "Perhaps I should have wired to let you know there was no reason to come today."

"You could have." He took a step closer and caught her fragrance, floral and delicate but far sweeter than her spring bouquet because of her own unique scent underneath. She shifted on her feet, as if she might dart toward him or side-step away. "But if I'd known you were here, I would have come anyway."

"I wished to see you too."

As it always did, the sight of her, her scent, the sound of her voice, lit him up inside. Warming every cold, dark corner of his soul. For some reason, he couldn't bring himself to say all he needed to while they were in the office, where he was ever reminded that she was a Ruthven, and he was no more than her family's employee.

"Would you come with me?"

She took his hand immediately and stepped forward, threading her fingers with his.

"Into a darkened alley for more lessons in fighting?" she asked with a saucy grin.

"We'll save that for another time." He let go a smile, and the freedom of doing so was a strange kind of bliss.

She stared at his mouth in dumbstruck fascination. "You definitely need to do that more often."

Gabe waited while she retrieved her coat and bag from his office, resisting the urge to adopt her habit of fidgeting. His body fizzed with frantic vigor, not unlike what he'd felt before entering a fight. Though this was worse. He'd readied himself for every round of fisticuffs, but he never felt prepared for his encounters with Clary. She surprised him every time.

He was a novice with her. He'd never conducted a proper courtship in his life.

Steady, man. He wasn't courting her. Not yet. Would he ever deserve that privilege?

First, he had to tell her the truth. No, that wasn't right. First, he had to find the courage to confess it.

CHAPTER SEVENTEEN

"Do I get a hint about where you're taking me?" Clary had to pick up the edge of her skirt to keep up with Gabriel's long stride. They'd been walking for what seemed like an hour, and he clearly knew where he wished to take her. Yet his pace was so quick, he was in danger of leaving her behind. She reached for his arm. "Are we in a terrible hurry?"

He stopped in front of her and glanced up at the storm clouds overhead.

"I don't mind a bit of rain." Clary didn't care if they were caught in a downpour. She sensed Gabriel wished to tell her something important. The frown pinching his brow hadn't eased since they'd left the office.

"I thought we'd head to Regent's Park." He tucked her hand against his arm. "Just a bit farther."

"Are we going to the zoo?"

"Not today." He grinned down at her, and the lines of his brow smoothed.

She liked the sound of *not today*. There was promise in it. An implication that there would be more days together.

More hours spent traipsing through London at each other's side. When she tightened her hold on his arm, his grin deepened, as if mirth was easy for him now. As if he was an entirely different man than the stoic office manager of Ruthven's.

When they reached the park's green, he led her to a bench set back from the main path. He indicated the seat, but Clary was too full of nerves to sit.

"Perhaps we could speak over there." Clary pointed to an oak tree set deeper within the park.

He led her over with two of his fingers hooked around two of hers, and she could feel that his hand was shaking ever so slightly. Once she was standing with her back to the broad tree trunk, he began pacing in a circle around her, as if she was holding up a maypole.

"You asked me last night why I was in Whitechapel," he finally began. "I was looking for someone." He stopped in front of her, looked into her eyes.

The pain she saw there made her want to reach for him, but she didn't want to stop him from saying more. He drew in a deep breath, his gaze never leaving hers.

"I was looking for my mother."

"You were raised in Whitechapel."

"That detail doesn't seem to surprise you."

"It's your accent."

"I worked years for this accent," he insisted, enunciating every word as if he was biting off each consonant.

Clary chuckled. "Helen noticed. She says she could hear the Cockney underneath, yearning to get out. She's from Bethnal Green. Her father was from Whitechapel."

Gabriel's eyes widened. "She's not Abraham Fisk's daughter, is she?"

"Yes, that was her father's name."

He smiled, a flash of white, and then a lovely sound rumbled in his chest. Like thunder breaking from far off and rolling ever closer. Finally, the chuckle burst out, and Clary found herself transfixed. She was sure he'd laughed before but never while she was near. The sound was intoxicating, infectious, and she found herself chucking too. Then she realized she had no idea what was so amusing.

When he caught his breath, he said, "Fisk was a scoundrel of the first order. A terrible gambler, a cheat, and an outrageous charmer. My mother used to say he could peddle water to a drowning man."

"Did you find her last night?" Clary regretted her question, because Gabriel's face fell before he looked away from her, casting his gaze toward the far edge of the park.

"No, I didn't find her." He gazed down at her again. "But I encountered someone else. A man I wished never to see again." He swallowed and closed his eyes a moment. "A man who used to own me."

Clary shook her head, an involuntary reaction to the denial she felt ringing in her soul. "No man can ever own another."

Gabriel stepped away, turned his back on her a moment and then returned. Drawing closer. Close enough to touch her, but he didn't. "My mother worked for him. She ran up a debt when I was young and offered me in payment. I stole for him, lied for him, fought for him. On the street and in the ring." His mouth stretched in a horrible mockery of a grin. "I was one of his thugs. And when I became his best brawler, he only allowed me to fight in the prize ring. Men bet on me like I was a terrier in a rat pit."

He lifted a fist between them. "That's where I got the scars."

Clary stroked a finger across his knuckles, then lifted her hand to trace the line near his mouth and the jagged slash near his brow. "But you got away and made yourself a success in business. You're not a brawler anymore."

"Aren't I?" Gabriel unclenched his fist and let his hand fall to his side. "I was a beast back then. Feral, he used to call me. I ran away, so he put me in a cage for a while." He lifted a trembling hand, stroked his fingers along her cheek. "I wish I were half the man you think I am."

"I've always known there was more to you. Secrets you kept locked away."

"More than a boring, rule-bound man. Isn't that what you thought of me?" He slid a finger under her chin and lifted her gaze to his. "Don't fool yourself into thinking I'm what you see before you. A fine suit and elocution lessons don't change what a man is at his core."

"I know who you are." Clary pressed closer, until the buttons of her shirtwaist clicked against the buttons of his shirt.

"You don't know all of it yet." He dragged in air as if it hurt to breathe. Hands clenched into tight fists, he faced her. "Men died, Clary. They died because of my fists." He swallowed hard, tendons straining in his neck as if the rest was stuck inside him. "The fight didn't stop when a man was bested. Rigg insisted we fight on." Shaking out his hands, he flexed his fingers before curling them into fists again. "Two men I fought never recovered from their injuries. Onlookers came for blood. That's what we gave them."

"Gabriel." The whispered word was meant to soothe him, but her voice had turned quavery. The horror of it welled in her chest—grief for him and the men he'd fought and those who loved them.

He deflated once the confession was out, broad shoulders sagging as his fists unfurled. When he finally raised his head to look at her, he wore the starkest, saddest expression she'd ever seen. "Now you know who I am. What I've done."

"I admire you more because of what you've overcome."

He laughed, but the sound came out rusty and bitter. When he pulled away from her, she let him go.

"You're confounding me with those girls at your school." He began pacing around the tree again, his voice fading and rising as he passed her. "Some sad East End charity case just waiting for the benevolence of a well-meaning spinster or noblewoman."

"I'm neither," Clary said, unable to resist pointing it out.

"And I'm not a waif to be redeemed." He came to stand before her and smirked. "There were nights I loved fighting, Clary. The shouts of the crowd, the sawdust under my feet, the iron tang of blood on my tongue." He shoved a hand through his hair, disheveling the perfect waves. "Some nights, I still hear and smell and taste those moments, as if they're calling to me." With a hard jerk, he squared his shoulders, as if he could shake off the past. "But I don't want to go back. I want to make a different kind of life."

"Gabriel, you *have* made a different life." Clary offered him a rueful grin. "One in which you've been burdened with mentoring me."

He stepped closer, bracing a hand on the patch of tree trunk above her head, another planted near her waist. "I don't want to mentor you. I want to—" He swept a hungry gaze across her lips.

"What?" Clary lifted onto the toes of her boots. "Don't you dare stop now."

With agonizing care, he slid his fingers along her jaw, caressing her cheek with the pad of his thumb. Then he slid his fingers into the pinned hair near her nape. He tilted her head and lowered his own until he was a hairbreadth from claiming her lips.

"I want what I should not. To touch you. Kiss you." He feathered a tantalizing kiss at the corner of her mouth and then bent to whisper near her ear. "Have you for my own. I want *you*." The heat of his mouth against her ear set off goose bumps across Clary's skin.

"Yes," she whispered. She couldn't manage more because Gabriel bent to kiss her neck, and she could only feel. Could only relish the strange elation of having him against her, his hands on her, his breath heating her skin. Strange, the odd combination of comfort and agony she felt in his arms. She wanted more, always more. To get closer, to know him deeper, to get past the maddening control he imposed on his emotions. Especially now that he'd shared his past, when it clearly pained him to do so.

When he lifted his head, she tugged at his lapel, pulling him down for a kiss. One deep, tempting taste of him, and he straightened.

"I'll ruin you," he said in a low, husky voice that did nothing to encourage her to think of propriety or etiquette or a thoroughly compromised reputation.

"Take me home," she urged him.

"Where your brother can challenge me to a duel?"

"Duels are outlawed, and Kit is only familiar with theater weaponry," she teased. "Besides, they're not at home. They've gone to visit friends and plan to attend the opera this evening."

His gaze burned even in the dim afternoon light, and she longed to wrap herself in that heat. She'd meant what she'd said to him at Ruthven's. She wasn't afraid of him. Not of how much she wanted him or of the hunger with which he seemed to want her. For once her in life, she wasn't alone in feeling too much, wanting too much.

"If I take you home"—he dragged a thumb across her lower lip—"there won't be any turning back from this."

"Turning back has never been my way."

"I don't deserve you." He drew one finger down the row of buttons on her shirtwaist, and Clary gasped. Her body was sensitive, attuned to his touch, throbbing for more. His hand stilled when he reached her belt; then he stretched his fingers, flattening his palm across her waist. "There's more you don't know."

"Tell me while you're walking me home."

He chuckled again, a low rumble that echoed with a pleasant tickle in her belly. "I do adore your tenacity."

"Then let me demonstrate for you." Clary latched her hand with his and started off toward the edge of the park. When she glanced back, he cast her a gaze of such naked admiration the quivering in her belly turned to anticipation.

Clary Ruthven rushing off to her ruination was a magnificent sight. She seemed to have no notion or care that her hair had slipped half its pins and that he'd loosed a quarter of the rest with his eager fingers. She looked wild, like a woodland sprite, and a wanton one at that.

Then the rain started. A few intermittent drops at first, and he shucked his overcoat to hold the fabric above her head. She merely laughed and bolted ahead, tipping her head up to the sky, as if the cool drops were a gift from heaven.

Even when the rain began bucketing down, she seemed content to allow the shower to drench her hair and clothes. She was truly unlike any woman he had ever known, and he had no idea how he'd been lucky enough to win her affection.

Rain fell harder, faster, until the downpour made it hard to see. Gabe led Clary to a row of shops along Marylebone Road, and they ducked underneath an obliging awning. "We should wait until the rain lets up."

"Shall we get a cup of tea to warm up?" She stretched onto her toes to scan the various shops along the road, and then her eyes ballooned wide.

Gabe knew the very establishment that had caught her notice. "Have you ever been?"

"Never, though I've always wished to go."

Curling his hand around hers, he said, "Then let me make at least one of your wishes come true."

They waited until the line of pedestrians passing had thinned and then started back out into the rain, picking up their pace to join the growing queue outside of Madame Tussaud's waxworks. One umbrella-carrying lady nearly poked Gabe in the eye, and a gentleman tried to steal their spot in the queue when the newspaper he held over his head melted in a heap of soggy paper pulp around his shoulders.

Finally, Gabe paid for their tickets and led Clary inside.

"Where's the Chamber of Horrors?" he asked the usher.

The man pointed them toward a separate room off the main display, and Clary nearly danced toward the entrance. On the threshold, she turned and reached for Gabe's hand.

"Thank you," she said when he drew up beside her, "for indulging my cutthroat tastes."

He wished he could give her a lifetime of what she wanted. That he could devote every day to making her smile at him, as she was now. The satisfaction of all he'd accomplished— escaping his past, earning honest wages—paled in comparison to the simple joy of bringing Clary Ruthven pleasure. As he followed her into the dark, shadowy room done up like a dungeon, he tried to focus on the macabre tableaus and not on the other ways he wished to pleasure her.

"The marker says this is the actual guillotine blade used to behead Marie Antoinette," Clary whispered with an almost reverential tone. She shivered as she took in the gleaming metal but then turned a beaming smile on him in the darkness.

He savored the feel of her hand in his, the easiness of being near her, her gasps of surprise or hums of interest as they proceeded through the displays. She moved quickly, missing nothing but taking in every detail with swift efficiency. She was too full of energy to linger. Her fingers sometimes twitched against his, and Gabe wondered if she was wishing for paper and her drawing pencils to capture the scenes before them.

One of the final tableaus bore the title *The Six Stages of Wrong* and was clearly meant to convey a moral lesson. Life-size figures portrayed the downfall of a man, from temptation to guilt to the bitter end of a scaffold's rope.

Gabe's skin itched. Once upon a time, it was a fate for which he feared he was bound. Others thought the same about him, cursing him to the gallows or worse. A fate, by any standard of law and fairness, he probably deserved. Not to mention most of the people he'd associated himself with while under Rigg's thrall.

After a moment, he realized Clary had unlatched her hand from his and was examining the very last wax figure, a poisoner and his victim bride. She returned to him, drawing near until they were closer than many of the other couples passing through the exhibit.

"Now will you take me home?" Her tone was soft, as bewitching as the gleam in her violet eyes. Most enticing of all, she asked the question with absolute certainty. She knew what she wanted. And she didn't doubt his answer.

As he followed her from Madame Tussaud's, he cast one final glance back at *The Six Stages of Wrong*. He'd escaped the fate he deserved. Now the question was whether he could be worthy of the one he'd been given. He wanted to be worthy of Clary as much as he'd ever wanted anything in his life.

He hailed a cab when they emerged from the waxworks, unwilling to wait another moment to be alone with her.

Inside the confines of the carriage, she leaned against him, and he willed himself to be patient. Not to pull her onto his lap and take down her hair and kiss her until she was breathing as hard and fast as he was.

"Your muscles are tense and tight," she mused as she placed a palm on his thigh.

"Vixen," he said, pressing a kiss to her temple, inhaling the fragrant scent of her damp hair.

"Am I?"

If he she moved her hand any farther, she'd discover precisely how much her nearness drove him mad. Gabe breathed a ragged sigh of relief when the cab pulled up along the pavement in Bloomsbury Square. As he helped her down, he took in the whitewashed facade. His gut clenched with guilt.

"Let's go someplace else." He wanted her, desperately, but her brother was his employer. Gabe had done awful things in his life, but it hadn't completely dulled his sense of right and wrong.

"For now, this is my home, and I have every intention of welcoming you inside." With a flirtatious grin, she added, "As long as you promise not to flee as you did last winter."

After they stepped inside, she started for the stairs, and Gabe caught her hand to pull her back. "I left because of you that night."

"Because of me?"

"You shocked me."

She nibbled her lower lip. "I can't recall anything awful that I did, though sometimes I do blurt an opinion and only regret it later."

"My reaction to you shocked me. When we first met, you were a girl of sixteen."

"And you loathed me."

"You were…vexing. But when I saw you last year, you'd become an irresistible woman." Gabe slipped a hand around her waist. "Beautiful, clever, vibrant. I couldn't take my eyes off you."

"But…you left." She leaned into him, creating an enticing friction between her chest and his. "Quite abruptly, as I recall."

He chuckled and found laughter was becoming easy, especially with her. "Your sister suggested we dance together. As you now know, I had no idea how to dance. And even if I'd managed, having you in my arms would have made it impossible for me to hide my reaction to you." Sliding a hand to her bottom, he pressed her closer.

She wiggled against him and smiled. "Come upstairs." As she reached for his hand, a woman cleared her throat.

Gabe whirled on the woman, pushing Clary behind him.

"May I bring refreshments for you and your visitor, Miss Ruthven?" The old lady's scowl raked him from brow to boot.

"No, thank you. I won't require anything else this evening, Mrs. Simms," Clary said with a tone of authority he'd rarely heard her employ. "Now," she said, once the woman had turned on her heel and departed down the hall, "come with me."

Gabe ignored the gnaw of guilt as he followed her upstairs, focusing on the sway of her hips, the bounce of flaxen waves down her back. Once he closed the bedroom door behind them, he took her in his arms and bent to kiss her neck, her cheek, her lips. She let out a low, erotic moan as she opened to him, letting him taste her with his tongue.

She was heaven in his arms. Everything he wanted. Precisely what he needed. He loved her boldness, her honesty, the hunger in her eyes that burned as fiercely as his own.

She began working the buttons of her shirtwaist, watching him as if she never intended to let him out of her sight.

And where would he go? This. Right here. This moment with her was all he wanted. This moment made everything that came before fade away.

When she got to the buttons midway down her chest, she lost interest in her own clothes and reached for his necktie. He kissed her cheek, her nose, her forehead as she worked the knot, then kissed her lips as she tugged the fabric, with a long, sinuous tug, from around his neck.

He took over unfastening the maddeningly tiny buttons of her blouse, telling himself not to tear the delicate fabric. Below her blouse, her lush breasts spilled over the edge of her corset, but her thin chemise hid far too much of her soft skin her from his view.

"You're like a thrice-wrapped present."

She laughed against his mouth before pressing a kiss to the scar at the edge of his upper lip. Like a skilled seductress, she drew her fingers down his bare chest. "Be quick, then, and unwrap me."

His fingers fumbled as he reached the last buttons of her blouse. Hard and aching, he only knew he wanted the barriers between them gone, so he could kiss every bare inch of her.

Clary only stoked his eagerness. Raining kisses against his face, sifting his hair through her fingers. Then she reached for the fastening of his trousers, and he clenched his teeth to stop himself from tearing her corset in two.

"Gabriel," she breathed against his mouth as her nimble fingers worked. He gasped when she brushed her hand against him. Rather than shy away, she drew her fingers gently along his cock, exploring, biting her lip when she drew a hiss of pleasure from him.

"You're driving me mad," he told her before pushing the edges of her corset back and dipping his head to take one taut nipple in his mouth, sucking her through the gauzy chemise.

"Gabriel," she said again, sinking her fingers against his scalp. He took her moans as encouragement, tugging and pulling until he got the chemise free of her skirt and over her head.

"So lovely." He wanted to look and memorize every inch, but he wanted to taste her too. He reached back to work the hook of her skirt, then her petticoat, easing both down the generous swell of her hips. He bent his knees and hunched as he guided the fabric, drawing his fingers across her thighs, knees, calves, until the garments pooled at her feet.

She bent to roll her stockings down, and he pressed up on his haunches to kiss her. Only her drawers hid her from his view.

"Take them off," she urged, planting her palms on his shoulders.

"I fear I'll tear them."

"Then do."

He tried to be careful as he pulled at the knotted ribbon, but when it wouldn't give way, he pulled the light cotton apart. Plump smooth thighs and a glorious thatch of burnished bronze curls were worth buying her a thousand new knickers. "You're the most beautiful thing I've ever seen. Exquisite."

"I want to feel you," she said in a breathy whisper. "I want you to teach me everything."

Bracing a hand on each of her soft, warm thighs, he leaned in and kissed her belly, stroked his thumbs nearer her curls. "Clary." He was ravenous to taste her, to be inside all of her delicious energy and heat, but he told himself to go slow.

"Hurry," she urged at precisely the same moment, and he chuckled against her belly.

He lifted a hand to cup her mound, parting her slick folds with one finger. She bucked against him, and he slid deeper. As he stroked, he bent to taste her. The honeyed sweetness made him shiver. He angled his tongue deeper, laving the velvety flesh until she dug her nails into his skin.

"It's too much," she said. "I'm falling."

"I'll catch you, sweetheart." Gabe stroked her deeper, gazing up to watch the wonder in her eyes. "I'm right here. I'll never leave you."

She gasped and shuddered against him, clutching at his hair, tipping her head back against the door, bucking against his finger. Finally, she looked at him, her eyes lust-glazed, her hair hanging in a wild gold bramble around her face. "What happens next?"

Gabe smiled and straightened, hooking an arm under her knees to lift her against his chest. "Now I take you to bed."

Laying her head against this shoulder, she let out a long, satisfied exhale, as if she'd happily doze there, but when he set her on the bed, she cocked a brow at him.

"Your trousers must go," she commanded.

Edging forward on the bed, she shoved the loosened fabric down his hips, hooking his drawers with her thumbs, and pulling those along too. When his cock sprang free, she offered him the most erotic smile he'd ever seen. Then she reached out, shaping the length of him with her hands.

"Clary," he said in warning, though the words emerged as a plea.

"The statues in museums are wildly misleading." She grinned up at him, as she continued to stroke. "I must draw you like this."

"I won't be like this for long if you keep touching me." He knelt on the bed to kiss her, and she released him with a little groan of frustration. "Lay back, love."

She fell back onto the bed, her long hair spread around her, and she was so lovely his whole body burned to be inside her. He again told himself to go slow. Despite her wonderful boldness, he suspected Clary was innocent, and he'd not been with many women himself. He'd never much liked being touched before Clary. Never cared to be truly intimate with anyone. Now he wanted nothing so much as to be close to her, to strip away every lie he'd ever told, to lose his forced control, to be unfettered with her. To hold nothing back.

As he stroked a hand up her leg, she parted her thighs, lifting her arms to urge him closer. "I need your heat," she said huskily.

He positioned his body over hers, eased himself between her legs, rocked against her slickness. Bracing on his elbows, he feared crushing her if he let her take his weight. But she was having none of his hesitation. She wrapped an arm around his shoulder and whispered, "Closer," before lifting for a kiss. When she bucked her hips, he breached her an inch, and she broke their kiss with a gasp.

"I don't want to hurt you," he said against her neck. "We must go slow."

"I hate slow," she pouted. Gabe took her plump lower lip between his teeth, before taking her mouth. He stroked her with his tongue and eased himself against her, rocking ever so slowly, nudging deeper with every thrust. When he lifted to gaze down at her, to ensure she was all right, she lifted her hips. "More," she whispered, before lifting her hips and drawing him deeper.

Sweeping her hair aside, he planted a hand on the bed beside her head, arching up to gaze into her eyes as he thrust deep. She nodded as if urging him on, and he built a rhythm as she stroked a hand down his chest, clutched at his shoulder, let out a delicious gasp as he slipped inside her.

He was lost. Clary was all that mattered. She was the bounty he was ever seeking, the reward for which he'd been searching all the ugly miserable days of his life. She was a bigger slice of heaven than he could ever deserve, but he would never get enough. Somehow, some way, he had to keep her. Love her every day, as she deserved. Pleasure her every damned night, as many times as he was able.

"Faster," she hissed, his insatiable beauty.

When she twisted her head on the pillow, he dipped down to catch her pink taut nipple against his tongue.

"Please, Gabriel, don't stop." She bucked out of rhythm to his thrusts, drawing him deeper. Then she let out a lusty moan as her sweet body spasmed around him.

"I won't, sweetheart," he rasped, lowering himself against her chest, as the unbearable agonizing bliss of his release built.

She turned her head to kiss his neck, flicking her tongue out to taste him. "I love you," she whispered against his skin.

Gabe jolted at the words. He craved them, needed them, and resisted their strange unsettling effects. Then his release tore through him, a violent rapture that turned his vision black but for flashes of light, like fireworks bursting across a night sky. He buried his face against Clary's neck, rolled to his side, and pulled her with him. She curled against him, soft, warm perfection in his arms.

He didn't deserve her. He never would. But he couldn't bear to lose her either.

Chapter Eighteen

Clary awoke to a cloudy-dusk light. A breeze, fresh with the scent of rain, wafted in from her open bedroom window. She reached out for Gabriel, but he wasn't beside her—though the sheets were still warm, as if he'd just stepped away. His clothes were still pooled on the floor too, except for his trousers and shirt.

Sitting up, she wiped the blurriness from her eyes and slid to the edge of the bed. Strange parts of her body were sore, but she didn't regret a moment she'd spent with him. Yawning, she stretched her arms over her head and smiled. Her first thought was to find him and do it all over again.

A sound drew her attention to the window. Shouting, angry voices. Altercations were rare in Bloomsbury Square, especially out in front of the row of houses for all to see.

Rushing toward her wardrobe, she grabbed a dressing gown and tied the belt at her waist as she made her way to the window.

Down on the street, Gabriel stood arguing with a little boy. He fisted his hand in the child's shirt front as he shouted at him.

Pushing the curtain aside, she slid the window up, and ducked her head out. "Gabriel."

He either didn't hear her or chose to ignore her call. Without bothering to find her boots, she started downstairs. Gabriel burst through the front door, pushing the boy along ahead of him. The child had a colorful vocabulary and seemed determined to expend every foul word he knew denouncing Gabriel's rough handling.

"'E'll 'ear o' this, ye can bet a crown, and 'e'll bury ye in the Thames, you bleedin' rotter."

Gabe released the child, and he stumbled forward, straightening his ragged old frock coat as if it were Bond Street's finest.

"Well, I never." Kit and Phee's housekeeper stood near the stairwell, eyes gaping, a hand covering her mouth. "Miss Ruthven, this is most unusual."

"Mrs. Simms, some tea in the drawing room, I think." Clary caught the child's eye. "And milk?"

He cocked an eyebrow.

"And biscuits?" The boy shot her a crooked grin.

Gabriel stepped toward her and placed his hand on her arm, caressing up and down in a comforting gesture. "Let me deal with him. I don't want you involved with this."

Clary leaned to get another look at the boy. He was eyeing the trinkets on the hall table, making a stealthy grab for a porcelain box. She cleared her throat, and he settled the box back on the table without a backward glance.

"If the matter of this boy involves you, then it's a matter that involves me," she told Gabriel. "You said in the park that there'd be no going back."

He wasn't happy with her tenacity. She could see the flicker of irritation in his gaze, but he relented, slipping an arm around her back and clapping his other hand on the boy's nape. He led them both into the drawing room and closed the door.

"Those biscuits comin' soon?" Almost the moment the boy's words were out, Mrs. Simms rolled a tea tray into the room, ducking back out as quickly as her legs would carry her.

Clary poured two cups of tea and lifted a pitcher of milk toward the boy.

"If you please, miss. Ever so kind, you are." He settled his gangly frame on Kit and Phee's lavender couch, flicking his grimy frock coattails out behind him.

She served him biscuits on a pretty blue-and-white plate and milk in a teacup, and he dipped his head in haughty thanks, as if he were a nobleman taking his afternoon repast.

"Which of you would like to tell me what's going on?" Clary rested on a settee cushion and took a sip of tea.

"Brought a proposition to 'is nibs, and he took a huff, 'e did." The boy shoved an entire biscuit in his mouth. Crumbs tumbled down his chest as he chewed. "Wouldn't let me get a word in h'edgewise. Would ye, guv?"

"What proposition?" Clary asked both of them.

Gabriel, who'd been pacing around the room, finally took a seat beside her, tipping her cushion toward him with his bulk. A bit of milky tea sloshed onto her finger. When she winced, he gently took her cup from her hand and lifted her finger to his lips. "Does it burn?" He blew against her over-warm digit.

"I'm all right." Except for the fact that she never liked being fussed over, yet somehow adored his tender ministrations. "Tell me about the proposition."

The boy yanked a dirty square of folded paper from his coat. "Right 'ere. Plain as day. Never took the time to read a word, did ye, guv?"

Clary retrieved the note and began unfolding the edges. Gabe's large hand came crashing down over hers, crumpling the paper. "It's from the man I spoke to you about. I want nothing to do with him or this child, who's one of his messengers."

"Slander!" the boy shouted. "I work for meself and for whoever's got a bob to send a message."

Gabe leaned toward him. "I'll give you half a bloody sovereign to forget this address. Forget you ever spoke to me. Forget your way back to my doorstep."

The boy scooped up the remaining biscuits and shoved them in his trouser pocket. "Done," he assured Gabe. "No message for Rigg, then?"

After digging in his pocket, Gabe flipped a gold coin in the air. The boy bounded forward and caught the shiny disc in his palm. After lifting the half sovereign to bite the edge, he cast Gabe a satisfied grin and shoved the bounty in his coat pocket. "Best be on me way," he said.

Clary scooted forward to see the boy off.

"Let me." Gabe placed a hand in her lap to stop her. At the threshold, she heard him call to the child. "I do have a message for Rigg. Tell him to burn in hell."

Smoothing the paper out on her lap, she tried to make out the words. The ink had run on the sodden page.

"Did you ever hear the story about curiosity and a cat?" Gabe's deep voice called to her from the doorway.

"He says he wishes to pay you to fight."

"Of course he does." He came into the room and closed the door behind him. "How much does he offer?"

"One hundred pounds."

Gabe snorted. "And what's my share to be? A few shillings?" He lowered himself to the settee beside her again, carefully this time, though she held no cup of tea. Stretching an arm out along the furnishing's back, he lifted a hand to stroke her hair.

"Says here that the one hundred pounds is your share, in victory or defeat." Clary placed a hand on his thigh and smiled when his muscles jumped under her touch. "Did he always pay you so much?"

"Never. At first he gave me nothing. Food, a cot to sleep on. I was paying off my mother's debt for years. Then, when I began prize fighting, he'd give me just enough to pay for a decent meal, a bit of mischief. Never enough to save or better myself." As he spoke, he gathered her unbound hair in his hand, slipping his fingers underneath to stroke the sensitive skin of her nape.

Clary's body pebbled with gooseflesh, and heat pooled between thighs. He leaned closer to nuzzle her neck, cupped her cheek, and lowered his mouth to hers for a kiss. She forgot the note, the child, everything but the tantalizing taste of him.

"How long before they're home?" He slid a hand inside her dressing gown and cupped her breast in his palm.

"Hours."

He smiled and kissed her again. Then he stood and reached for her hand. Clary led the way, and when they reached her bedroom and locked themselves inside, she pushed Gabe against the door and stood on her toes to kiss him. He groaned when she teased at his lips with her tongue, reaching around to grab her backside and lifting her against him.

Turning with her in his arms, he gently pushed her back against the door and reached down to part her dressing gown and settle her legs around his waist.

"Is it possible...like this?" she asked between kisses.

He was hot and hard between her thighs, and she wanted to try.

"Yes," he said, breathing against her mouth, "but I want to take you to bed." He settled her back on her feet.

Clary smiled, sidestepped past him, and dashed for the bed. "Ow!" Her bare foot came down on some obstruction beneath their pile of discarded clothes, and she hobbled to a chair near the fireplace.

Gabe rushed forward and knelt to take her foot in his hand. "There's no cut, just redness."

"What did I stumble on?"

He patted the piles of clothing—her black skirt and shirtwaist, his gray waistcoat and overcoat—and stalled as he shaped an object with his fingers. Pushing the garments aside, he lifted his coat, and a chess piece thudded to the carpet.

"A little knight." Clary retrieved the glowing marble horse head from Gabe's palm. The stone had substantial heft and had been carved with detail and care. "Where did you get this?"

Still down on his knees, he lifted two fingers to pinch the skin between his brows. "In the gutter. Where I came from."

"Gabriel." Clary reached for him, but he leaned away from her and got to his feet.

The horse head was a token, a reminder, jostling Gabe from a dream.

This joy, this luxurious bliss of Clary and contentment and thoughts of a future with her was a figment. A fantasy he'd let spin too far.

"When I found the piece," he told her, "I thought I'd discovered treasure. That marble seemed fine and delicate, a piece of beauty when everything around me was ugly. I believed the trinket was the only piece of beauty and goodness I'd ever possess." He cast her a stark gaze. Realization enveloped him like the bitter smoke of Rigg's cheroot, snuffing out the foolish hopes he'd let kindle into an inferno. "I never dreamed of someone like you."

"And now you're stuck with me." She smiled as if she believed what he'd told her in the park. That there was no going back. Apparently, she'd taken his words as a promise rather than a warning.

"I can't give you what you deserve." And he'd bring her misery. Pain. That little imp he'd found outside her door meant that Rigg knew exactly where to find her. Gabe had let his guard down and led the devil to her door. God, what had he done?

He stared at the chess piece in her hand, but he couldn't meet her gaze.

When she stood and approached him, Gabe backed away.

"All I want is you," she said in a tone of utter certainty. Her eyes shone with a love he longed to grasp, to hold on to.

"You don't know me, Clary." With a shaking finger he pointed at the chess piece clutched in her fingers. "I'm a guttersnipe who found a bit of beauty and wished to keep it for my own. I was selfish then, and I was selfish tonight."

Selfish, thoughtless, reckless. He hadn't changed a bit since the day he'd found the knight floating in flotsam. She was all he wanted, and he'd taken what she offered without any noble thought of doing what was right or protecting her.

"This was a mistake, Clary." Nausea welled up. He hated hurting her. He wanted so desperately to keep her from all the dangerous parts of his past, but now he was the one causing the pain shadowing her eyes. Still, he had to make her see. "This can't ever be between us."

"You care for me. I know you do." Panic threaded her tone. "I've only just found you. Don't do this." After drawing in a breath, she reached for him. "Gabriel, I love you."

Her words lit him up inside with a warmth that spread to fill up every dark space. But she didn't know the rest. And when she did, she'd take the words back. Sidestepping away from her touch, he confessed, "I lied to you, Clary. To your whole family."

Swallowing back tears, she insisted, "I don't care where you came from. Neither will they." She pressed a fist to her chest. Gabe longed to go to her, to take back the pain he was causing. But he couldn't. He'd only bring her more pain to replace whatever he soothed away.

"No man is perfect," she said quietly, in the determined tone he loved. "Not even my father thought so. That's why he wrote books telling men how to behave."

Ah, yes, Leopold Ruthven. The shadow of that blasted man had loomed between them from the moment he'd met her.

"How well did you know your father?" Gabe strode to the window and looked out onto the darkening sky. "Did you know what he did with his leisure hours?"

"The last thing I care about is my father's predilections." She came up behind him, and he ached to turn and take her in his arms. To hold her and kiss her and love her again, to forget truths and lies and live only for this moment. "I overheard bits and pieces from Kit and Sophia's discussions about him," she said. "He kept women, I believe. A mistress, maybe more than one. And he had a fondness for Gaiety Girls."

"He had a fondness for whores." Bracing his hands on the window frame to keep from reaching for her, he glanced over his shoulder. "I'm sorry to speak that way to you."

"I'm not a child, Gabriel. How do you know of his... interests?" The truth began to dawn on her, little by little. Her eyes widened, her kiss-stung mouth parted. "He came to Whitechapel."

"Regularly." Gabe faced her, leaning his backside against the sill, arms braced across his chest. "One of Rigg's girls was a favorite. She loathed him. Complained about him. Blackmail isn't hard when men wish to keep their sins a secret."

"Blackmail?"

"You're far too clever to think your father lifted me from the fighting pit to manage Ruthven's out of kindness. Or some philanthropic impulse." Gabe shook his head, a sad grin lifting the edges of his mouth. "He wasn't like you. Good and charitable. He didn't have your generous heart."

His voice had gone as cold and empty as his soul. He couldn't stay near her. If Rigg came for him and threatened to harm her—

She approached slowly, reaching for his half-buttoned shirt, clenching the fabric in her hands as if she had no intention of letting go.

"I don't care," she said tentatively, as if fearing he'd bolt. Tension radiated between them. Need and fear and a desire like he'd never felt. "Whether you blackmailed my father or lied your way into a job. You did what you needed to do to survive." One step closer, and she moved between his spread thighs. Her floral scent made him dizzy. The warmth of her body made his mouth water. He knew how she tasted, knew how it felt to sink inside her sweetness. That was all he wanted. Nothing more. Just her.

"You're a good man." Clary lifted a hand and ran her fingers along the stubble framing his jaw.

Gabe nuzzled against her fingers, captured her hand, and pressed a kiss to the center of her palm, licking her skin, memorizing the flavor and texture. "Everyone's redeemable in your eyes, aren't they? Your girls at Fisk Academy, the ragged little messenger boy, a man who used to find satisfaction in beating other men senseless." With both hands cradling her head, he held her steady. "What if I'm not redeemable? What if you wake up a month from now, a year, a decade on and wonder what you've done to bind yourself to a man like me? What if I can't give you what you deserve? What if I disappoint you?"

"I can't tell the future. I've never visited a soothsayer or gazed into a crystal ball. I only know what I feel for you and what you feel for me."

From the moment he'd met her, she'd lingered in his thoughts. Now she was prepared to give him more. All her passion and devotion. But he didn't deserve any of it. Not yet. Perhaps not ever.

"I only want to be with you," she said.

He wanted the same, but he had to let her go. Standing, he took her in his arms. She melted against him, pressing her cheek to his chest, where she'd be able to hear his heartbeat galloping. He pressed a kiss against her hair and stroked circles across her back. "You're the most extraordinary person I've ever known." The only woman he would ever want. And he cared for her enough to want more for her than he could give. "And you deserve better."

It was agony to untangle himself from her and start toward the door. He paused only to retrieve his waistcoat, neckcloth, and overcoat. He collected the crumpled note from the messenger boy too. Let no part of him remain to remind her of a decision she would no doubt regret.

"Don't do this, Gabriel." She remained at the window, but she quivered, on the verge of movement. She reached for him, opening her hand, urging him to come back and take it.

He couldn't. He kept on. Three more miserable steps to the threshold.

At the door, he stopped and gripped the handle so hard his knuckles burned. "I want you as I've never wanted anyone, Clary. But I care for you enough to spare you the misery I'd cause."

Then he did the hardest thing he'd ever done in his life. He left behind the woman he wanted as much as he wanted his next breath. And he knew instantly that she'd kept a part of him with her. His chest was hollow, burning, as if the devil's fingers had raked inside and torn out his heart.

Clary stomped toward the door, but she couldn't find the breath to call him back. Her throat hurt. Her whole body ached. In the center of her chest, the pain came in throbbing waves, as if someone was pulling her corset tighter, inch by agonizing inch. But her corset still lay on the floor, abandoned where it had fallen when Gabriel helped free her from its stifling embrace. That moment seemed days past rather than hours ago. How had so much happiness dissolved so quickly?

Striding toward the fireplace, she scooped up the chess piece, twisting the tiny horse head in her fingers. Such a finely carved trinket to be a harbinger of heartbreak. The moment he'd seen the knight, her joy had come crashing down around her. After smoothing her fingers over the smooth marble, she wound her arm back and flung the chess piece across the room.

When the trinket hit the window glass, a crack formed from its impact, fracture lines spreading out as the knight clattered to the wood floor below.

Her heart was fracturing too. The pain of it stole her breath.

After what they'd shared, she'd felt safe. Happy. Content as she'd never been. She could still taste his kiss. Her body still ached from their lovemaking. *Gabriel.*

Tears came streaming down her cheeks. She swiped them away on the arm of her dressing gown, but more came.

Would he come back to Ruthven's tomorrow? Pretend what they'd shared hadn't changed everything?

She couldn't imagine a moment of pretending she didn't love Gabriel Adamson, let alone a lifetime.

CHAPTER NINETEEN

Clary had no reason to worry about facing Gabriel on Wednesday morning.

He wasn't at Ruthven's, though Kit was, and she'd rarely seen her brother shaking with the kind of rage his office manager inspired.

"No indication!" Kit shouted as he slammed a hand on top of Gabriel's desk. "Not a single word of forewarning. After eight years of service, how bloody dare he?"

"May I see the note?" Clary retrieved the piece of foolscap and began pacing. The sentiments in Gabriel's flawless italic handwriting were familiar. Nearly word for word the same letter of resignation she'd found discarded in his dustbin. Except that he made no mention of Wellbeck's, only of his plan to move to a new situation. And unlike the previous letter, this one included no offer to remain until a replacement could be found.

Effective immediately were perhaps the two most painful words she'd ever read.

Did he truly plan to never see her, speak to her, again? What of Daughtry, who lived to serve him, and the clerks, who looked up to him, even if they made light of his dour management style behind his back?

She lifted the resignation letter again and read the final paragraph. His only mention of her. "I pray Miss Ruthven continues in her mentorship with Daughtry. She is talented, clever, and possesses an instinct for leaving everything she touches better than she found it. I wish her every success." Clary squinted, wishing she could find more between the precise strokes of his pen. Some hidden message just for her. Some indication that all that had passed between them wasn't so easily dismissed.

"Any ideas?" Kit prompted, his voice steadier than the tirade she'd been listening to for a quarter of an hour. "He certainly thinks highly of you." He gestured disgustedly at the letter.

"Mr. Daughtry has been here longer than Gab—longer than Mr. Adamson. He can take over his duties until we find a replacement." The word *replacement* tasted awful on her tongue. They might find another man to sit at his desk, but she could never imagine another managing the many functions of Ruthven's as he had. And with as much ruthless efficiency.

"Will you stay on?" Kit's question cut into her thoughts. "You could continue your mentorship, as Adamson suggests and then..." He shrugged and tipped his head as he assessed her. "Would *you* be interested in managing Ruthven's?"

Clary opened her mouth but no words would come. All that truly interested her at the moment was speaking to the man who belonged behind that desk. And the first thing she'd do would be to lead him outside the office and straight back to the shelter of that leafy oak tree in Regent's Park, where he'd vowed that taking the step they had would mean there was no retreat.

"Not immediately, of course," Kit continued. "Go on learning as much as you can. But according to Mr. Daughtry, you fit in here. Everyone adores you, and I did think you seemed to be enjoying the publishing business."

"Yes." She'd fallen in love with the place, the processes, and the man who ruled over every aspect of Ruthven's operation. "I'll consider a larger role, but not yet. I still wish to be involved with Fisk Academy, and I haven't given up on my magazine project."

Kit filled his lungs in a long, drawn breath. When he exhaled, the punishing line of his shoulders seemed to ease, his gaze softened, and a grin pulled up the corners of his mouth. "No, you rarely give up on anything, do you?"

If only believing in something, and someone, was enough. If she could bring Gabriel back with the power of her faith in him, he'd already be at her side, but that clearly wasn't sufficient. Not until he believed in himself. What would that take?

"Clary?" Kit's face had scrunched into grim lines. "Do you know something you're not telling me?"

She stared down at Gabriel's note until the black letters merged into a blurry mess. She was the worst liar in England. But how could she confess the truth to her brother? He'd speak of her ruin and reputation and probably wish to force Gabriel to marry her.

"I simply wish I knew why," Kit mused as he scratched at his temple. "Did you know I gave him an increase in salary a few weeks ago?"

"No, you never told me."

Now it was Kit's turn to duck his head and stare at the blotter on Gabriel's desk as if the square of black was the most interesting sight in the world. "Just before he began mentoring you."

The stretch of days felt like a lifetime now. As if she'd lived more vibrantly, been more alive, in that collection of hours than all the years before. She'd fallen for and lost the only man she'd ever loved. And she still wasn't sure why he was gone.

Kit shifted uncomfortably in his chair, and the truth of what he'd done came to her like sunlight spearing through the clouds.

"You paid him to mentor me in the hope I'd be too busy to go to the East End." The irony almost made her laugh, though the familiar tickle in her chest never came. Only a constant ache lodged there. "Did you know he's from Whitechapel?"

"Adamson? No, Clary. You've heard him. He has an accent sharp enough to cut glass." Kit guffawed. "I imagine the little upstart went to Eton or Harrow. Father wouldn't stomach anything less for his precious publishing enterprise."

"But he did, Kit. Father did many things that I suspect would surprise both of us." A painful knocking started in her head, and she swiped a hand across her brow. "Gabriel's history isn't mine to tell."

"Yet clearly you're privy to his past, and I'm not." Her brother had a gaze that saw deep, behind whatever facades people erected. He cast her one of those searching gazes now. "My God, if he's taken advantage of you in any way—"

"No, he never took anything from me I didn't willingly give." Body, heart, devotion, love—there was so much she wished to give Gabriel. Now her feelings for him were a tangled knot. His departure devastated her. Was it only Friday when he'd held her hand at the waxworks? Made love to her as if it was all he ever wished to do? She hated how easy it had been for him to walk away. But if he came striding into Ruthven's at that moment, there was no place she'd want to be but in his arms.

"Clary?" Kit had spoken her name more than once while she'd been lost in thoughts of Gabriel. "What are you saying?" He clenched a fist on the desktop. "Tell me he hasn't touched you. R-ruined you."

Clary walked calmly to the edge of the desk, remembering how she'd walked into the V of Gabriel's thighs. Washed paint from his forehead. Slid her fingers through his hair.

"Clary, tell me the truth."

"I love him." Mercy, it felt good to say the words aloud again. Especially to Kit. She was tired of keeping secrets from him. Exhausted with secrets all together. "Maybe I did from the first moment I saw him in this office. I never forgot Gabriel, even after four years at Rothley. Some part of me knew he'd come back into my life." Her voice quavered to admit it. She hadn't even admitted that much to herself. "I knew the path I was on would lead me to him."

Standing and coming around from behind the desk, Kit laid a hand gently on her arm. "You're rambling, sweet."

Softly, in his brotherly tone, he cajoled, "Just tell me what he did to you. If he...ruined you."

"That's an ugly word. An ugly sentiment." Clary couldn't bear to look at him. Not because she was embarrassed, but because he wasn't listening to a word she'd said. "I told you, Kit. I love him." Finally, she lifted her head, confident and clear on that one certainty above all else. "I regret nothing."

He nodded, and for a moment she thought he understood. That he heard her and had some sense of what Gabriel meant to her. Placing a hand her shoulder, he offered her a mournful pinched-brow look. "I'm sorry I entrusted you to his care, Clary. I thought I could trust him. Now I fear I'm going to have to kill him."

"Mr. Wellbeck will see you now, Mr. Adamson." Talbot, Wellbeck's spindly-limbed managing editor, swept a hand toward the offices of T. J. Wellbeck.

Gabe rose to his feet, straightened the lapels of his suit, and strode into the spacious room.

"Have a seat wherever you can find one." A white-haired man sat behind a room-spanning desk, inspecting a document through pince-nez glasses, and gestured toward a collection of chairs, most of which were overflowing with folders, documents, and books.

Gabe found a bare seat and pulled the chair closer to the cluttered desk.

"Tell me who you are again?" Wellbeck quizzed, finally casting his squinty gaze over the edge of his document.

"Gabriel Adamson, Mr. Wellbeck. Former manager and editor at Ruthven Publishing." Gabe cleared his throat to push away the razor-sharp scratchiness that hadn't eased since his last words to Clary. As if his body was determined to remind him that if he was going to speak, his words should be to her. "You did offer me a position a few weeks ago, sir. And several months before that."

"Ah, yes." Wellbeck settled back in his chair and piled his hands one on top of the other. "*Former* manager of Ruthven's, you say? Have they dismissed you?"

"No, sir." This, Gabe had known, would be the sticking point. "I have resigned my position."

"Without first securing another?" Wellbeck huffed and fluttered his hands in the air before dropping them on a pile of correspondence. He rifled through and plucked one particular letter from the stack. "According to this letter dated…" He peered up.

"About a month ago, sir."

"Precisely. A month since one Gabriel Adamson sent a rather curt, artless refusal of our offer. Never to be heard from again, I presumed." He dove his nose toward his desk, and his heavy-lidded eyes bulged in Gabe's direction. "Yet here you are."

"Is the position you offered still available, Mr. Wellbeck?"

His head bobbed up and down on his neck. "The position remains vacant."

Gabe let out the breath he'd been holding. There was no burst of relief in his chest, loosening knots, or easing of the jagged pain there. But Wellbeck's news brought a marginal lessening of the fear he'd known since leaving a resignation letter on his desk at Ruthven's before anyone else arrived. He'd been desperately tempted to remain and wait for Clary. If she did come. Perhaps she planned to stay away to avoid him. He couldn't blame her. Whatever she felt today—regret, hatred, anger—he couldn't blame her for any of it.

He hoped one day to be able to earn her forgiveness. He dreamed of one day deserving her love. But there'd been no question of his remaining at Ruthven's. He'd broken the trust of her family. Taken advantage of the forced nearness of her mentorship.

Gabe realized the old man was staring at him, glaring as he waited for him to speak again. "Mr. Wellbeck, I would be very much obliged if you would allow me to accept the position now."

After a long sniff and a purse of his thin, dry lips, the man's face stretched in a grin. "No," he pronounced with decided satisfaction in his bulging eyes.

"No? But you did say the position is unfilled." Gabe leaned forward in his chair. "I assure you, Mr. Wellbeck, I am the man to fill it. I have nearly a decade of experience earned at Ruthven's, where I managed every aspect of the enterprise." Sitting up, Gabe squared his shoulders. On the question of his aptitude for this role, he had no doubts. With Ruthven, he may have wheedled and connived to get a chance at employment, but in this case, he had every qualification the publisher could require. And then some.

"The answer remains the same, young man. A most emphatic *no*. I gave you a chance. Several of them, if my aged brain does not fail me. You snubbed your nose at us every time." The man flicked his fingers at Gabe, as if he wished he could snap like a magician and make him disappear. "Now you make the absurd decision to leave your post before you've secured another and expect us to fill the gap. It won't do, Mr. Adamson."

Wounded pride. Gabe knew that bitterness all too well. But if Wellbeck expected him to grovel or beg, he would wait a long while. Gabe's begging days were over. As were his days of demeaning himself to win favor with men who wished to lord their power over him.

"I'm sorry to hear that, Mr. Wellbeck." With a glance around at the chaos in the man's office, he added, "Wellbeck's would have benefited from my skills in management and organization." Standing, he lifted his chin and cast the man a smug grin. "Now another publishing house will enjoy the advantage of my experience." He executed a curt half bow. "Good day to you, sir."

As he started for the door, he heard the old man grumbling to himself.

"Wait, Adamson. Stop right there, young man."

Gabe stopped on the threshold to indulge Wellbeck. Mostly because once he'd stormed from the man's offices, he had no real notion of where to go next.

"You would do well to curb your arrogance, boy," Wellbeck said, with equal arrogance. "Rumor is you're rather fierce in your management methods, but every man must bow to his betters. You're far too young to have earned your brand of smugness."

Give the man coal-black eyes, some grime in his wrinkles, and a lit cheroot in his mouth, and he'd look a bit like Rigg. He certainly sounded like the old puppet master. Rigg loved nothing better than to lecture others on how best to bend themselves to his will. To hell with both of them.

"Did you hear me, boy?"

He was six and twenty and had long ago tired of being called *boy*. "I heard you, Wellbeck. Now if you'll excuse me, I need to find a job."

Walking out of Wellbeck's felt as if a binding had been loosed. A relief not to be under that bitter man's control but also a terrifying freedom. He had no job. No prospects. And the woman he longed for was probably a few buildings away, hearing of his abrupt departure from Ruthven's. His feet started the familiar path toward the office, and he forced himself to turn back.

He'd promised Sara he would meet her and Thomas Tidwell for lunch after his meeting, and if he wished to be the kind of man who deserved Clary, he needed to begin by keeping his promises.

CHAPTER TWENTY

"**H**ow bleedin' dare ye?"

"If you don't lower your voice, we'll be kicked out of my favorite coffee shop." Gabe lifted a hand but didn't dare touch his sister. She was bristling like an angry badger. "Sara, I can explain."

"I'm going to start charging you thruppence every time you say those words to me." She slashed a hand toward him across the table. "Or any man, for that matter."

"What can I do to calm you down?"

She took an angry sip of coffee, belting the hot liquid back and slamming the mug down onto the table. "Start by telling me why you crept behind me back to make some *arrangement* with Thomas." Before he could answer, she added, "Didn't you think he'd wish to marry me without you bribing him to do the deed?"

"I never bribed him. And I didn't creep behind your back." Gabe gripped the back of his neck before taking another swig of black coffee. "As your only living male relative, it's not unusual that I would wish to arrange a dowry on your behalf."

Sara snorted and glared at him. "You speak like we were born in Belgravia. I wager there's never been a King girl wot had a dowry paid for her."

King was their father's name. Adam King. He'd been killed in the prize-fighting ring, according to their mother, but Gabe didn't possess a single memory of the man. As their mother told the tale, he died the year of Sara's birth, when Gabe had just turned two.

"Well, I'm content to start a new tradition. And you mustn't direct your ire at Tidwell for expecting me to assist with getting you two off to a good start. He has high hopes, your man. Plans to be a solicitor one day."

"He is ambitious," she conceded, "but he says we must wait on you before arranging our wedding and new lodgings. Not sure I like that he must have my brother's money afore he'll be my husband."

"I asked him to wait." Gabe leaned closer to whisper. "Before I knew about the babe. You two should start out with as much as you can. Consider the blunt a wedding gift."

" 'Twould be happy to, if Thomas weren't determined to have the sum before we wed."

Gabe had stopped by the bank and withdrawn nearly every pound to his name. He lifted the notes and coins from his inner coat pocket and laid them on the table between them.

Sara dove toward the pile and clasped her arms over the cash as if a gang of pickpockets were at her back. "Are you mad, Gabe? A man doesn't flash his coin in public. Especially when he's carrying such a pile."

Gabe placed his hand over hers. "This is Knightsbridge, Sara. I think we're safe." Lifting her hands, he gathered the notes and coins and placed neat piles in them. "Now, take this and get yourself to the registry office. Tell Thomas I'll send more as soon as I'm able."

"And you've still enough for rent at the boardinghouse?"

He offered her a smile that felt stiff and unnatural on his face. "This month's rent is paid. I'll find more for next month."

"Find more?" As she stuffed the money into her pockets, her brow pleated in a fretful crease. "Won't your wages be coming next week?"

Gabe raised his mug to drink the gritty dregs of his coffee. "I quit my job at Ruthven's. Another will come along." He heard the lie in his tone. There wouldn't be another assistant as loyal as Daughtry, nor an employer as willing to trust his judgement as Kit Ruthven. There sure as hell would never be another Clary Ruthven.

"This has to do with the daughter." Sara's fingers were cool as she reached for his hand. "You told her the truth, didn't you? About Rigg and what you did to get your position at Ruthven's?"

"She deserved the truth."

"I cannot disagree." Settling back, she placed her palms against her belly. "I'm only sorry she couldn't find forgiveness in her heart."

"Clary has more forgiveness in her heart than anyone I've ever known," he retorted. And too harshly.

Sara's eyes widened. "Clary, is it? Goodness, you took my advice, then? Told the young lady what you felt for her?"

Gabe scrubbed a hand across his face. "She knows what she means to me." Yet he hadn't said the three words to her that she'd said to him. *I love you.* Because he wasn't at all sure he could back up the words with actions. Clary had every inch of his rotten heart, but could he give her all that a loved one deserved? Could he provide for her? Protect her from his past?

"And yet you still gave up the post that changed everything." Sara ducked her head to catch his gaze. "You did enjoy your work, didn't you?"

"Every single day. I relished having a purpose of my own choosing. Knowing that the money in my pocket had been fairly earned, and no one had to bleed for my earnings."

"Then why did you give her up?"

Gabe wasn't sure whether his sister had referred to his job at Ruthven's or the woman he loved. "I got them both by lying. Clary didn't know the truth of who I am the first time I touched her. She sure as hell didn't know I'd blackmailed her father for a job." He hunched over his coffee cup as he would a mug of beer or a glass of rotgut gin, inhaling the fumes, considering whether he could manage another cup. "I don't deserve her, Sara. I'm not sure I ever will."

"Codswallop." She pointed an insistent finger at him. "You listen here, brother of mine. We don't choose whom we love, and we don't choose where we're born or to whom. Her father was a right bastard, according to Rigg's girls. Our mother was little better. What does any of that matter now? You love the girl. If she loves you, go to her, Gabe. Marry her."

He gazed at her with his head tipped down. "I have no job, sister of mine. No means of paying my rent next month. Where would we live, me and this lady to whom I want to give the world on a silver platter?"

"Has she no money?"

"She was as happy as I to receive her wages at the end of the week." He waved Sara's eagerness off. She'd chosen the worst possible moment to start being impractical. "Clary is independent. I'm not sure she'd considered marriage. To anyone." That thought made him want to smash the table and chairs in front of him into a thousand pieces. Of course another man would come along who'd want her. Woo her. Another man who'd be able to offer the kind of life Gabe couldn't.

He clenched his fists and glared out the window toward Ruthven's. How long until some other gentleman caught her eye? A clever man, well bred, with lined pockets and manners that didn't slip when irritation stoked his ire.

"What will you do, Gabe? You've backed yourself into a corner."

He thought long and hard, of items he could sell, money he could borrow and from whom, skills he might barter.

"There's a way out." He lifted the crumpled note from Rigg out of his inner coat pocket. "A hundred pounds for one fight."

Sara snatched the paper from his hand, reading the message quickly. "No, Gabe." She shook her head emphatically. "Don't even think of going back to 'im." She tore Rigg's message in two, and then in halves again, and again, just as Clary had torn his rejection letter and stuffed the tattered pieces in his pocket before pressing her palm against his chest. A twinge of pain and a rush of heat warmed the spot as he remembered her teasing grin. "I won't let you go back there," Sara said as she let the pieces rain down on the tabletop like grungy bits of snow.

"It's now or never, Sara. This will get Rigg off my back and put money in my pocket. Then I can start again, find a job on my own merit." He scrubbed a hand over his face. "Maybe then I can deserve her."

Clary signed the invoice a clerk had placed before her. "You know where these books go?" she asked the young man.

"Yes, miss. Been expecting this shipment for months."

"Good." She handed him the signed document. But rather than leave Gabriel's office, he waited with his hands crossed in front of him. When he caught her eye, he jerked his head toward the shelf of ledgers behind her head.

"Boss usually notes the bill number, date, item, and amount in the blue book, miss."

After retrieving the heavy ledger, she opened the book to where a thin strip of grosgrain, no wider than a shoelace, had been used to mark the last entry. Gabriel's immaculate script stared back at her, and a little catch pinched her throat.

"Thank you," she said to the young clerk as she entered the details. "I wouldn't want to ruin his records before he returns."

The young man shot both brows up in surprise. "Is he returning, miss?"

"I certainly hope so."

When the clerk had gone, she replaced the ledger, ran a finger gently over the others to align them, and sagged into Gabriel's chair. She placed her palms carefully on the armrests, aligning her hands where his would have laid. *Where are you?*

Kit had departed in the morning, and the rest of the day had stretched on, feeling like one of the longest of her life. Not because she was stuck behind a desk. She rather liked the busyness of attending to all of the many matters that would have come before Gabriel in a given day. She'd been so busy during the lunch period that Daughtry had brought her a sack lunch and a cup of tea from the shop down the street. Of course, she'd taken special care not to spill crumbs or leave a ring of tea on Gabriel's blotter.

She was ever aware that the space was his. Now, sitting in his chair, she understood the satisfaction of the orderliness he'd created for himself. There was a comfort in knowing where each item she needed was and replacing them to that exact spot when she was finished with them. The single day wouldn't transform her into a tidy person, but she understood the allure of tidiness better than ever before.

The allure of Gabriel's scent was one she'd always recognized, and he permeated the room. The scent was somehow greater now that he was gone. She'd press a hand to the chair's leather, and the smell of his sandalwood shaving soap would come wafting up. Or she'd reach for a document in his vertical cabinet and catch a whiff of his clean-laundered smell.

"Good evening to you, miss," Daughtry said as he entered to place a piece of paper at the edge of the desk. "The daily." He pointed a wrinkled finger at the document. "Boss required me to provide a daily tally of who attended work, timeliness, productivity, and the progress of various projects under way."

"Thank you, Wilbur." Clary collected the sheet and scanned the information, though her eyes began to blur with tears she refused to shed. Daughtry's sympathetic gaze stayed on her, and she was tempted to crumble and confess her misery to the kindly old man. Tempted, but she wouldn't let herself burden him or anyone else. "Good night to you, and convey a hello to Mrs. Daughtry."

"Of course, miss." He waited an extra moment, as if expecting, or hoping, she would come around and tell him the rest of the story. From Kit, he and all the rest of the workroom staff had heard a curt recitation of Gabriel's letter and nothing more. Finally, when she said nothing, Wilbur Daughtry turned and started for the front door. As he headed out, he called back to her. "Young lady to see you, miss."

Clary stood and peered through the open door. A young woman she'd never seen before stood just inside the workroom. Daughtry spoke quietly to her, even patted her on the arm, and then departed, locking the door behind him with a decided snick.

"Hello," Clary called to the lady. The moment she came out from behind the desk to greet her, the young woman rushed forward. Clary gasped when she came into the gaslight of Gabriel's office.

Cool blue eyes. Pitch-black hair.

"Sara?" Clary questioned as her heartbeat kicked into a canter. "Miss Adamson?"

"The name's King, actually. Soon to be Tidwell, if I have my way." Gabriel's sister stepped close to greet Clary. "And you're Miss Clarissa Ruthven. A real beauty, you are, and the cleverest girl in England, if my brother's to be believed."

That was a looming question for Clary. Was Gabriel Adamson to be believed?

"Please sit, Miss King." Clary scooted one of the visitor chairs close to the other, turning the furnishings so that they almost faced each other. She didn't wish to converse with the woman from behind Gabriel's desk. "I wish I could offer you refreshment."

The young woman planted a hand on her belly in the way she'd seen other women do when they were increasing with child. "A bit unsettled today. Wouldn't take anything if you did." Tall but much thinner than her brother, Miss King moved with much more frenetic energy, and she flitted around the office, submitting every inch to a thorough inspection before taking the seat Clary indicated. "Looks very much like Gabe, it does. Neat as a pin. He's always hated dirt and muck and mess. Even when we were living in the midst of worst of it."

"I'd like to know more about his upbringing," Clary said as she settled beside Sara. She perched on her chair, turning to face the young woman who bore such a striking resemblance to her brother.

"Would you, indeed? I suspect you'll have a fine time of it, trying to get more details from Gabe. As much as he hates mess, he loathes thinking about the old days more." Sara waved at her. "If he's told you anything at all, then he must adore you. Never speaks of what he's been through to anyone."

Clary had a sense his history was far darker than the horrors he'd confessed, though she found it difficult to imagine much worse than a child being caged.

"Would you mind if I'm blunt and sharp this afternoon, Miss Ruthven? There's no time to waste." She leaned forward, and Clary could see that her skin was pebbled with perspiration. "I've come to plead with you. I think you're the only one who can stop him."

Clary shook her head. If only she had that power, he'd still be with her. He'd never have walked out of Kit and Phee's front door and left her behind.

"Yes, miss," Sara insisted. "Now hear me out. He's gone to Whitechapel. I rue the day I ever mentioned our mother to him a few weeks ago. He went back to find her, when he hadn't stepped foot in that godforsaken place for years." She bowed her head to stare at the floor a moment before meeting Clary's gaze again, her eyes beseeching. "Please, miss. You must help me stop him. He's gone to fight for Rigg."

Ice filled her veins, and Clary shivered. "No, he wouldn't do that." The shivering wouldn't stop. From her feet to her forehead, she quivered as if she'd been dunked in the icy depths of the Thames. "He hates that man."

"He hates the notion of losing you more." Sara shook her head. "You see, he has nothing. He's given us, my Thomas and me, all his savings for a dowry."

"Congratulations," Clary told her, still unable to make sense of what she'd been told. "But how could Gabe think of going back to fighting?"

"He needs to pay his rent, Miss Ruthven. Find employment, the honest way." She shrugged and rubbed a hand over her belly. "Says he hopes to win you back some day."

"Win me back?" Clary stood and prayed her shaking body would keep her upright. "He left me, Miss King. Resigned his position here. He didn't lose me. He left me."

Sara stood too. "Men aren't always easily understood, and what they call logic, we might call rubbish. But Gabe hasn't stopped thinking of you for a single second, I vow that to you." She laid a clammy hand on Clary's arm. "The old devil's offered Gabe as much as he'd earn in a year for one fight in the pit. Gabe thinks he needs that money to have you."

Clary could recall the sodden feel of the messenger boy's note in her hands. Gabe hadn't even wanted her to read it. And he wouldn't have gone back into that life of horrors willingly. Unless he felt trapped, with no other choices.

If he'd only come to her, they could have found a solution together.

"I'm hoping that fierce look in your lavender eyes means you'll help me."

Clary patted the young woman's hand where she still had a hold on her arm. "Of course, I will."

"Tell him the money means nothing to you," Sara pleaded. "Even if it's a lie. I know as well as most that money matters a great deal, but say anything you must to dissuade him from this terrible course."

"The money doesn't matter to me." Her body stopped quivering, and Clary pressed a hand to where her heart was beginning to thump with something other than the misery she'd felt since parting from Gabe. "And I'm terrible at lying," she told his sister, "but I do have another idea."

CHAPTER TWENTY-ONE

Gabe waited in the shadows, watching dusk turn to darkness over Whitechapel. He'd spent an hour in the Ten Bells, nursing a single pint of dreadful ale and confessing his misery to a man he'd never met before today. Just his luck that the man would turn out to be one of H Division's wily plainclothes detectives.

Now he stood in the dark, awaiting the devil.

The behemoth appeared first. He lurched down the pavement, scanning for any mischief ahead. Then Rigg came along, with his other thug in tow, heading into one of his favored establishments, a whorehouse cum gambling den that none but his closest associates were allowed to enter via this alleyway entrance.

"Rigg," Gabe called to the demon.

The behemoth and the other thug sprang into action, one palming a cudgel, the other raising the barrel of a pistol that gleamed in the moonlight.

"Go inside, boys," the old man told them. "Tell 'em to prepare a spot for me at the table, while I conduct a nice tête-à-tête with my Ragin' Boy." After sweeping his beady gaze from one end of the alley to the other, as if he could see in the darkness, he smiled across at Gabe. "Got my message, did ye, boy?"

"An offer I couldn't refuse."

"Quite right too." Rigg started toward him with a gangly strut, swinging his cane. "More where that came from, boy. Always more blunt to be 'ad."

"I want the funds first. Then I'll fight."

The old man flashed him a snaggletooth smile. "That's not 'ow it works, my son. Ye know that better than most."

"The rules have changed," Gabe told him, widening his stance, muscles tensed, keeping one eye peeled for more thugs. Rigg never traveled alone. "Blunt first. Fight second. Then I want a bounty if I win."

A rusty sound emerged from Rigg, then higher, a see-sawing cackle. He leaned on his cane and bent at the waist, guffawing out a wretched sound, like metal scraping metal. Then, in a flash, he straightened and pressed a blade to Gabe's throat. "I make the rules 'ere, son. Always 'ave. Always will. Ye forgot yerself if you fink I'll take me orders from a guttersnipe."

Gabe held his hands up and considered how deep Rigg could slice him in the time it would take for Gabe to get his hands around the man's scrawny neck.

"A hundred, in victory or defeat. That's my offer, boy. Take it as it stands, or scarper off back to your high-kick girl."

At the mention of Clary, Gabe's vision clouded with crimson. He jerked up and arched back, knocking Rigg's knife arm away. He grabbed the old man and spun him, lashing a forearm across his neck. He squeezed the arm that held the knife until the metal switchblade clattered to the ground.

"I'm stronger than you, old devil. I always have been. I should have killed you when I was in my prime."

Rigg laughed again. "Kill me, and you won't ever see yer hundred pounds," he squawked past Gabe's hold.

The old man was shockingly frail. Gabe could feel his bony body under the layers of soot-grimed clothes. One squeeze, and he had no doubt he could snap the devil's neck and snuff out the life of one who'd caused others so much misery. It would be justice, but it would be cold-blooded murder. He'd never be able to face Clary. Sweet, good, loving Clary, who thought everyone was redeemable. Hell, she'd probably offer Rigg a cup of tea if she ever met the blighter.

If Gabe had anything to say about it, she never ever would.

He lifted his arm, and Rigg stumbled forward, planting his palms on the brick wall ahead. A moment later, he whirled on Gabe, his cane pointed toward him, a blade protruding from the end. "Fight or go, boy. Choose yer fate."

"One fight, and I'm finished."

Rigg lowered his cane and sneered. "We shall see, boy. I wager one taste of blood and pain won't be enough. Ye always were a bloodthirsty brute."

Gabe couldn't deny the charge. But that was his past. He'd left that part of himself behind. This single dive back into hell, and he would go back to making a better life for himself. This chapter could be closed, once and for all.

"Where?" Gabe asked the devil.

"One o' the usual places. Behind the Crossroads this time."

The pub was a vile place, but the yard behind was large enough to accommodate hundreds of spectators, though some of Rigg's fights had attracted as many as a thousand. People came from all parts of London, and farther, to view the brawls. Visitors paid the lodging house proprietors for a room, not for the night but for an hour. For a spot where they could look out a window or get a good view from the rooftops. That was the power of bloodlust.

"The hour?"

Rigg slid a cheroot from his pocket and took the time to strike a match against the bricks and light the end before offering an answer around the burning length of his wretched cigar. "The witchin' 'our, of course."

Gabe gave one downward jerk of his chin, shoved his fists in his pockets, and started back toward the Ten Bells. In the end, he hadn't been fool enough to engage in this venture alone, and he needed to tell his compatriot where he'd be and when.

Four hours after leaving Ruthven's, Clary and Sara were cold, miserable, and on the verge of panic. They'd visited Sara's old acquaintances, houses of ill repute, gambling dens, and a lodging house where a crotchety old woman barked at them to leave and never come back. Nivens, Sara said she was called. Gabe and his sister had once lived in the old woman's dilapidated lodging house just a few blocks from Fisk Academy.

Clary thought of the school and Helen and the girls at Fisk more than once as they traversed the handful of square miles that constituted Whitechapel, but she dared not peek her head in or lead Sara to their door. Tonight, she was about dangerous business, and she didn't wish the threat to touch any of them.

"Almost at me wit's end," Sara said in an exhausted voice.

They chafed their hands as they huddled across the street from one of the most notorious pubs in Whitechapel. The Ten Bells had been associated with the Ripper murders a decade earlier. A few of the victims were known to frequent the establishment, and one visited the very night of her heinous murder. Many suspected the culprit must have partaken at the pub too, perhaps choosing his victims from among its patrons.

"Shall we go inside?" Clary asked Gabe's sister.

"Nothing in me wants to, except for the hope of hearing word of this bleedin' fight." Sara peered through the glass of the establishment. "Not a fit place for a lady such as yourself, Miss Ruthven, but I fear we've got to try."

Clary needed no more encouragement. She started across the road and tipped her head back to make sure Sara followed. They hooked arms as they stepped inside, drawing the notice of several men, who grunted and offered compliments and lewd suggestions. Sara led Clary straight to the bar, waving to catch the barman's notice.

"Wot can I get ye, ladies?" the affable man said as he approached.

Clary slid a coin across the counter, keeping it covered with her palm. "Information, sir."

He ducked to see the coin, and she lifted her fingers to reveal a crown. The man whistled as one brow shot up. "Tell you anything you like, miss. Wot you need?"

Sara planted an elbow on the bar. "Word's floatin' 'bout a brawl. Rigg's boy. Where and when?"

The barman eyed them both dubiously. "Eager for blood, are ye, ladies?"

"I have cutthroat tastes," Clary told him. "Do you know anything about a fight this evening?"

He gestured toward her hand and the coin below. She slid him the crown across the bar.

"Might do," he said after pocketing the money. "Stroke o' midnight. Back o' me rival's establishment." He nudged his chin left. "West a mile. Edge of Whitechapel. The Crossroads."

"I know the place," Sara whispered eagerly to Clary. "Let's go."

Starting down Whitechapel Road, they walked until Clary's feet ached and the muscles in her legs burned. A few times, Sara stopped to catch her breath, patting and rubbing her belly before continuing on.

"Are you with child?" Clary finally whispered to her.

The young woman gulped before casting her a defensive look. "And what if I am?"

Clary offered her a soft smile. "Then I offer you felicitations and insist we get out of here as soon as we can."

"Believe me, I'll drag the fool out of this stew by the scruff of his neck if I have to." Sara picked up the pace. "I only wish Thomas were here to help us, but I didn't wish to wait any longer before coming to find you."

"Is Thomas your husband?"

Sara's face lit in a smile. "He soon will be."

A few more steps, and Sara grabbed Clary's wrist. "That's it. Just up ahead."

The building housing the pub was taller than most. Light spilled out onto the pavement from its many windows, along with the music of accordions and raucous laughter.

"We should go 'round back," Sara advised. "If Gabe's come early, that's where he'll be to prepare."

Finding a side lane several buildings down, they proceeded to an alley that ended abruptly at a high wooden fence that enclosed the yard behind the Crossroads pub.

"How do we get inside?" Clary asked as she scanned the wood for any opening or loose slat.

"We knock," Sara told her as she lifted her fist to rap on the wood. A moment later, four slats several feet away parted, and an enormous man stuck his head through.

"Rigg sent us to see to 'is man," Sara told him boldly.

The man raked her with a leering gaze. "How about you see to me first, luv?"

Sara sauntered over, and Clary followed close behind. "Let us in," she told him, "and we'll negotiate."

The man cast a gaze at Clary and licked his beefy lips. "Two at a time is just to my taste." He pulled back the linked slats farther, leaning in close as Sara and Clary stepped inside.

Sara pulled Clary away from the man and leaned in to whisper in her ear. "Go and find Gabe. Convince him we must leave here. I'll distract this one."

"He's too big and too vile. I can't leave you alone with him." There was little point in finding Gabe and convincing him of her love if she allowed harm to befall his sister. She knew him well enough to know he'd never forgive her.

"I've got a blade in my boot and another stuffed in my corset." Sara glanced back at the randy gatekeeper. "I'm not afraid to use 'em. Now go," she said with a shove to Clary's arm. "Find him so we can get out of this miserable place."

Clary walked quickly across the yard, attempting not to draw the notice of the men clustered around various spots inside the walls. Some stood smoking, others sat in chairs, as if awaiting the fight. Still others worked on stringing long lines of rope around the space, creating the fighting ring itself, she assumed. Up ahead, she saw light inside the open rear door of the pub, and to the left, another area, covered with a tarp but not part of the building itself. She ducked toward the shadowed space, and the air whooshed from her lungs.

At the far end of the tarpaulin shelter, Gabe moved in the dim light of a lantern. Bare from the waist up, he jabbed at a bag that hung from a beam overhead.

She ran toward him, and he pivoted at the sound of her footfalls.

"Clary?" he rasped.

He caught her as she slammed into him, holding her tightly in his arms. She plastered herself against him, linking her hands behind his back, unwilling to let him go. When he tipped her chin up to gaze into his eyes, she saw the same relief that was singing through her body.

"What the hell are you doing here?" He tore off the padded gloves he wore and took her face in his hands, which were wrapped mummy-tight in strips of fabric. "You need to leave here."

"I'm not going anywhere without you."

"Clary—"

"Gabe, listen to me. Sara is here. We need to find her and go."

He cast a gaze over her head. "Where is she?"

"With the gatekeeper, but I don't want to leave her with him for long. Please"—she latched her hand around his and urged him to follow her—"let's go."

But he didn't budge, no matter how she pulled. "I need to do this, Clary."

She shook her head until it ached. "You need to come home with me. I need you."

He let out a breathy chuckle. "I'm not sure you've ever needed anyone."

Striding closer, she confessed, "I never expected to, but now I do."

"The money from tonight—"

"I don't care about Rigg's money, and we'll have plenty of our own." Clary wound her arm through his. "Wouldn't you rather have my money than his?"

When his brows tented in confusion, Clary stepped away from him, casting a glance back toward the spot where she'd left Sara. Apparently, the gatekeeper had gotten her a chair. She sat just inside the walls of the yard. He stood nearby, seemingly engaged with her in friendly conversation.

"Clary, please take Sara and go. I can't do this if I'm worried about you two."

"Then don't do this at all." Reaching for Gabe, she said, "I know this isn't the place or time, but I have a proposal for you."

A horn blasted the air, and then a man's low shout echoed around the yard. "The moment has come, ladies and gentlemen."

"It's time," Gabe said ominously. He hauled her into his arms, then quickly released her. "Go. Now. Don't look back. Take my sister and get out of here."

"I love you." She wouldn't convince him. He was determined. She could see it in his eyes.

His expression changed, softening, warming. She saw a bit of the Gabe who'd kissed her, made love to her as if she was all he ever wanted.

"Ragin' Boy," the announcer shouted through his bullhorn, "returns for the bloodiest fight of his life."

Gabe's head snapped up. Thunder came into his eyes, and his muscles bunched as he shifted and tensed. He slammed a fist into the opposite palm. Began bouncing on his toes.

"Wot 'ave we 'ere, then?" A dark, gravelly voice came from behind, and Clary wheeled around to find a thin, bearded man leering at her. A lit cheroot at the corner of his mouth let off wisps of smoke.

Then he was gone. Her view of him cut off as Gabe planted himself in front of her, nearly knocking her off her feet.

"Yer name's been called, boy. Up in the ring with ye." An evil, rasping chuckle emerged from the man. "I'll keep yer lovie entertained."

Gabe glanced at her over his shoulder and mouthed one word: Go. He said more with his eyes. They were bleak. Cold. In another man, she'd call them cruel. The look told her that he would brook no arguments. That he didn't wish to know about her proposal or why she'd come. That declaring her love again hadn't changed his intentions one whit.

He didn't want her here. Perhaps he no longer wanted her at all. But he clearly intended to fight.

The odious man—Rigg, she guessed—scooped up Gabe's gloves and led him toward the ring, slapping his cane against Gabe's back to urge him on faster.

Gabe tugged his gloves back on, waited while Rigg tied the laces, and then lifted the rope to duck underneath. Once inside the ring, he glanced back at her. A fleeting moment. She could read nothing in his gaze but seething anger.

A burly man approached from the edge of the yard. "Rigg says yer to sit up front." He hooked a massive hand under her arm and began to haul her off.

"No, thank you." Clary brought her boot down on his foot, yanked her arm from his grasp, and searched the yard for Sara. The crowd had thickened, bodies packing in, shoulder to shoulder. A hand shot up through the crowd, and Clary glimpsed Sara's dark hair and pale face. She picked up her skirt and ran toward her.

"We should get out of here," Sara told her.

"And leave Gabe?"

The crowd let out a raucous roar, stomping their feet and waving fists in the air.

Sara stretched onto her toes to see over the sea of hats and bare heads. "It's too late," she said miserably, "the fight has begun."

Chapter Twenty-Two

She was walking away. Gabe told himself that was good. It's what he wanted. Clary and Sara and the baby needed to get to safety.

He hated that they'd come into this ugliness to find him. Hated that Clary had seen him here among the thugs and brutes. Hated pushing her away and causing more pain.

God, he'd missed her. A few hours apart, and he'd ached for her every damn minute.

He could smell her floral scent on his skin.

But other smells swarmed in. Scents that hadn't changed after all these years. The sweat of a hundred bodies. Liquor spilled and guzzled as the audience gaped with eager eyes. Sawdust, gritty and pungent, beneath his boots.

The sounds were the same too. The shouts of the crowd, the dancing gait of his opponent's shuffling feet, Gabe's own blood rushing in his ears.

He'd never met his opponent before this night. The boy was too young, too fresh-faced to have spent much time in the ring.

There was a typical Rigg cruelness to it. As if the devil had thrown him a puppy to batter.

An angry puppy. The young man gnashed his teeth and glared at Gabe as they waited for the call to begin.

Gabe understood. These moments before the violence began were when a fighter stripped down. Peeling away thoughts of the woman he loved and the life he wanted. This was a time to bore down to basics and tear one's opponent apart. Not with fists. Not yet. First, he took a man to pieces in his mind. The body before him didn't have a name. There was no wife or family or lover watching from the sidelines. His opponent became an obstacle. A threat to his existence. A marauder who'd take everything if he could.

For Gabe, besting this young man who was slavering to rip him limb from limb, would be a ladder out of the chaos and muck.

Forever.

Rigg took over the bullhorn, rasping through the mouth-piece in a smoke-deep roar. "Do yer worst, boys. Who craves a bit o' blood?"

The crowd let out an earsplitting cry of enthusiasm, begging for the coming blood sport.

Gabe's opponent danced straight toward him, assessing his speed and movement, before stepping back. The young man was light on his feet, and Gabe guessed he outweighed the boy by several stone.

The first blow came at him fast. He ducked and feinted left. The boy was quick, but Gabe was quicker.

He was older too, and his body immediately reminded him of the fact. As he circled the boy, shifting and diving to avoid two more jabs, muscles pulled and stretched. Twinges of pain shot across his back, and his bruised temple began to throb.

"Hit me," the boy demanded. "Do something, you bastard." He was dancing about so eagerly that he was already breathless.

Gabe didn't mind letting the kid tire himself out.

"Kill him!" someone shouted from the crowd.

Others joined in. "Bash 'im."

"Do the rotter's head in."

"Blood! Blood!" The chant swept across the bystanders in a wave, more voices added until the word became a crescendo.

The boy obeyed and came at Gabe with a series of swift, hard left, right punches.

Gabe took one, ducked another. Then he miscalculated and caught a punch straight to his jaw. He stumbled back. The boy was far stronger than he looked.

Scrawny bastard.

Blood rushed over his tongue. Old impulses sparked. Fury tangled with fear. Hunger twisted with hate. Shifting on his toes, he lunged forward and delivered a low cut to the boy's midriff. Stepping back, he waited for his opponent to shift and landed another punch to the lad's clean-shaven cheek.

The boy stumbled, shaking off the daze of his strike. Dizziness. Spots of black. Bells ringing in his ears. Gabe knew exactly what he was feeling. He'd learned to fight after being beaten by bullies far better at brawling than he was.

The boy spit blood into the sawdust, slammed his gloved fists together, tucked his head, and came at Gabe like a wild bull. A daring move but worth every ounce of energy spent if it got one's opponent off his feet.

Unfortunately for the lad, Gabe anticipated the blow. Planting his feet wide, he took the boy's weight as all the air rushed from his lungs. But he was still standing, and that's what mattered. He hooked an arm around the boy's shoulders as their bodies crashed together.

When his opponent tried to retreat, Gabe held him in place and delivered one quick jab to his ribs.

The punch had virtually no effect. Twisting away, the boy straightened to his full height and slammed a quick blow to Gabe's face.

The strike caught him off guard. Gabe ducked away, but the boy saw his confusion. Saw his advantage. And swung again. The next blow caught Gabe in the temple. The spot where Rigg's thugs had bashed him thoroughly. The spot Clary had cleaned so tenderly.

The thought of her cleared his mind. Chased the pain from his body. He had a purpose in this ring. He needed to get through this bout, see this night to its end, and get her back in his life.

The boy came at him again, and Gabe caught him low. Midriff, ribs. Two quick jabs. Left, right. The boy bent from the pain. Gabe hooked his jaw and sent him back on his arse.

Sawdust burst up, and Gabe tasted the wood pulp on his tongue.

As the boy bounced up on his feet, baring his teeth at Gabe like a rabid dog, a murmur swept the crowd, rolling toward them like thunder. Louder. Shouts mixed with cries of outrage.

"Scarper!" someone shouted into the bullhorn, "The rozzers is 'ere."

Bodies moved in snarled clusters, hats toppling, arms flailing as some got pushed out of the way to make room for others.

As the crowd thinned, Gabe spotted the detective he'd met at the Ten Bells. The man tipped his bowler Gabe's way, then nudged his chin toward the edge of the yard.

Two burly coppers had clapped Rigg's behemoths in irons. Rigg himself had been swarmed by four uniformed constables—one in front, one in back, a man on each side. The detective knew as soon as Gabe mentioned Rigg's name that he'd stumbled on the biggest catch of his career.

Gabe realized his opponent was still standing beside him when the boy's gloves thudded into the sawdust. "You can be done with him now," he told the boy. "Rigg. Whatever he had on you, he doesn't own you anymore."

"All this just to snitch on 'im." There was no recrimination in the boy's tone. Just a thread of admiration. A grin lifted his bruised cheek as he watched a copper secure the irons around Rigg's wrists. "Wot if someone worse comes along to replace 'im?"

"Could there be worse than Rigg?"

"Nah, you're right. Ain't nobody worse."

"Do you have a job?"

The boy slapped a fist against the opposite palm.

Gabe side-eyed the boy. "A proper job, I mean."

"Not sure I'm cut out for proper."

At the boy's age, Gabe didn't think he could change either. But he'd taken the opportunity Leopold Ruthven offered in lieu of payment. "If you change your mind, I'll give you a chance for honest work. Ruthven Publishing. Southampton Row. Come and find me."

As he climbed from the ring, he stopped in his tracks and realized what he'd said. Mercy, those blows had turned him dotty. He couldn't offer anyone a job. He didn't even have employment of his own.

But he would. He was free now. He could wash himself clean of this life and pursue what he wanted most.

Clary. He scanned the crowd for her and felt a strange mix of regret and relief when he couldn't find her. Perhaps, for once, she'd taken his advice and gotten herself and Sara to safety. Perhaps they'd gone to Fisk Academy. He'd go there as soon as he settled one last score.

Striding toward the cluster of constables, Gabe tossed his gloves away. He felt the rush of the fight ebbing. His pulse began to steady. His breath came in even bursts. And pain came on with a vengeance. There wasn't a part of his body that didn't ache.

Still, he squared his shoulders, stood up tall, and clenched his fists as he approached the circle of policeman surrounding Rigg. The H Division detective strode over and gave his constable a nod. The burly young man backed away and shot Gabe a grim look.

There was no cheroot in Rigg's mouth now. No smirk under his grizzled mustache. Only hate burning in his black eyes. "Never knew you to be a rat, boy."

"You never knew me at all." Gabe lifted his arm, wound back, and planted a facer on Rigg's nose.

The devil didn't even wince. Blood gushed down over an evil, snaggletoothed smile.

"I'm done with you, old man." Gabe turned and jerked a satisfied nod toward the detective.

He stumbled across the trodden grass. Fatigue and weariness set in. It was over. This part was done. Now the rest of his life could start.

A few stragglers remained, loitering around the yard. He bumped into one woman, who waggled a finger at him. "Terrible fight, son. Not enough blood."

He moved past her and another feminine voice called out of the darkness. "Are you ready to hear my proposal now, Mr. King?"

Clary. He'd never been so happy to see anyone in his life. Nor so irritated that she remained among this raucous mess.

"Sara's fine," she assured him. "She's waiting for us at Fisk with Helen and the girls."

He pivoted toward her and came closer. He longed to have her in his arms, but he could see the hesitation in her eyes. He'd hurt her. He had so much to make up for.

"About this proposal." He stepped toward her and grazed his knuckles across her cheek. "If you're going to mention your ladies' magazine again—"

"Marry me." The two words were far easier to get out than Clary imagined they'd be. They'd been bubbling inside her since she'd set out for Whitechapel with Sara.

Even when Gabe told her to go. Even while she watched him fight, the two words remained lodged inside in her heart, waiting to get out.

He stood dumbstruck and silent before her, mouth gaping, eyes wide, not a sound emerging from him. Then he finally choked out, "What did you say?"

"I asked you to marry me. Maybe I phrased it wrong," she teased. "Gabriel, will you marry me? Please."

"You needn't do this out of desperation," he finally said. "The fight is over. There won't be anymore. I don't need you to save me."

"Perhaps I'm saving us both."

"You've never wished to marry. You long for your independence."

She couldn't deny his claims, though she'd never been wholly averse to marriage. Only doubtful that anyone would come along to make her wish for such a commitment. Most of all, he was right about her desire for independence. She still craved the freedom to do as she wished, to pour her energy into worthy causes, to make a difference. But now she wanted Gabriel too.

"Do you intend to quash my independence, convince me my charities are foolish, and my politics are pointless?"

"I would never want to change you, Clary." Earnestness filled his gaze, then a glint of mischief lit his expression. "I'm not sure I could if I tried."

"No, you couldn't. So you'll have to accept that I love you. I know what I'm saying and what I want. And I should warn you, I never give up."

He grinned at that.

"Will you?" she asked softly, because she needed him to say *yes*. She ached to know he wanted her. That he would commit his heart, his life, to her.

"Yes, love." He wrapped his arms around her and lifted her off her toes for a kiss. A searching, hungry joining that left her breathless, almost making her forget where they were and how awful this night had been. When he set her back on her feet, he cupped her cheek against his palm and said, "But I can't leave here yet."

Panic swept in to steal all the bliss. "Why on earth not? Gabe, whatever money you wish to collect, we don't need it. My dowry will give us a decent life for years to come."

"It's not the money." He scanned behind her, gripped her shoulders, and turned her body so that she could see across the yard. "I came tonight to catch the spider in its web." He pointed to a gathering of men at the far edge of the yard. "Those men are coppers. Undercover detectives." His breath warm against her nape, he added, "I've told them everything about Rigg. What I did for him. About his schemes and associates. Where to find his vaults of stolen goods. Where the bodies are buried."

Clary swiveled and pressed her hand against his chest. His heart beat hard but in a steady rhythm. "Will they charge you with anything?"

"No, but I've agreed to testify in court." He smoothed a hand down her arm. "I'll make enemies by ratting on Rigg. But I've agreed to help the Met catch all they can. They've asked to take a formal statement at Leman Street station tonight."

"Then I'll go with you."

"No."

Clary let out a shaky breath. "Is that your answer to my proposal?"

He pulled her into his arms, stroked a hand down her back, and lowered his mouth to hers. Clary kissed him hungrily. Hours apart had been far too long. When they were both breathless, he rested his head against her forehead.

"*That* is my answer." He kissed her again. "I love you." Another kiss, deeper, sweeter. "I want to be your husband."

"Then take me to the station with you." Her stubborn, determined chin jutted out, and he ducked his head and kissed her there too.

"No, love," he whispered against her skin. "I may be the last man who deserves it, but you'll have to trust me." He kissed her again but too quickly. A taste when she craved more. Then he led toward the road in front of the Crossroads pub. "Go to Fisk and tell Sara all is well. I'll come and join you when I'm done at the station. This will be over before you know it."

"And then we can begin?"

"Yes. I cut my ties to all of this tonight. Nothing here can haunt us anymore." He smiled. "Now we can pick up where we left off."

CHAPTER TWENTY-THREE

Over Kit's protests and Sophia's offer to host their wedding at the Stanhope estate in Derbyshire, Clary insisted on a simple wedding. As quick as possible and with minimum fuss. Except for her dress. She did spend at least one sleepless night turning a simple cream silk gown into a glittering, organza-strewn masterpiece. For the ceremony itself, she and Gabe agreed on the nearest registry office.

They suggested to Sara that a double ceremony might be in order, but Gabe's sister had been so eager to tie the knot with her groom that she refused to wait while Gabe and Clary obtained a license. A day after Sara and Thomas's registry office wedding, Helen let Clary know that Nathaniel Landau had proposed. But they weren't keen on a double wedding either.

Dr. Landau's family had decided the couple deserved nothing less than an elaborate ceremony, and Nate's aunts and uncles and cousins were making their way to London for the nuptials, some coming from as far as America.

The fifteen days leading up to their own wedding was agony. But when they joined hands before the registrar, with Kit and Phee serving as witnesses, all the wait was forgotten. Gabe's gaze lit with happiness, though his jaw tightened when Clary smiled up at him.

"You're sure about this?" he whispered, one glossy black brow arched.

"Once I fix on a course, I rarely change my mind."

He grinned and lowered his head so that they were a hairbreadth apart. "But you're also impulsive. Perhaps you've rushed into this too quickly."

"I'm also impatient, so quickly suits me perfectly."

Lifting a hand, he swept her veil aside to stroke the edge of her jaw. "You suit me perfectly, Clary Ruthven."

The registrar, a slight, pale man, cleared his throat. "Then may we begin?"

The vows were read, and Gabe repeated them in a clipped, sharp accent, enunciating every word with loving care. Clary got caught up in watching his eyes, the cool blue warming as she said her vows, shifting from love and happiness to a heat she felt kindling inside her. When they reached the part regarding obedience, Gabe chuckled, and the registrar quelled him with a stern frown.

A moment later, they sealed their promises with a kiss, and Clary forgot that Kit and Phee were watching. The registrar tapped his toe, waiting impatiently for them to be done so that he could move on to the next couple.

Clary forgot everything but Gabe. She only knew he was in her arms, right where she wished him to be. She deepened the kiss, and he responded instantly, wrapping a hand around her waist to pull her body snug against his. He snagged her veil in his hand, and pins popped from her coiffure, but she didn't care. She kissed him again. And once more for good measure.

Kit and Phee offered hugs and well wishes and reminded them of the celebratory dinner party Sophia and Grey were hosting later in the evening. Nate and Helen would be there, and Sara and Thomas too.

"We'll be there," Gabe promised.

Clary's throat was still too full. In fact, her whole body felt stretched, buoyant with joy and anticipation. She wanted to savor every moment as Gabriel's wife, yet part of her wished to rush forward to the next day with him and the next. Most of all, she couldn't wait for the night, when she would have him all to herself.

"To Ruthven's next, wife?" he asked as he tucked her arm into his and smiled down at her.

They'd agreed to Daughtry's request that they stop by the office and allow him and the clerks to offer them well wishes and celebrate their nuptials in some small way.

After handing her up into a hansom cab and helping to wrestle the many layers of her gown and petticoats into the carriage, Gabe climbed up beside her and immediately began unfastening the buttons of her gloves as the vehicle rolled toward Ruthven's. Once he had her arms free, he lifted one hand and then the other for kisses.

"A new scent," he said as he applied his tongue to where her pulse hummed in her wrist.

"Orange blossom for weddings."

"So you do attend to etiquette after all."

"Just this once," she said on a gasp when he leaned close to kiss her neck. Clary braced her hand against his thigh and felt the hard length of him through his trousers. She moved her hand closer, running her fingers over his heat.

He groaned against her neck as she explored. "Perhaps we should skip Ruthven's and go home."

Clary lifted her hand and turned to kiss him. "We can't. We promised Daughtry." Another kiss, and she took care where she placed her hands. "Besides, it's a short ride."

Gabe drew in a sharp breath as he straightened. "Feels like forever to me."

Yet a moment later, the cab pulled to a stop in front of Ruthven's, and Daughtry stepped onto the pavement as if he'd been watching for their arrival.

"Oh, happy day," he shouted, clapping his hands.

Gabe stepped down first and helped Clary—and her enormous gown—out of the carriage. After allowing Daughtry a quick embrace, they entered the workroom to the whoops and cheers of the clerks inside. Someone had engineered a bucket of confetti to be strung from the ceiling and the whole fluttered around them as they stepped deeper into the room.

Clary laughed and tried to catch a few squares of the light paper as it floated down. Gabe watched her with a smile, though when she turned to him, he feigned a glower. "Someone will have to clean up all of this, you know."

One of the clerks laughed, and Gabe pointed at him. The boy he'd bested in the ring a couple of weeks earlier had been hired on as their newest clerk. "I elect you for cleanup duty, Simkins."

"Yes, sir," the young man said with a mock salute.

Another leaned in and chimed, "Does that mean you're boss of Ruthven's again, sir?"

Clary took Gabe's hand in hers. "He certainly is." She ignored Gabe's arched-brow gaze. The matter was one they'd yet to fully resolve. He freely admitted how much he missed Ruthven's, but then guilt would rise up, and he'd insist on finding employment on his own. Though she hadn't worked out all the details with Kit, Gabe had at least agreed to resume his role for the time being.

Clary had ideas about what might come next.

"The tea shop has spoiled us today," Daughtry said behind them as he gestured toward the spot near the work-room where they'd brought a table out, covered the length in a pretty lace-edged cloth, and decorated every inch with platters and teacups and plates. In the center sat a large silver urn, steaming at the top, and Clary could smell the tea shop's signature Earl Grey brew from across the room.

"Shall we tuck in?" she asked the gathered clerks, and they headed off to fill plates in reply.

Gabe never took his hands off her as they chatted, partook of tea and sandwiches, and accepted well wishes from each and every man. Clary was grateful for his breach in etiquette, relishing the way he rested a hand on her lower back or linked his fingers with hers.

When the last employee filed out and they'd locked the doors behind them, Gabe led her into his office. The door had been shut, and when they pushed inside, the scent of books and leather and a faint whisper of his cologne made Clary smile.

"All is just as I left it," he said wonderingly.

"I made sure of that." She squeezed his hand. "As far as I'm concerned, this is your space and no one else's."

"In that case, I'm welcome to do whatever I like in here?"

"Of course." Though if Clary had her wish, the row of *Ruthven Rules* books would be the first to go.

Judging by the structure of the workroom, they could probably expand the walls of the office to make the space bigger. Which fit quite nicely with her idea. "Actually—"

"Come here, wife," he said from where he'd planted himself against the closed door. He'd shed his suit coat, waistcoat, and tie, folding them neatly on the visitor chair, and he'd unfastened the top buttons of his shirt.

The patch of skin between his parted white collar made her mouth water. She went to him, lifted onto her toes, and kissed the spot, dipping her tongue into the hollow at the base of his throat to taste his skin. He made quick work of her coiffure, gently easing out pins and collecting them in his palm. He laid them on top of his folded clothes before running his fingers through her tresses. When his hand slid down the length of her hair, he didn't stop. Cupping her bottom, he pulled her against him.

"Here? In the office?"

He caught her bottom lip between his teeth before soothing the nip with kisses. "Here. Now."

Turning, he stepped with her until her back was against the wall and settled her on her feet. Kneeling down, he eased her gown up. She shivered as he dragged his fingers up her legs, slipped the ribbon of her drawers, and pulled the gauzy garment to her feet. Clary reached back and unlatched the hooks of her double petticoats, and Gabe tugged the fabric until the cotton pooled between them.

When he stood and lifted her again, her body began to pulse with aching need just where she could feel him hard and hot against her middle. Trusting him to hold her, she wrapped her legs around his waist.

He groaned as he took her mouth, stroking his tongue inside her.

"Love me like this," she told him.

His lips found hers again as he delved a hand between them to unfasten his trousers. Breathless, on fire, heat sizzling through her veins, Clary waited for him to fill her. For some mad reason, they'd adhered to propriety since her proposal, exchanging only kisses and caresses, but this joining with him was what she craved. She would never get enough of being this close to him.

"I have a better idea," he said hoarsely, shifting to carry her to the edge of his desk. He settled her down gently and then, in one violent sweeping motion, removed everything else from his desktop. The metal tray protested with a clatter, his beloved fountain pen spun like a top, and his blotter landed with an unceremonious thud.

"Who are you?" Clary teased. "And what did you do with my husband?"

"Your husband's here," he said as he gathered her skirts and wedged himself between her spread thighs. "And I never wish to part from you again."

"Promise?" she gasped as he nipped at her neck while he slid against her.

"Forever, Clary," he vowed as he joined with her, lifting her thighs to his hips as he thrust deeper. "I love you." He pressed his forehead to hers as he built a rhythm, caressed her bare shoulders, pushed her bodice low to cup her breast. "I love you," he repeated as he claimed her mouth.

Clary pulled so hard at his shirt, buttons popped free. She needed to feel him bare beneath her fingers, stroke her hands across his skin, get close to him. He took her mouth, kissed her cheeks, her nose, her neck, as he took her on his desk. When he nipped her earlobe between his teeth and whispered with heated breath, "Tell me you're mine," something in her sundered. She was floating, melting in bliss, clinging to him, one hand on his back, her other threaded in his hair.

She came against him, squirming and shuddering, and telling him, vowing with her body and soul, "Gabriel, I'm yours."

"You're mine," he vowed before burying his face against her neck and groaning out his release.

Afterward, he fussed over her, settling his suit coat over her shoulders, fetching her a cup of tea from the urn in the workroom, looking at her with a worry she didn't wish to see in his eyes.

"What is it?" She slumped down into his desk chair.

"I'm not sure I'll ever be able to concentrate on work in this room again." He lifted a hand, and she came to him, letting him settle into his chair and pull her down onto his lap.

"About that—"

He burst into robust laughter before she could manage another word, and she pressed a hand to his chest, relishing the reverberation of his amusement as it echoed in the room.

"Promise me you'll laugh more often."

After a kiss on her nose, he said, "With you by my side, I fully expect my days to be filled with laughter." He grinned. "Except at the office, of course. Don't wish to ruin my reputation with the lads."

Clary pushed at him playfully, and he settled his hands around her hips.

"Now, tell me what's whirring in that brilliant mind of yours. I can almost see the wheels turning when I look in your eyes."

"Well…" Clary drew a circle with her finger on his chest. "This is assuredly your office."

He pursed his lips and glanced at the desk's edge where he'd made her shudder in pleasure. "Perhaps it's ours now."

"That is exactly my idea! What would you say to…" She paused and assessed him. "Managing Ruthven's together?" The words emerged as a question, her tone uncertain, hesitant.

Gabe drew in a long breath and narrowed an eye at her as he exhaled. "Will you require tea and biscuits at every meeting?"

"Probably."

"And waste time assuring dreadful writers that they can improve and flood our postbox with more stories?"

"I might."

He frowned and stared at the ceiling. "Will you douse yourself with ink on occasion?"

"You married a rather accident-prone woman," she teased, pushing the placket of his shirt aside to draw her fingers across his bare chest. She gripped a few strands of soft hair and warned, "You did vow to love me forever. There's no going back now."

Following her lead, he tugged her bodice down, slipped his fingers past her corset and chemise, and stroked her nipple until she was taut against his fingers. "I have no desire to be anyplace but here with you. I'm never going back," he vowed as he stroked her. "And forever won't be long enough for how much I love you."

Clary shifted in his lap and felt him stiffen beneath her. She reached down, eager to shape the length of him with her hand. He only let her touch him a moment before lifting her in his arms and settling her back on his desk. He flipped up her skirt.

"Again?" she said as she eagerly worked the fastenings of his half-buttoned fly.

"This will be our office, won't it, Mrs. King? We can do whatever we like after business hours."

EPILOGUE

Clary bounced on her toes as the craftsman worked. He tolerated her exuberance well, casting only a few irritated glances over his shoulder as he carefully painted the letters. Gilded this time, not simple black.

"He's back!" Daughtry shouted across the workroom.

"Hurry," Clary urged the man with the paintbrush.

He heaved a weary sigh and applied the last swipe of paint on the frosted glass. With a wagging finger, he turned to instruct her, "No touching for an hour."

Clary stifled laughter. Apparently, he knew nothing of her or her husband. They couldn't keep their hands off each other for a quarter of an hour, let alone sixty minutes. But she nodded at the serious man. He meant the paint, of course, not what Mr. and Mrs. King got up to in the office after everyone went home for the day.

As one of the clerks presented the painter with a check and led him out the rear exit of Ruthven's, Gabriel entered the front door, a box with baked goods balanced in one hand and a bouquet of fat summer roses in the other.

His grin pierced her with the sweetest burst of pleasure in her chest. Six months on from their wedding day, he still wore a look of wonder when he spotted her across a room, as if he was seeing her for the first time and quite liked what he beheld. Clary was still getting used to anyone looking at her with such naked appreciation. Most of all, she loved that Gabriel didn't hide his feelings for her anymore.

In fact, she had become the moderate, cautious one at times, stopping him when he was ready to wrap her legs around his waist. He'd take her against the front door of Ruthven's if she'd allow him to.

Several times, she'd been quite tempted to let him.

"Is there still hot tea?" he asked as he strode forward and pecked a kiss on her cheek.

Tea had now become less a luxury and more of a necessity. The sink in the rear of the building, which previously had been used for washing printing plates or for the clerks to clean up after a spill, was now employed to draw water for tea. They'd installed a gas-fueled hob, which allowed them to keep hot water for beverages on hand throughout the day.

"Simkins has just made a fresh pot," Clary informed him. None of the clerks minded who made the brews, as long as the supply was kept up.

Gabe scanned the workroom for the young man and nudged his chin up in approval. "Good man, Simkins."

The clerk grinned as if he'd just been acknowledged by the queen.

"Notice anything different?" Clary said suggestively as she stepped back to lean against the doorframe of their office.

Gabe spun in a circle, casting his gaze around the office, and then faced her. "No. Should I?"

Clearing her throat, Clary edged up onto her toes and perched a hand on her hip nearest the door. "Nothing at all?"

He twisted his mouth as he stared at her, then drew his gaze down her body, slowly, that hungry look she adored turning his eyes a darker blue.

"Up higher," she urged.

Tipping a wicked grin, he fixed his gaze on her breasts before licking his lips.

Clary shivered. She knew what those lips could do. "Higher," she growled, only barely resisting shoving her hand in the air and drawing a line underneath where the craftsmen had written their names on the frosted glass of their shared office door.

"Ah," Gabe finally said, "you've changed your hair." He clucked approvingly before leaning close. "Though to be honest, I prefer it hanging loose down your naked back or gathered in my hands while I—"

"The door," Clary said on a frantic whisper to keep him from setting her body aflame in front of their entire staff. And Daughtry.

Taking a step back, he lifted his hand to his mouth. "Hmm," was all he uttered—then a maddening "I see," before he finally looked down at her and let go a smile that lit up the room. "It's perfect."

"Do you think so? Truly?"

Their names were printed, one on top of the other.

GABRIEL KING
&
CLARISSA RUTHVEN KING

Gabe had settled on using his true surname, determined to keep clear of the shadows and live without fear of Rigg, who'd been sent to Newgate, or his cronies, many of whom had shared his fate. After Gabe's sworn testimony, others came forward, confessing their parts and implicating Rigg in crimes far and wide, even beyond the East End.

Clary wished to keep her maiden name as well as adding Gabe's. She refused to view their marriage as a loss of any part of herself. Gabe had only enriched her life, broadened it, brought her more happiness than she ever imagined she could find by binding herself to another.

Gabe led her into their office, which had been expanded to twice its size and included a movable partition for times when they met with authors or vendors separately. Today the partition was hidden away, and the curtains had been pulled back to allow the bright summer sun to flood the room with its light.

"Many appointments today?" he asked her.

Clary lifted the watch pinned to her fuchsia shirtwaist. "The girls are due to arrive to work on the first issue of *The Ladies' Clarion*. I can't believe we go to print in a week. After that, I have only one appointment, but it's not for another hour. It's the sentimental-story lady. I wished to meet her, and she's promised to bring more stories. You?"

"Daughtry and I are meeting with a new printing-press vendor. The man promises his machine is faster and cheaper to operate." Gabe glanced back at her. "He's not due until after lunch." Standing before their closed door, he examined the freshly painted letters of their names. "I like the way the ampersand touches both names, connecting them," he said.

"I asked him to do that and to add those extra flourishes to the letters."

He took in the gilded swirls and smiled back at her. "Of course you did." Turning, he took two long steps to close the space between them. "I've never a met a woman less able to avoid a flourish."

"Is that a complaint?"

"It couldn't be. I have none where you're concerned." Gabe leaned closer, and Clary pushed a palm against his waistcoat.

She'd warned him about being too intimate in the office, especially when the clerks and Daughtry were on-site. But she never chastised him with much vehemence when he crossed the invisible line of propriety.

"Do you know what else I like about our names on the door?" he asked as he nuzzled her cheek.

"Tell me," she whispered.

He placed a chaste kiss on her cheek and another close to the edge of her mouth. "They are stacked rather suggestively, don't you think?" Slipping a hand around her waist, he bent her back until she had to reach for his shoulders to keep from tipping.

"You mean, you on top and me underneath you?"

He nodded, drawing his stubbled cheek against hers. "Mmm, precisely." Straightening to his full height, he cast her a devilish grin. "Though I must admit"—he tightened his hand at her back, pulling her hips snug with his—"I do quite like when you're on top."

"Do you?" Clary snaked a finger between the buttons of his shirt to feel his warm skin against hers.

"Tonight," he said, catching her hand in his and pressing her palm over the spot where his heart beat steady and strong. "I promise to show you just how much."

Don't miss any of the Ruthven siblings' romances in
Christy Carlyle's Romancing the Rules series!
First up, keep reading for an excerpt to Kit's story,

RULES FOR A ROGUE

Kit Ruthven's Rules (for Rogues)
*#1 Love freely but guard your heart, no matter
how tempting the invader.*
*#2 Embrace temptation, indulge your sensual impulses,
and never apologize.*
*#3 Scorn rules and do as you please.
You are a rogue, after all.*

Rules never brought anything but misery to Christopher
"Kit" Ruthven. After rebelling against his controlling father and
leaving the family's etiquette empire behind, Kit has been breaking every one imaginable for the past four years. He's enjoyed
London's sensual pleasures, but he's failed to achieve the success
he craves as London's premier playwright. When his father dies,
Kit returns to the countryside and is forced back into the life
he never wanted. Worse, he must face Ophelia Marsden, the
woman he left behind years before.

After losing her father, Ophelia has learned to rely on herself.
To maintain the family home and support her younger sister, she
tutors young girls in deportment and decorum. But her pupils
would be scandalized if they knew she was also the author of a
guidebook encouraging ladies to embrace their independence.

As Kit rediscovers the life, and the woman, he left behind,
Ophelia must choose between the practicalities she never truly
believed in, or the love she's never been able to extinguish.

He always searched for her.

Call it perversity or a reckless brand of tenacity. Heaven knew he'd been accused of both.

Pacing the scuffed wooden floorboards at the edge of the stage, Christopher Ruthven shoved a hand through his black hair and skimmed his dark gaze across each seat in the main theater stalls of Merrick Theater for the woman he needed to forget.

Damn the mad impulse to look for her.

He was a fool to imagine he'd ever find her staring back. The anticipation roiling in his belly should be for the play, not the past.

Finding her would be folly. Considering how they'd parted, the lady would be as likely to lash out as to embrace him with open arms.

But searching for her had become his habit. His ritual.

Other thespians had rituals too. Some refused to eat before a performance. Others feasted like a king. A few repeated incantations, mumbling to themselves when the curtains rose. As the son of a publishing magnate, Kit should have devised his own maxim to repeat, but the time for words was past. He'd written the play, and the first act was about to begin.

Now he only craved a glimpse of Ophelia Marsden.

The four years since he'd last seen her mattered not. Her bright blue eyes, heart-shaped face, and striking red hair had always distinguished her from other women, but Kit knew they were the least of the qualities that set her apart. Clever, stubborn to the core, and overflowing with more spirit than anyone he'd ever known—that's how he remembered Phee.

But looking for her wasn't mere folly; it was futile. She wouldn't come. He, after all, was the man who'd broken her heart.

As stagehands lit the limelights, Kit shaded his eyes from their glare and stepped behind the curtain. The thrumming in his veins was about the play now, the same giddiness he felt before every performance.

Hunching his shoulders, he braced his arms across his chest and listened intently, half his attention on the lines being delivered on stage, half on the pandemonium backstage. He adored the energy of the theater, the frenetic chaos of actors and stagehands rushing about madly behind the curtains to produce rehearsed magic for the audience. Economies at Merrick's meant he might write a play, perform in it, assist with scene changes from the catwalk, and direct other actors—all in one evening.

Tonight, though, beyond writing the words spoken on stage, the production was out of his hands, and that heightened his nerves. Idleness made him brood.

Behind him a husky female voice cried out, and Kit turned to intercept the woman as she rushed forward, filling his arms with soft curves.

"There's a mouse!" Tess, the playhouse's leading lady, batted thick lashes and stuck out a vermillion-stained lower lip. "Vile creatures. Every one of them."

"Tell me where." Kit gently dislodged the petite blonde from his embrace.

"Scurried underneath, so it did." She indicated a battered chest of drawers, sometimes used for storage, more often as a set piece.

Kit approached the bulky wooden chest, crouched down, and saw nothing but darkness and dust. Bracing his palms on the floor, he lowered until his chest pressed against wood, and he spied the little creature huddling in the farthest corner. The tiny mouse looked far more frightened of him than Tess was of it.

"Can you catch the beast? We can find a cage or give it to the stray cats hanging about the stage doors."

"Too far out of reach." He could move the chest, but the mouse would no doubt scurry away. Seemed kinder to allow the animal to find its own way to freedom. Kit knew what it was to be trapped and frightened. To cower in darkness covered in dust. His father hadn't shut him up in a cage, just a closet now and then, but Kit would be damned if he'd confine any creature.

Tess made an odd sound. Of protest, Kit assumed. But when he cast a glance over his shoulder, her gaze raked hungrily over his legs and backside as he got to his feet.

"The little thing will no doubt find its way out of doors, Tess. Not much food to be had here."

Tess took his attempt at reassurance as an invitation and launched herself into his arms.

She was an appealing woman, with tousled golden curls, catlike green eyes, and an exceedingly ample—*Ah, yes, there they are*—bosom that she shifted enticingly against his chest, as if she knew precisely how good her lush body felt against his. Without a hint of shame or restraint, she moved her hands down his arms, slid them under his unbuttoned sack coat, and stroked her fingers up his back.

"Goodness, you're deliciously tall."

Kit grinned. He found female praise for his awkward height amusing, since he'd been mercilessly teased for his long frame as a child. In a theater world full of handsome, charming actors, his stature and whatever skill he possessed with the written word were all that set him apart.

"You're like a tree I long to climb," she purred. "Feels so right in your arms. Perhaps the gods are telling us that's where I belong."

Tess wasn't merely generously built. From the day she arrived, she'd been generous with her affections too. Half the men at Merrick's were smitten, but Kit kept to his rule about avoiding intrigues with ladies in the troupe. Since coming to London, he'd never sought more than a short-lived entanglement with any woman. He relished his liberty too much to allow himself more.

"Perhaps the gods are unaware you're due on stage for the next act," he teased, making light of her flirtation as he'd done since their introduction.

"Always concerned about your play, aren't you, lovie?" She slid a hand up his body, snaking a finger between the buttons of his waistcoat. "I know my part. Don't worry, Kitten."

The pet name she'd chosen for him grated on his nerves.

"The music's risen, Tess." Kit gripped the actress's hand when she reached toward his waistband. "That's your cue."

"I'll make you proud." She winked and lifted onto her toes, placing a damp kiss on his cheek. "You're a difficult man to seduce," she whispered, "but I do so love a challenge." After sauntering to the curtain's edge, she offered him a final come-hither glance before sashaying on stage.

"Already breaking hearts, *Kitten*? The evening's only just begun." Jasper Grey, Merrick Theater's lead actor and Kit's closest friend, exited stage left and sidled up beside him. With a few swipes across his head, Grey disheveled his coppery brown hair and loosened the faux silk cravat at his throat. The changes were subtle, but sufficient to signal to the audience that his character would begin a descent into madness and debauchery during the second act. Having explored many of London's diversions at the man's side, Kit could attest to Grey's knack for debauchery, on and off the stage.

"I'm sure you'll be more than happy to offer solace. Or have you already?" Choosing a new lover each night of the week was more Grey's style than Kit's, though both had attracted their share of stage-door admirers and earned their reputations as rogues.

Grey's smirk gave everything away. "Whatever the nature of my private moments with our lovely leading lady, the minx is determined to offer you her heart."

"Bollocks to that. I've no interest in claiming anyone's heart." The very thought chased a chill up Kit's spine. Marriage. Commitment. Those were for other men. If his parents were any lesson, marriage was a miserable prison, and he had no wish to be shackled.

Kit turned his attention back to the audience.

"Still looking for your phantom lady?" Grey often tweaked Kit about his habit of searching the crowd. Rather than reveal parts of his past he wished to forget, Kit allowed his friend to assume he sought a feminine ideal, not a very specific woman of flesh and freckles and fetching red hair. "What will you do if she finally appears?"

"She won't." And if he were less of a fool, he'd stop looking for her.

"Come, man. We've packed the house again tonight. This evening we celebrate." Grey swiped at the perspiration on his brow. "You've been downright monkish of late. There must be a woman in London who can turn your head. What about the buxom widow who threw herself at you backstage after last week's performance?"

"The lady stumbled. I simply caught her fall."

"Mmm, and quite artfully too. I particularly admired the way her lush backside landed squarely in your lap."

The curvaceous widow had been all too willing to further their acquaintance, but she'd collided with Kit on opening night. Having written the play and performed in a minor role for an indisposed actor, he'd been too distracted fretting over success to bother with a dalliance.

Of late, something in him had altered. Perhaps he'd had his fill of the city's amusements. Grey's appetite never seemed to wane, but shallow seductions no longer brought Kit satisfaction. He worried less about pleasure and more about success. Four years in London and what had he accomplished? Coming to the city had never been about indulging in vice but about making his mark as a playwright. He'd allowed himself to be distracted. *Far too impulsive* should have been his nickname, for as often as his father had shouted the words at him in his youth.

"How about the angel in the second balcony?" Grey gestured to a gaudily painted box, high in the theater's eastern wall. "I've never been able to resist a woman with titian red hair."

Kit snapped his gaze to the spot Grey indicated, heartbeat ratcheting until it thundered in his ears. Spotting the woman, he expelled a trapped breath. The lady's hair shone in appealing russet waves in the gaslight, but she wasn't Ophelia. Phee's hair was a rich auburn, and her jaw narrower. At least until it sharpened into an adorably squared chin that punctuated her usual air of stubborn defiance.

"No?" Grey continued his perusal of ladies among the sea of faces. "How about the giggling vision in the third row?"

The strawberry blonde laughed with such raucous abandon her bosom bounced as she turned to speak to her companion. Kit admired her profile a moment, letting his gaze dip lower before glancing at the man beside her.

"'That's Dominic Fleet." Kit's pulse jumped at the base of his throat. Opportunity sat just a few feet away.

He'd never met the theater impresario, but he knew the man by reputation. Unlike Merrick's shabby playhouse, known for its comedies and melodramas, Fleet Theater featured long-running plays by the best dramatists in London. Lit entirely with electric lights, the modern theater seated up to three thousand.

"What's he doing slumming at Merrick's?" Grey turned to face Kit. "Did you invite him?"

"Months ago." Kit had sent a letter of introduction to Fleet, enclosing a portion of a play he'd written but been unable to sell. "He never replied." Yet here he was, attending the performance of a piece that revealed none of Kit's true skill as a playwright. Merrick had demanded a bawdy farce. In order to pay his rent, Kit had provided it.

"You bloody traitor." Grey smiled, his sarcastic tone belying his words. "You wouldn't dare abandon Merrick and set out for greener fields."

"Why? Because he compensates us so generously?"

Though they shared a love of theater, Grey and Kit had different cares. Grey possessed family money and worried little about meeting the expenses of a lavish London lifestyle. Kit could never take a penny from his father, even if it was on offer. Any aid from Leopold Ruthven would come with demands and expectations—precisely the sort of control he'd left Hertfordshire to escape.

"You belong here, my friend." Grey clapped him on the shoulder. "With our band of misfits and miscreants. Orphans from lives better left behind."

Belonging. The theater had given him that in a way his father's home never had. Flouting rules, tenacity, making decisions intuitively—every characteristic his father loathed were assets in the theater. Kit had no desire to abandon the life he'd made for himself, just improve upon it.

"We came to London to make something of ourselves. Do you truly believe we'll find success at Merrick's?" Kit lifted his elbow and nudged the dingy curtain tucked at the edge of the stage. "Among tattered furnishings?"

"That's only the backside of the curtain. Merrick puts the best side out front. We all have our flaws. The art is in how well we hide them." Grey had such a way with words Kit often thought *he* should be a playwright. "Would you truly jump ship?"

"I bloody well would." Kit slanted a glance at his friend. "And so would you."

Merrick paid them both a dribble, producing plays with minimal expense in a building that leaked when it rained. Cultivating favor with the wealthiest theater manager in London had been Kit's goal for months. With a long-running Fleet-produced play, he could repay his debts and move out of his cramped lodgings. Hunger had turned him into a hack writer for Merrick, but he craved more. Success, wealth, a chance to prove his skill as a writer. To prove that his decision to come to London had been the right one. To prove to his father that he could succeed on his own merits.

"Never!" Tess, performing the role of virginal damsel, shrieked from center stage. "Never shall I marry Lord Mallet. He is the worst sort of scoundrel."

"That's my cue." Grey grinned as he tugged once more at his cravat and dashed back into the glow of the limelights. Just before stepping on stage, he skidded to stop and turned to Kit. "You'd better write me a part in whatever play you sell to Fleet."

With a mock salute, Kit offered his friend a grin. He had every intention of creating a role for Grey. The man's acting skills deserved a grander stage too.

Kit fixed his gaze on Fleet. He seemed to be enjoying the play, a trifling modernized *Hamlet* parody Kit called *The King's Ghost and the Mad Damsel*. He'd changed the heroine's name to Mordelia, unable to endure the sound of Ophelia's name bouncing off theater walls for weeks. Months, if the play did well.

After his eyes adjusted to the stage-light glow, he pointlessly, compulsively scanned the crowd one last time for a woman whose inner beauty glowed as fiercely as her outer charms. He wouldn't find her. As far as he knew, Phee was home in the village where they'd grown up. When he'd come to London to escape his father, she'd insisted on loyalty to hers and remained in Hertfordshire to care for him. All but one of his letters had gone unanswered, including a note the previous year expressing sorrow over her father's passing.

He didn't need to reach into his pocket and unfold the scrap of paper he carried with him everywhere. The five words of Ophelia's only reply remained seared in his mind. *"Follow your heart and flourish."* They were her mother's words, stitched in a sampler that hung in the family's drawing room. Kit kept the fragment, but he still wondered whether Ophelia had written the words in sincerity or sarcasm.

A flash of gems caught his eye, and Kit spied Fleet's pretty companion rising from her seat. The theater impresario stood too, following her into the aisle. Both made their way toward the doors at the rear of the house.

He couldn't let the man leave without an introduction. Kit lurched toward a door leading to a back hall and sprinted down the dimly lit corridor. He caught up to Fleet near the ladies' retiring room.

"Mr. Fleet, I am—"

"Christopher Ruthven, the scribe of this evening's entertainment." The man extended a gloved hand. "Forgive me, Ruthven. It's taken far too long for me to take in one of your plays."

Attempting not to crush the slighter man in his grip, Kit offered an enthusiastic handshake.

"I want to have a look at your next play." Fleet withdrew an engraved calling card from his waistcoat pocket. "Bring it in person to my office at the theater. Not the one you sent. Something new. More like this one."

"You'll have it." Kit schooled his features, forcing his furrowed brow to smooth. So what if the man wanted a farce rather than serious drama? He craved an opportunity to succeed, and Fleet could provide it. "Thank you."

"If we can come to terms and you manage to fill my playhouse every night as you have Merrick's, I shall be thanking you."

Kit started backstage, his head spinning with ideas for a bigger, grander play than Merrick's could produce. Never mind that it had taken years to grasp the chance Fleet offered. Good fortune had come, and he intended to make the most of it.

As he reached the inconspicuous door that led to the back corridor, a man called his name.

"Mr. Ruthven? Christopher Leopold Ruthven?"

Two gentlemen approached, both tall, black-suited, and dour. Debt collectors? The instinct to bolt dissipated when the two made it impossible, crowding him on either side of the narrow passageway.

"I'm Ruthven." Taller than both men and broader by half, Kit still braced himself for whatever might come. "What do you want?"

The one who'd yet to say anything took a step closer, and Kit recognized his wrinkled face.

"Mr. Sheridan? What brings you to Merrick's?" Kit never imagined the Ruthven family solicitor would venture to a London theater under any circumstances.

"Ill tidings, I regret to say." Sheridan reached into his coat and withdrew an envelope blacked with ink around the edges. "Your father is dead, Mr. Ruthven. I'm sorry. Our letter to you was returned. My messenger visited your address twice and could not locate you. I thought we might find you here."

"Moved lodgings." Kit took the letter, willing his hand not to tremble. "Weeks ago."

"Your sister has made arrangements for a ceremony in Briar Heath." Sheridan lifted a card from his pocket and handed it to Kit. "Visit my office before you depart, and I can provide you with details of your father's will."

The men watched him a moment, waiting for a reaction. When none came, Sheridan muttered condolences before they departed.

Kit lost track of time. He shoved Sheridan's card into his coat pocket to join Fleet's, crushed the unread solicitor's letter in his hand, and stood rooted to the spot where they'd left him. Father. Dead. The two words refused to congeal in his mind. So many of the choices Kit made in his twenty-eight years had been driven by his father's wrath, attempts to escape his stifling control.

Now Kit could think only of what he should do. Must do. Look after his sisters. Return to Briar Heath.

He'd leave after speaking to Merrick. Any work on a play to impress Fleet would have to be undertaken while he was back home.

Home. The countryside, the village, the oversized house his father built with profits from his publishing enterprise— none of it had been home for such a very long time. It was a place he'd felt shunned and loathed most of his life. He'd never visited in four years. Never dared set foot in his father's house after his flamboyant departure.

As he headed toward Merrick's office to tell the man his news, worry for his sisters tightened Kit's jaw until it ached. Then another thought struck.

After all these years, night after night of futile searching, he would finally see Ophelia Marsden again.

Turn the page for a look at Sophia's happily ever after in

A STUDY IN SCOUNDRELS

Sophia Ruthven is the epitome of proper behavior. On paper at least, as long as that paper isn't from one of the lady detective stories she secretly pens. She certainly isn't interested in associating with the dashing Jasper Grey, the wayward heir to the Earl of Stanhope, and one of the stage's leading men. But when she learns Grey's younger sister Liddy has gone missing, she can't deny her desire to solve the mystery…or her attraction to the incorrigible scoundrel.

Responsibility isn't something Grey is very familiar with. On the boards and in the bedroom, he lives exactly how he wants to, shunning all the trappings of respectability and society. Grey knows he should avoid the bewitching Sophia, but he's never been able to say no to what he wants. And having Sophia in his arms and his bed is quickly becoming the thing he wants the most.

As Sophia and Grey's search for Liddy continues across the English countryside, can this scoundrel convince a proper lady that he's actually perfect for her, or will their adventure leave them both heartbroken?

Sophia Ruthven never intended to plaster her palm against the man's shapely backside.

In fact, she hadn't intended to encounter the Earl of Westby at all. True, she had stolen into the man's private study. But his sister, Lady Vivian, who'd invited Sophia to speak at her weekly ladies' book club tea, insisted her infamous rake of a brother was not at home.

How could Sophia have known that a simple request to use the ladies' washroom would lead her past the half open door of the earl's study? Who could blame her for succumbing to the mingled aromas of smoke and book leather wafting out of the room?

The chance to inspect a notorious scoundrel's lair was simply too tempting a prospect to ignore.

Purely for research purposes, of course.

For months, Sophia had been working on a story about her fictional lady detective, Euphemia "Effie" Breedlove, but the details weren't right. Her rakish villain lacked verisimilitude.

A sheltered upbringing in the countryside had provided few opportunities to observe scoundrels firsthand.

Now her hand was pinned between the room's dark wood paneling, a firm muscled posterior, and the green velvet curtain she'd hidden herself behind. The man and his companion had burst into the room as Sophia stood inspecting the items on the earl's desk. Thankfully, the long drape-covered bay window had been near enough to offer concealment.

"Now. Right here on my desk. You've kept me waiting long enough, sweetling." The man's husky tone drew a moan from the young lady, interspersed with the squelching sound of wet kisses. Who gave with such fervor and who eagerly received, Sophia couldn't be sure.

But she was sure of one thing. The feminine voice beyond the curtain belonged to Miss Emmeline Honeycutt, a fellow guest at the ladies' tea. Sophia had been introduced to the girl not half an hour ago. She guessed her to be quite young, not many years older than her own seventeen-year-old sister, Clarissa. She couldn't stand by and allow the girl to ruin herself.

Shifting her hand, she pushed at the heated swell of the man's derriere.

"What's that?" He stilled, pressing his weight against Sophia's palm. "We don't wish to be caught out, little minx. Seems we must wait a bit longer. You should get back to my sister's gathering."

After a few moments of whining protest and what sounded like the thud of dainty feet stomping thick carpet, Miss Honeycutt retreated with the swish and click of beaded fabric. When the study door slid shut, Sophia reached up to stifle a sneeze. She couldn't get the taste of the earl's pungent cologne off her tongue. Spicy and overly sweet, the scent was laid on so thick it tickled her nose.

"You can come out now, whoever you are." His voice had taken on a hard edge, as firm as the contours of his backside. Not at all the warm murmur he'd offered Miss Honeycutt.

Thankfully, he'd moved enough to free Sophia's hand, but she still hesitated a moment before pulling back the curtain and facing the man she'd read the worst sort of stories about in the gossip columns.

With one push at the drapery, she managed a step forward, keeping her chin up and back straight, lest he think her as brazen as the young woman who'd just left his arms.

"My lord, I can explain…"

But she was apparently going to have to plead her case to an empty room. He'd gone, leaving her with nothing but flame-filled cheeks and the knowledge that, in future, she needed to stem her raging curiosity and keep out of scoundrels' private spaces.

A clock chimed over the mantel and panic set in. She'd been gone too long. Even longer than the silly girl who'd nearly given herself to the earl on his desk.

Starting toward the door, she tripped on the velvet drapery clinging to her ankle.

A vice grip enclosed her wrist to keep her upright. No, not a vice. A hand, large and long fingered, and exceedingly strong, judging by how her own fingers had begun to numb.

"Lord Westby."

With his dark clothing, the man blended into the room's shadows. He'd been watching without her sensing him at all.

Cursing her flawed powers of observation, Sophia snatched her arm from his grip. He released her and she quickly righted herself, yanking her boot from the drapery and moving toward the center of the room.

"You're a foolish woman," he whispered, "but I suppose men forgive that once they get a look at your face." He stalked toward her until he was close enough for her to see the glint on his obsidian eyes. Moving slowly, he began circling her like a predator, deciding how he wanted to begin consuming his prey. "And those breasts."

"I must return to your sister's tea, my lord."

"You should have considered as much before hiding away in my study." He drew closer, looming at her back. As his damp breath rushed against her neck, the cloying sweetness of his cologne caught in her throat and burned her eyes.

"I allowed my curiosity to get the better of me, my lord." Sophia started toward the door. "A mistake I shan't repeat."

Westby came around to stand before her, blocking her progress.

Sophia studied the scoundrel for the first time. Dark hair, coal-black eyes, and an arrogant smirk above a strong, squared jaw. Symmetry and sensuality conspired to give the impression of male beauty, as long as one ignored the coldness of his gaze and the cruelty in the set of his mouth.

He seemed to enjoy her perusal. Lifting his arms out at his sides, he urged, "Do your worst. How may I satisfy your curiosity? With a body like that"—he fixed his gaze on the overly ample bosom she'd spent most of her life trying to bind and conceal—"satisfying you would be no burden."

Sophia took his fixation on her breasts as an opportunity to escape. She started past him, gathering a handful of her skirt to keep from tripping on her hem. By the time she reached the study door, he'd sprung into action, rushing up to slam a palm on the panel above her head and pin her against the wood.

"Don't you want a taste before you go? One kiss to remember me by?" He drew his fingers across her cheek and chills raced down Sophia's spine. "I certainly want to taste you," he whispered, his lips hovering near her ear. "Are you the flavor of honey, like the shade of your hair? Or strawberries, like the flush in those perfect lips?"

Blood raced in her veins, flooding her cheeks, heating her chest and neck and the tips of her ears. Her skin pulled taut, muscles cramped.

She'd never been kissed, but she'd been this close to a dangerous man once before.

Flirtation and seduction meant nothing to Westby's sort. But to Sophia, her first kiss was more than an item to tick off the list of all that she'd yet to experience in life.

She still hoped for marriage and even had a prospect in mind. Research for her book was not worth forfeiting favors to a blackguard who reeked of oversweet cologne.

"I've been gone too long," Sophia insisted. The rush of blood in her ears wasn't enough to block the ticking of the clock. Why had no one come to look for her after all this time?

Lord Westby tucked a hand around her waist, twisting her to face him. With one brusque slip of his hand, he palmed her breast, pushed until he'd pressed her back against the door.

"I'll have a kiss before you go." Westby hooked a hand around her neck, sliding his fingers into her pinned hair.

She was on the verge of stomping her foot as Miss Honeycutt had done, but forcefully and on his toes, when Westby dipped his head. A current of shock rioted through her when he swept his tongue across the seam of her lips.

She recoiled, pressing at his chest with one hand and lifting the other to swipe across her mouth. Something had to eclipse the soppy wetness of his tongue, like a warm slug slithering across her lips.

"You do taste like honey," he enthused.

He tasted like cigar smoke and the rose water he'd apparently licked off the lady he'd been kissing moments before.

"Enough of this nonsense, my lord. Let me go." She twisted her body, pushing at him with her hip to create distance between then.

When she finally had the man at her back and the study door latch in her hand, he gripped her arm and whispered, "Did you hear that?"

Somewhere in the house a woman raised her voice. A man shouted in reply, though Sophia couldn't make out his words. Heavy footsteps shook the floorboards, louder as they continued, growing closer to the earl's study.

"Get behind the drape." The earl shoved her toward the window. "Don't look at me like that. You were quite content there a moment ago."

Sophia loathed his dictatorial tone and rough handling. She rubbed at the spot where he'd left a bruising sting around her arm.

"Look, you little fool," he growled, "a forced marriage will never be my fate. And I trust you don't wish to ruin your reputation entirely. Get behind the damned curtain."

Sophia scowled at him as she sheltered behind the velvet drapery. The moment she drew the fabric across her body, the study door swung open.

"Winship?" the earl called out. "Good God, man, it's been an age. I wasn't sure you were still among the living."

"That must be why your housekeeper was so reluctant to admit me." The visitor's voice was as rich and smooth as warm honey. But there was more underneath, a note of barely leashed ire.

"Well, you're here now. Care for a scotch?" Westby seemed oblivious to the thread of fury in the man's tone.

The clink of crystal indicated the earl had turned his attention to the liquor trolley. Sophia sensed the other man moving, the rustle of clothing and thud of his footsteps as he circled the room.

"Did you rip this ribbon off a lady, or did she offer it as a token?" The visitor's voice was humming with anger.

Westby let out an ugly bark of laughter. "Let the fripperies fall where they may, I always say."

Sophia held her breath. She needed to hear the stranger speak again. Something about his voice was oddly familiar.

"You bloody knave, where is she?" He no longer attempted to hide his anger, and Sophia no longer doubted his identity. Westby might call him Winship, but the man's appealing voice gave him away as Jasper Grey, her brother's theater friend.

"What the blasted hell. I don't—" The earl began to sputter before his words cut off, followed by a sickening wallop of flesh colliding with bone.

"Phyllida is besotted with you, as you well know. Tell me where she is, and I'll consider letting you live." Mr. Grey's tone had tempered to a deadly calm.

"Liddy? What business would I have with your sister? Check the bloody nursery."

A struggle ensued, grunts and movement, then the thud of a body hitting a solid piece of furniture. The desk?

"Where is she, Westby?"

"I have…no"—the earl's voice emerged on a breathless choke, as if something, or someone, was cutting off his air—"idea."

"In that case, letting you live seems far too generous."

Sophia fumbled with the drapery, trying to disentangle herself. Westby deserved a walloping, but Mr. Grey would suffer far more if he assaulted a powerful aristocrat.

"Mr. Grey!" she shouted and finally found an opening in the thick fall of velvet fabric.

Both men froze when she emerged. Westby lay atop his desk, face pink with exertion, as Jasper Grey leaned over him, a muscled forearm braced across the earl's throat.

Mr. Grey was just as she recalled him, tall and lean, with tumbling chestnut hair and striking gray eyes, as cool as a January breeze.

"Miss Ruthven?" The infamous actor squinted at her. "What the hell are *you* doing in this bastard's study?" He scowled down at the earl, then straightened and faced her.

"I had no idea you possessed such wretched judgement, Sophia."

"And I had no idea murder came so easily to you, Mr. Grey."

They both cast a glance at the Earl of Westby, who'd sat up and begun clawing at his necktie to loosen its folds.

"There, you see. He's alive. I'm not quite a murderer yet."

"What in heaven's name is going on?" The earl's sister skidded to a halt in the study doorway. "The housemaid nearly fainted."

Sophia scooted into the recess of the bay window, hoping to escape notice.

After an assessing glance at her brother, Lady Vivian turned her gaze on Mr. Grey, a grin curving her lips. "Winship," she purred as she approached, "why are you in such a state? Come and have tea with us to soothe your nerves. We've missed your company at Westby House."

This Sophia remembered about Jasper Grey too. The man had a way with women. Not only did they buzz about him, but he seemed to exude a calming effect too. On the day she'd met him, he'd turned an angry woman into a fawning, cooing fool with a few sweet words. The second time she'd seen him, as lead actor in one of her brother's plays, his effect had been even more potent. Ladies in the audience swooned and the clamor to visit him backstage ended with one young woman crying over her trampled hat.

Now Lady Vivian wore the same look other ladies did around him—a sort of blissful, awestruck hunger.

"Leave us, Viv," the earl commanded in a rusty bark. "Close the door behind you."

She shot her brother a look of concern and offered their visitor another simpering grin before doing as Westby instructed.

When Sophia emerged from the window nook, Mr. Grey lifted his arm, and Westby shrunk back as if to avoid a blow.

"Let me take you out of here." Mr. Grey crooked his fingers, bidding her to come toward him.

"You," the earl began, scooting a safe distance away before shoving a finger in the air toward Mr. Grey, "get out of my house. Immediately." He turned his attention toward Sophia, skimming her face before gaping at her breasts. "Do return another time for your kiss."

"I—" Offense and protest perched on the tip of her tongue, but Grey spoke over her.

"Don't speak to her, Westby." He extended his hand as if he expected her to take it. As if he expected her to allow him to make her decisions.

"I will choose when to depart, Mr. Grey." She'd had enough of high-handed men for one day. Never mind that she shouldn't have been snooping in the earl's study in the first place.

"The man is a wretch." He flicked his gaze toward Westby. "An utter scoundrel. A certifiable scalawag."

"I"—the aristocrat cleared his throat—"am standing right here."

"And you cannot deny a single claim."

The earl frowned but offered no rebuttal. "What's become of you, man? A few years on the stage, and you lose all sense?

If you were anyone else, you'd be clapped in irons for assaulting me." He rubbed a hand across his jaw where an abrasion bloomed in shades of red and blue. "We were friends once."

"We were never friends, Westby. You're an arrogant sod and have no respect for the fairer sex."

The earl chortled. "Says the man who's bedded half of London's fairer sex."

Sophia thought she spied a patch of pink on the high cut of Mr. Grey's cheek, but the look he cast her was tinted with more pride than humility. Lifting his hand again, he petitioned her. "Come with me, Sophia. Please."

"I can't simply leave." Sophia owed Westby nothing, but she couldn't say the same for his sister. "Lady Vivian invited me. What shall I tell her?"

"Nothing," Grey said quietly. "Returning to the drawing room will raise questions you won't wish to answer." He tipped his head toward the earl. "Westby will direct the housekeeper to say you fell ill and called a cab to take you home."

"Will I?" Westby asked with arch haughtiness.

Mr. Grey cast him a hard stare, and the earl stomped across the rug. With a dramatic sigh, he yanked his study door open. "Anything to get you out of my house, Winship."

Sophia didn't take Mr. Grey's offered hand, but she moved past him toward the door. For however long she remained in London before returning to the countryside, she suspected her days of receiving invitations from the aristocracy had just come to a crashing end.

"This isn't the time for worrying about etiquette," Grey said, close behind her, a hand heavy at her lower back as he guided her through the door. Once she was across the threshold, he turned back. "Not a word about Liddy to anyone, Westby. If you hear word of her whereabouts, wire me immediately."

"You truly have no idea where your sister is?"

Sophia couldn't detect any concern in the earl's tone for the sister of a man he claimed had once been a friend.

"No." Grey's jaw tensed, his hands tightened to fists against his thighs. "But I will find her." He spun away from Westby and started past Sophia.

For a moment she thought he'd storm out of Westby House without her. Then she felt his fingers, warm and insistent, tangling with hers as he reached for her. He paused in the hallway, waiting for her to respond.

She felt a tremor across his skin. His hands were shaking.

Sophia clasped her fingers around his and let him lead her quickly toward the front door.

ABOUT THE AUTHOR

Fueled by Pacific Northwest coffee and inspired by multiple viewings of every British costume drama she can get her hands on, *USA Today* bestselling author **CHRISTY CARLYLE** writes sensual historical romances set in the Victorian era. She loves heroes who struggle against all odds and heroines who are ahead of their time. A former teacher with a degree in history, she finds there's nothing better than being able to combine her love of the past with a die-hard belief in happy endings.

Discover great authors, exclusive offers, and more at HC.COM.

Dear Reader,

I hope you liked the latest romance from Avon Impulse! If you're looking for another steamy, fun, emotional read, be sure to check out some of our upcoming titles. Historical romance fans are in luck because we have two great new titles this winter!

First up, we have another male/male romance from Cat Sebastian coming in December! IT TAKES TWO TO TUMBLE launches Cat's brand new series, Seducing the Sedgwicks, and it's a steamy story of a country vicar who is asked to help wrangle the children of a stern but gloriously handsome sea captain…the two men can't seem to keep their hands off each other!

In January, we have a delightful, charming debut novel from Marie Tremayne! LADY IN WAITING features a runaway bride who takes a position as a maid in a lord's household.

He's incredibly tempted by his new servant, but he knows they can never be together due to class differences…or can they? You don't want to miss this fantastic first book in Marie's Reluctant Brides trilogy!

You can purchase any of these titles by clicking the links above or by visiting our website, www.AvonRomance.com. Thank you for loving romance as much as we do…enjoy!

Sincerely,

Nicole Fischer
Editorial Director
Avon Impulse